BROKEN
TRUST

WSJ & USA TODAY BESTSELLING AUTHOR
JAYMIN EVE
USA TODAY & INTERNATIONAL BESTSELLING AUTHOR
TATE JAMES

Copyright © Jaymin Eve & Tate James 2019

All rights reserved.

First published in 2019.

Eve, Jaymin | James, Tate

Broken Trust: Dark Legacy #2

No part of this book may be reproduced, stored in a retrieval system or transmitted in any form or by any means, without the prior permission in writing of the publisher, nor be otherwise circulated in any form of binding or cover other than that in which it is published and without a similar condition, including this condition, being imposed on the subsequent purchaser. All characters in this publication other than those clearly in the public domain are fictitious, and any resemblance to real persons, living or dead, is purely coincidental.

Cover design by Tamara Kokic

Book design by Inkstain Design Studio

BROKEN TRUST

To all the fucked up girls who love fucked up boys.
This is for you.

Chapter 1

I couldn't stop shaking. My hands trembled to the point where my toothbrush clicked against my teeth as I tried to brush them.

It had been eight hours since I'd shot a man in the head.

Eight fucking hours since my entire life was ripped to shreds.

Again.

Losing my parents was still the worst moment of my existence, but the betrayal of Beck, Dylan, Evan, and Jasper ranked a close second.

"You okay?" Dante asked, perched in the bathroom doorway. He still looked rough, but I'd patched up most of his injuries, and in general, he was dealing much better than me. We were back in his Jersey apartment. I'd taken his car—which had been out in the woods, after he was lured there by Beck—and then driven at stupid speeds all the way back here.

Spitting out the paste, I rinsed my mouth. "No. Just … not fucking okay."

He moved closer, and when his image joined mine in the mirror, it was clear how much paler than normal I was. Dante had bronzed, inked-all-over skin, and I looked like I'd never seen sun in my life.

"The first kill is always the hardest, Riles. Give yourself time."

Bile rose in my throat, and I tried to swallow, but everything burned.

"I ... I don't even want to touch that statement," I told him hoarsely. "But I have to ask ... have you actually killed someone before? More than one someone?"

I turned my back on the mirror—it was revealing way too much of my pain and sadness, and I wanted to properly see Dante's face when he answered.

He examined my features, like he was searching for something, before he nodded, expression serious. "Yes. I have."

A huge gust of air burst from me, and I clenched my fists to stop them from shaking.

Dante continued. "I should have told you earlier—I'm a little more involved in the gang life than I've previously let on. I was trying to keep you out of danger. Funnily enough, the Grims were the least of my worries when it came to you."

I wanted to laugh, because it was ironically funny, but I just didn't have the heart for any emotion like that.

"What are you going to do?" Dante asked me softly, the green of his eyes darkening as anger filled them. "This is a fucked up situation, Riles, and while I will help in any way I can..."

He trailed off because we both knew there was really nothing he could do to help me.

I shrugged. "They own me now, so I have to play the game."

Beck and the others had made that perfectly clear. There was only one way out. My brother, Oscar, had taken that route, but I was not at that place yet.

"And Beck?" Dante asked, and I was surprised that he didn't sound as fucked off as he usually did when mentioning the heirs. "What are you going to do about him?"

Laughter finally burst from me, harsh and cynical. "Beck is dead to me. He used me. Made me care about him. All the time he's been playing the long game for Delta. If I knew any of this shit was coming, I would have bailed long ago and just kept running for the rest of my life."

Now I had blood on my hands. I was trapped.

That knowledge made it hard to breathe.

"One day you will control a portion of the most powerful company in the world," Dante reminded me. "You can make them all pay then."

I nodded, having already thought about that myself. It was my most fervant hope that one day they would regret inviting me into their world. I just had to figure out how to do it all without getting Dante killed. He was the one person I still trusted and loved. Even Eddy was iced from my life now.

Dante and I crawled into his bed, and I put the television on. Silence was the enemy, and thoughts had to be banished before I lost my mind. Snuggling down into the familiar sheets, breathing in the familiar scent, I could almost pretend for a moment that my life hadn't completely gone to shit.

"You know you can stay here as long as you need," Dante said sleepily, turning on his side to see me better. "But what are the odds that Delta won't hunt you down?"

I wished I could just stay here forever. With Dante. And pretend the rest of those fuckers didn't exist. Dante was right though, they were never going to let me fade away. The entire fucking point of me shooting a man was to have leverage to hold over my head.

"Like I said, they own me now, but I'm going to make it as difficult as I can for them," I decided, pushing my hair back so it was across the pillow.

Dante reached out and took my hand, squeezing it gently before he rolled back the other way and almost instantly fell asleep.

Bastard had always been able to do that.

Meanwhile, every single time I closed my eyes, all I could see was the jerking of the Huntley dude's head when the bullet went through. The spatter of his blood as it coated so much of the room behind him. The thud as the gun slipped from my hands and hit the ground. Beck's face as he lowered his own weapon, freeing Dante.

Those images were permanently branded in my brain. On my soul.

"You want something to help you sleep?" Dante murmured, not quite asleep like I'd thought.

I shook my head. As badly as I wanted oblivion, I was scared to let myself be vulnerable again. Drugs or alcohol were going to be a rare occurrence in my life, because this new world I was part of was dangerous and cut throat.

Dante's breathing got really deep, and I was relieved that he was finally resting. He had so many injuries, sleep was the best thing for him. Meanwhile, I continued to stare at the ceiling, too tired to even cry.

My heart hurt so badly, like the fucking thing had been stabbed and was slowly dying. It was so much more than the fact I'd had to kill someone. I'd lost four guys who I'd been counting as friends … as more than friends. Family.

My phone lit up again from the bedside table, and I ignored it. It had been going off all night, messages and calls, over and over, non-stop, until eventually Dante suggested I turn it off. I couldn't bring myself to do that; instead, I put it on silent and just left it there to torture myself.

I wanted so badly to know what they were saying. So badly.

But I was too angry.

A loud banging on the door had me jumping about a foot in the air. Looking over, I was surprised to see Dante remained sound asleep. He desperately needed it, so I didn't wake him. Stumbling out of bed, I pulled the shirt down from where it had crept up. I wore only Dante's shirt and some clean panties that I'd thankfully left here and he'd washed for me.

Creeping out of the bedroom, I tiptoed through his living room and stood behind the door.

Somehow, before they even spoke, I knew who was out there. I could feel that energy they carried, like an extra spark or presence that most people didn't have.

"Butterfly, I know you're in there." Beck's low voice drifted through to me.

I dropped my head against the wood, and the tears which had been absent since I'd taken someone's life finally appeared.

"Please open the door," Dylan added.

"Go away," I whispered, exhaustion and tears choking my words. "Just leave me alone."

Please. I was silently begging.

"We want to explain," Jasper said, and his voice was rough, "We ... we can't have this conversation out in the hall."

Anger rose up in me at their pleading tones. "That's not my problem, Jasper," I snapped. How *dare* they? How dare they try and guilt me into forgiving them after what they'd just forced me to do. "Fuck off. All of you.

You're dead to me."

I squeezed my eyes tightly shut, fighting against the hot tears which spilled down my cheeks regardless. I couldn't deal with them right now. Not when their betrayal was so fresh.

There was a long pause, but I wasn't dumb enough to think they'd left.

"Butterfly." Beck exhaled heavily and there was a wooden thump like his forehead was pressed to the other side of the door like mine was. "That's not how this works. You're one of us now, for better or worse."

The matter-of-fact cast to his words boiled my fury higher, and I embraced it. It was an unhealthy coping mechanism, but once again, I found myself much preferring to welcome the anger than dwell on the pain.

Clenching my teeth, I flipped open the locks, stepped back, and whipped the door open so quickly Beck almost tumbled into the room. Off balance, he staggered back a few steps then glared at me in confusion.

"What the fuck, Butterf—"

"Stop." My voice was like ice, and I blocked the doorway, making it clear they weren't welcome to enter. "Never call me that again. I am not some fragile bug with pretty wings for you to pull off." I cast a disgusted look at Beck—desperately ignoring the pangs of agony in my chest when I noticed the dark pain etched across his face. It was just easier not to look at him, so I whipped my furious, sickened eyes over the other three.

"You got what you needed. My shackles are locked down and filed away in your revolting vault, so let's cut the bullshit. You used me. You deliberately formed this ... fucked up bond between us, all so I wouldn't question shit until it was too late."

Tears choked me and I swallowed past them, grasping onto that burning hot anger.

"I'll do what's required as a Delta successor, but nothing more. We're not *friends*, and we're certainly not…" The words stuck in my throat and my gaze involuntarily returned to Beck. His broad chest heaved as he sucked a deep breath to speak, and I held up a palm to silence him even as my gaze dropped to the ground. "Like I said, you're dead to me. Lose my number, I'll see you at the next forced Delta meeting."

I stepped back, grabbing the door and slamming it in their sorry faces before any of them could find the words to respond. Or maybe they just had nothing to say. My days of naively believing they were good people—that they were just the product of their upbringing—were done. Those four had played me like the pawn they'd first accused me of being, and I felt nothing but shame and betrayal for it.

My shaking fingers flipped the six deadbolts closed and I stepped back into Dante's warm embrace. I didn't know how long he'd been there, but the second his arms closed around me it was like the floodgates opened. My whole body shook with sobs as I buried my face in his bandaged chest, and he just stood there stroking my hair. Exactly the pillar of strength I needed when my whole world was crumbling around me.

Chapter 2

Every day, one of the guys showed up outside Dante's apartment building. It started the morning after they'd shown up to "apologize" and I'd slammed the door in their lying faces. Dylan appeared in the doorway of the walk up across the road. I spotted him from the window as I brushed my teeth and flipped him off. He'd just folded his arms, leaned on the wall, and *grinned* at me.

The next day was Evan. The next was Jasper.

The whole time I stayed at Dante's they maintained this routine. *Watching* me… Like I was a flight risk. They weren't wrong. Not a day passed that I didn't think about the fake IDs in Richard Deboise's office. But if I fled … what would happen to Dante? To Eddy? Not to mention the worry that those IDs wouldn't work now that they had video footage of me murdering someone? My face wasn't going to change.

I was fucking trapped.

"Who's on guard duty today?" Dante asked as I stood at the living room window, staring out absentmindedly while my fingers tangled in the dirty, off-white net curtain. His words startled me, and I jumped slightly as I turned to face him.

He was holding out a mug of coffee and I took it from him with a grateful smile. "Um, Dylan, again."

Dante quirked a brow and leaned past me to peer out the window. He would see exactly what I'd just been staring down at. Dylan, in his usual spot, sitting on the steps of the old, abandoned laundromat across the road.

Dante gave a sarcastic little finger wave, and I didn't bother looking to see what Dylan's reaction was. As if Delta taking Dante, beating him half to death, then holding a gun to his head wasn't bad enough, now they were stalking us.

"Still no Beckett, huh?" My best friend said the words lightly, but I didn't miss the intense way he watched me when we made our way over to the couch.

I shrugged, like it didn't tear me up inside that Dylan, Evan, and Jasper had been outside—watching me—every damn day, but not once had Beck showed up. "Why should he do his own dirty work?" I murmured with a scathing edge.

Dante's jaw clenched, and his knuckles turned white on his mug, but I was too exhausted to press him for what he was thinking. Probably about how Beck had personally broken three of his ribs and he'd like to return the favor. I wouldn't mind lending a hand.

"Riles," he started, but stopped when his phone buzzed loudly on the coffee table. Mine had run out of battery days ago and I just hadn't bothered to charge it. What was the point?

Dante picked up his device and scowled at the screen before answering the call.

"Catherine," he drawled, making eye contact with me as he spoke, "How lovely to hear from you. We wondered how long it would take."

I gave him frantic *what the fuck are you doing* faces, but he shrugged and clicked the call to speaker phone just in time for me to catch my birth-mother's chilling response.

"Tell my daughter that she's expected to return to school tomorrow morning, or we will take action. I have been more than lenient, but enough is enough. This little temper tantrum has gone on long enough."

I scoffed a humorless laugh. "Or fucking what, bitch? You'll turn in that little snuff film to the police? All because I won't go to school? Fuck off."

Catherine laughed then, and it was one of the coldest sounds I'd ever heard. "You think that's our only card to play? Your stupidity astounds me, girl."

I met Dante's eyes over the phone he held between us, and ice formed in my belly. They'd already beaten him, and threatened to shoot him… Was there more? Maybe I was underestimating Delta.

"Here's what will happen," Catherine continued, her tone icy and uncaring. "You'll attend Ducis Academy, just like the good little Deboise heir that you are. You'll excel in classes, you'll keep your head down, and you'll stay out of trouble. When we require you to act in Delta's interests, you'll do so without question or argument. In return, I'll allow you to live outside the Delta compound. Stewart will source a suitable apartment for you, because frankly I'm sick of having you under foot."

I spluttered in confusion. "And if I don't?"

"Then I will personally break one of Edith Langham's fingers every day until you comply. It's your choice." She hung up then, and I scrambled off the couch. I just barely made it to the bathroom before the contents of my stomach began emptying into the porcelain bowl, hot tears stinging my eyes and streaming down my face as I sobbed and vomited.

Dante crouched beside me, his gentle hand stroking my hair out of my face and just *being there* for me. He always had been, but since Beck—and the guys—betrayed me, I was appreciating just how much Dante cared for me.

"They're fucking twisted," I croaked, after wiping my mouth on the wet washcloth he handed me. My whole body was trembling, and Dante just gathered me up in his arms, pulling me into his lap despite his own injuries.

"There's no denying that," he murmured back, his cheek pressed against my hair as I huddled closer into his warm body. "But if I've learned anything about living in a darker world—you'll never beat them, unless you become them. Is that really something you want to do? Damn your soul like that?"

I shuddered, my mind flashing back to the sound of the gunshot, the splatter of blood and gore, the heavy thump of the Huntley man's lifeless form hitting the ground. My recurrent nightmares. "Haven't I already?"

Dante let out a long sigh. "Not even close, Riles. Not even remotely close."

We stayed like that for a long time, until I started to worry I was hurting him and shifted to stand up.

"Hey," Dante murmured, catching my face between his palms and halting me. "You know I'll always have your back, right? You're not in this alone."

The way he stared at me ... it was intense, passionate, and a bit unnerving.

"I know," I replied with a tiny smile. "I guess I should get back to my gilded cage before Eddy pays."

Dante peered at me with that heavy gaze for another long moment before a switch flipped and a devilish grin slid over his face. "Not yet. Debitch said you needed to be at school tomorrow morning, which leaves tonight free."

I raised my brows, pulling back gently so that his hands left my face. "What did you have in mind?"

"Rabbit just got a new Supra that needs to do a test run. I'm sure he wouldn't object to you putting her through the paces at Widowmaker. Then when you're done with that, you can drive one of my cars in the actual race." His grin was sly, and excitement surged in me for the first time in *way* too long.

"That's tonight?" I bit my lip, thinking it over. Widowmaker used to be *my* race. It was only run twice a year and had a crazy high crash rate. I'd held first place for the last five races and I hated the thought of someone else taking my crown … still, I would have to attempt it in an unfamiliar car and I was carrying a shit load of mental baggage.

"The supra is tricked out with NOS…" Dante coaxed, and I groaned.

"Fuck," I sighed. "I can't say no to that." I scrambled up off the bathroom floor and held out my hand to help Dante up. He grunted as he held his ribs but gave me a tight smile to reassure me he was okay.

"I need something to wear," I commented as I reached for my toothbrush. I'd been wearing Dante's t-shirts and shorts for the past week and a half, seeing as I hadn't left the apartment. But I needed something more kick ass for Widowmaker.

Dante chuckled, shifting past me to grab his phone where he'd left it on the couch. "I'll call Serena. She'll get you sorted."

This time my smile was more genuine. If anyone could make me look badass—other than Eddy—it was Dante's older sister.

"**HOLY SHIT, IT'S BEEN SO** long, Riles!" Serena was a hugger. Over the years I'd grown used to her full bear hugs, and a part of me felt a tiny bit better when she squeezed me tightly.

"I know, so much shit has happened; it feels like ten years since I last saw you."

She led me across to the couch, and I marveled at the blue streaks in her black hair. Didn't matter that she was nearing thirty, Serena looked hot and sexy, with a rocker edge.

Her story could have been very different though because it sure as shit started out terribly. In high school she'd been the popular, pretty chick. Until her school's wide receiver knocked her up at eighteen and then bailed to leave her to raise their kid alone. Luckily her story had a happy ending when "diner guy," as we'd used to call him, finally got the balls to ask out the pretty waitress that he'd lusted after from afar. Turned out that Rob Laidner, who was a few years older than Serena, was a police officer on the other side of Jersey. But he still made the trip every morning to eat breakfast in her section of the small family diner where she worked.

They'd gotten married five years ago, and Rob was raising Dante's niece, Chloe, like she was his own.

I loved fairy tales. Pity mine was more of a nightmare.

"So, Dante's been filling me in a little, but he said the details were yours to share," Serena started when we were sitting. "So share."

When she wore that fierce face, she looked so much like her brother, that it was almost scary. "I trusted the wrong people," I said quietly. "They betrayed me, when they should have had my back. They hurt Dante."

I practically spat those last words, my anger rising again. Every time I started to miss those bastards, I just had to picture my best friend, bloodied and beaten with a gun to his head.

Serena didn't look surprised, and some might have thought her lack of concern about Dante was cold, but I knew that she had accepted his dangerous life long ago. I, on the other hand, continued to try and convince him it was time to get out of the Grims. I never wanted to deal with losing him.

"Dante doesn't seem that upset by it," Serena said, ruffling her hair up. "He said they were just doing their duty."

I let out a low grumbling sound. "I don't fucking get him. He hated them last month, but now he's almost … understanding and accepting of their bullshit. How could getting beaten and almost killed have taken him from hate to whatever he's feeling now?"

Serena shrugged, but it was Dante that answered. "Because I understand them better now," he said as he stepped in from the balcony. He'd been out there taking a phone call. "Beck took no joy in hurting me, and I too have been forced to do things I disagree with out of obligation. Sometimes life is about duty, and from what I can tell, your boys have had to perform for Delta most of their lives."

I crossed my arms stubbornly. "There is always a choice."

Dante shook his head at me. "You can't afford to be that naive any longer. You don't have the luxury."

I knew he was trying to remind me that I shot a guy because I didn't have a choice. But the truth was, I did have a choice. I could have turned the gun on Catherine, or Beck, or any of Delta. I could have turned the gun on myself and damned Dante as well. But I'd made the choice to shoot the

Huntley operative. The same way the Delta heirs had made a choice to *not* tell me about what I was facing and to take my best friend as collateral in a war he was not part of.

Beck chose to fuck me, all the while knowing he would have to betray me.

We all made choices. And now we had to live with them.

Serena jumped to her feet then, her torn up boyfriend jeans swishing around her slim hips. "Enough maudlin talk, let's get you sexy for this drive tonight."

She rushed back to the front door, picking up the overnight bag she'd dropped there. I pulled myself off the couch slowly, but there was a tingling sensation in my limbs that I only got when I knew I was going to race soon.

I needed this. I really fucking needed it.

Twenty minutes later I was dressed like old-Riley. Skinny black jeans, and black ankle boots. A deep red tank top that hugged all of my curves and was tucked into the jeans. Black leather jacket over the top and my hair tamed into a long mass of frizzless curls. Serena had makeup with her as well, and I lined my eyes dark and my lips were red to match my shirt.

"Fuck, Riles." Dante waggled his eyebrows appreciatively. "Lucky Beck isn't out on Riley Duty today, because he would be on you so fast your head would spin."

My fingers twitched at his words, and I worked very hard not to let the pain I felt show on my face. "I'll probably shoot him the next time he touches me. You said the first kill is the hardest, might be worth testing that theory."

Dante just smirked like he knew I was full of shit. I talked a big game, but shooting someone you cared about was very different to shooting an asshole that had attempted to kidnap you. And it had still almost broken me. Fuck Sebastian Roman Beckett. Fuck him to Hell.

Chapter 3

Dante had a few new cars, and I took my time looking them all over. He said I could choose the car and while none of them were my baby, my butterfly, they also weren't to be sneered at. The first I ran my hand gently across was a Porsche GT2, emerald green, and while I'd never driven one, I knew how stupidly fast it was. Next was an Audi R8, but it was the same yellow as Jasper's Lambo, and I immediately dismissed it. Too many bad memories there, including the race I'd won for him.

The third car was old school. Mustang '69 Fastback, it was cherry red, and I felt like that was a good omen for me tonight. I was rocking red all around.

"Thinking about going old school tonight, Riley girl?" Serena asked, her eyes running appreciatively across the Mustang.

I could never imagine any of the Delta heirs driving a car that wasn't built this year.

"Yep," I decided. "This is the one I'll drive in Widowmaker."

Dante grinned, and something told me that's the one he'd been hoping I'd pick all along.

"Ahh, I wish I could go with you," Serena said, her green eyes lit up with old memories. "But got to get home and cook my loves dinner."

I hugged her this time, and she chuckled in my ear. "Thank you," I whispered. "I appreciate you coming to my rescue."

My ribs protested as she squeezed me back. "Girl, you're family. You can come to me anytime you need something."

I was too choked up to say anything, but I hoped she knew how grateful I was to hear those words.

Serena left then, and I slid into the driver's side of the 'stang, flexing both hands on the wheel. I'd taken my black exoskeleton cast off a few days ago, and while my wrist felt a little weaker than usual, there was no pain. I was relieved to have full range of movement back.

"Ready to fuck shit up?" Dante asked, looking more alive than he had for days. His injuries were basically healed now, except for the ribs, and he apparently could handle that with no worries because I never even saw him flinch when he walked or breathed.

Dante hit the button to open his private underground garage, and I started the car, letting the rumble soothe me. For the first time since I'd been ambushed and forced to murder, tension in my chest eased, and I dropped my head back with both hands firmly on the wheel.

"There's nothing better than this," I moaned.

Dante pissed himself laughing, which I ignored to continue my Zen moment.

Before I even opened my eyes, I'd shifted her into gear, and slammed my foot on the accelerator. Dante's laughter turned into a whoop, the crazy bastard, because anyone else would have shit themselves. The Mustang didn't corner quite as smoothly as the last few cars I'd driven, which I'd have to keep in mind for a couple of the turns during the race, but she more than made up for that in pure power.

Sliding into the street, laughter burst from me as adrenalin and joy simultaneously filled me. "Fuck yes!" I shouted, swinging her around a corner, and slamming through the gears as I raced along the mostly deserted street. Dante lived in a quiet area, but we'd be downtown soon because I had to cross through the center of Jersey to get to Widowmaker.

We didn't talk much, cranking the music instead and letting the beats of Dre fill the silence.

That was until we were about a mile from the rendezvous point with Rabbit. Dante had been looking over his shoulder again, the third time in as many minutes, before his eyes locked on his side mirror.

"What?" I said, exasperated. I was dodging traffic at high speed and couldn't take my eyes off the road to see what had his attention.

"We have company," he said simply.

Taking a risk, I shot a glance in the rearview and a familiar Bugatti came into sight. *Muthafucker!*

Beck was one car behind me, and I'd missed him somehow.

"He was out of sight until just then," Dante said, knowing I was pissed. "I actually saw Jasper first."

The yellow Lamborghini was hard to miss, even though I had apparently done that as well. My focus had been in front of me, and I'd missed that there were four somewhat familiar cars following at varying distances behind me.

"Those fuckers picked the wrong chick to mess with," I said with heavy saltiness. "Hold on to your panties, Dante, we're going to lose us some Delta heirs."

Dante grumbled something about "not wearing fucking panties" but he took my warning seriously. His fingers threaded through the oh-shit handle, and he gave me a tight nod to show he was ready.

The corners of my lips pulled up in what was surely an evil grin, and with a quick glance in my mirrors and blind spots, I made my move.

"Fuck me," Dante exclaimed as he gripped the handle with white knuckles and pressed himself tighter into the seat to stop from being thrown around as I gunned the engine and whipped the steering wheel to the side.

The Mustang handled like a dream, jumping eagerly to my commands as I ducked and weaved between the traffic at close to three times the legal speed limits. My left wrist panged a little as I aggressively steered one handed while my right was busy shifting gears, but it was a good sort of pain. It reminded me of everything that had brought me to this point, starting with my parents' deaths.

"Whoa, Riles," Dante gasped as I narrowly missed a pickup truck when I shot through a red light without flinching.

I flicked a quick look at him, but was reassured to see a broad grin on his face. "Shit, Dante," I grumbled, focusing on my break neck driving. "Thought you were questioning my driving for a second there."

Dante made a strangled sound somewhere between a laugh and a groan, but I didn't dare take my attention from the road before me. It was like a maze, and my mind could see a clear path between the obstacles. I'd always been good at labyrinth puzzles, I could just *see* the pattern instantly, and this was no different.

Slamming down through the gears, I hooked a sharp left turn, hugging the curb so tight that my wing mirror missed a post box by an inch. This new road was clearer than the main strip I'd been on, and I risked a glance in my mirrors.

I'd shaken a few of them, but that offensively bright Lambo, and Beck's sexy fucking Bugatti were still holding their own.

"Fuck," I cursed. Of course Jasper was keeping up. Hadn't he told me that he *always* won that stupid rich kid race I'd run for him a few weeks ago? Even with his injuries, he was driving almost as good as me.

Almost.

I was better, though. He—and Beck—were just pushing me to try a bit harder.

"Brace yourself," I murmured to Dante, my sharp gaze snagging onto my next move and my body reacting on instinct.

I jerked the steering wheel to the side—just slightly—and gritted my teeth as the Mustang mounted the curb and we sped toward the worksite on the side of the road. I knew the second Dante figured out what I was doing because he sucked in a sharp breath and sat up straighter in his seat.

"Riley…" He barely got the warning out before my wheels gripped the half completed ramp and shot us up like we were a toy car on a hot wheels track. A wordless shout tore from my best friend's throat as we hit the top of the ramp and then…

Airborne.

It was only for a second, or less, but it was enough that when our wheels came down hard on the second level parking lot on the other side of the gap, my heart was pounding so hard it was practically jumping out of my shirt.

I wrestled control of my wheels again, fighting the steering wheel as we spun out, but in moments I was back in charge and shifting my gears smoothly to gun it out of there.

"Follow *that*, assholes," I muttered, grinning wildly as I peered in my rearview mirror and spotted a distinctive black sports car sitting stationary at the top of the ramp.

Dante started laughing then. A slightly unhinged, hysterical kind of laughter. "Holy fucking shit, Riley. God, I've missed you, girl."

I shot him a quick, manic grin as we peeled out of the parking garage and lost ourselves in the rabbit warren streets behind it. Beck and Jasper didn't stand a fucking chance of following us now. Dante and I knew these streets like the backs of our hands, and now that they didn't have us in their line of sight, they were screwed.

Confident that we'd lost them, I eased off the gas and merged back into the traffic of the main street leading us toward Widowmaker. That little exercise had been fun as shit, but it almost made us late. I could only thank the gods of muscle cars that we'd miraculously avoided police ... or did Beck and all his *powerful connections* have something to do with that?

"That was just a warm up," I told Dante with a smirk. "I still need to thrash some wannabe drivers at the race."

Dante grinned back at me, then whooped with excitement and turned the stereo up.

Chapter 4

A cool breeze sent a shiver through me as I leaned against Dante's Mustang and talked shit with Rabbit. I'd taken my jacket off to drive his Supra, but now that the adrenaline was wearing off I would need to hunt it out again.

"You okay?" Dante murmured, leaning in closer and peering down at me. The bruising on his face had lightened up to a yellowish green, and the shadows from the street lights hid the worst of it. Still, I'd heard him need to shrug off questions several times, blaming it on "business."

"Yeah, just cold." I gave him a smile, and he draped his arm over my shoulders, tugging me in close to the warmth of his body. "Thanks, heat bean." I chuckled, wrapping my arms around his waist and snuggling tighter.

Rabbit barked a laugh, and I frowned at him in confusion. "About damn time," he snickered, giving us a slightly sexual leer. "You've got the patience of a damn saint, my friend." He clapped Dante on the shoulder then swaggered away to chat with someone who had their head under the hood of his tricked out Supra. It had been a dream to drive, that was for sure, but I actually preferred the Mustang.

"What was that about?" I asked Dante, peering up at him from where I was tucked into his chest.

He just shook his head, not meeting my eyes. "Nothing. You all good for this race? That bit of fancy driving you did earlier probably wore down the tread a bit." He kicked one of the tires with his heel, but didn't release me from his embrace. In fact, he shifted a bit so that both arms wrapped around me and held me a bit tighter. "How's your wrist?"

I smiled at his concern. He was such a worry-wart sometimes. "I'm fine, my wrist is fine, the 'stang is fine. We'll nail this, just like every other Widowmaker I've run in."

Dante huffed. "Yeah, well that was when you were driving the butterfly."

I cringed at the mention of my—I mean, *Dante's*—car that I'd crashed. "I still owe you for that."

"Nope," he responded in a gruff voice. "She was always yours anyway. I had the papers put in your name years ago."

My jaw dropped, and I stared up at him. "What? When? Why didn't you tell me?"

He rolled his eyes, but there was a smug smile on his lips. "Because you would have pitched a fit and demanded I change it back. But she was always your car, so it felt wrong having my name on the papers." He shrugged, and his hands rubbed my upper arms. "You should get warmed up, the race starts in five."

I nodded, but hugged him tighter for a moment. He'd done so much for me over the years, words couldn't really express how much I appreciated our friendship. He hugged me back, kissing my head and pressing his face into my dark hair.

Then all of a sudden, he was gone.

"Beck, no!" I screamed in fury as he slammed Dante onto the hood of the Mustang and drew his fist back to punch him in the face. My voice froze him, but his thunderstorm gaze didn't shift from Dante. "Sebastian Roman Beckett, if you don't take your hands off Dante right this fucking second I will never forgive you for what you've done." My voice was low, trembling with anger, and my fists clenched at my sides.

Beck lowered his fist, but didn't let Dante go. "You're saying there's still a chance you will?"

Words failed me as my lips parted, but no sound came out. Beck's stormy gaze captured mine and held me immobile. "Let him go, Beck," I eventually said, ignoring his question. "Go back to Jefferson. You don't belong here."

He held my gaze for another heavy, tense moment. "Neither do you, Butterfly."

I flinched at his use of my nickname.

"Just fuck off, Beck," I whispered tiredly. "No one wants you here, least of all me."

His jaw tightened and his body radiated tension. Slowly, he released Dante's shirt from his iron grip and backed up a step. Call me psychic, but I guessed Dante's intentions and darted forward to grab him by the collar of his jacket before he could launch himself at Beck. Not that I gave a shit if Beck's face got messed up, but I'd seen that dangerous fuck in action. I stopped Dante to spare my friend any more injuries.

"Enough," I snapped at Dante, flicking my death glare at Beck and Jasper. "Dante, we have a race. Let's go."

Dante snarled a curse but followed me when I started heading over to where Rabbit was gathering the racers for a briefing. His hand rested on the small of my back, over the thin red fabric of my tank, and I shivered again. I still hadn't grabbed my jacket and the skin on my arms was pebbling with cold.

"Take your hand off her or I will fucking break it off," a dark voice threatened, and I whipped around to find Beck and Jasper right there.

"Try it," Dante sneered back. "Let's see how long it takes for you to win Riles over after you touch her best friend. *Again.*"

"Hey!" I barked. "That's enough. Briefing is for racers only, now *fuck off.*"

Jasper raised his hand, looking past me to Rabbit and Joe—the race organizer. "Hey, I'd like to race."

Joe gave Jasper a small frown, then leaned to the side to peer at Jasper's obnoxiously bright car. "Uhh ... who are you again? This isn't really a free-for-all."

"I'm friends with the Butterfly," Jasper replied with a cocky-as-fuck grin. He pushed his way past both Beck and Dante to sling his arm over my shoulders. "Right, babe?"

Joey's brows shot up at me. "You vouching for this rich kid, Riley?"

I shot Jasper a glare and shrugged out of his hold, even as a low growl of warning came from Beck. "Fuck no," I spat. "They're harassing me."

Jasper made an offended sound, and his face fell, but I just glared at him. Who the hell did he think he was, pretending like we were all buddy-buddy? They used me. *Played* me. We weren't friends. Not even fucking close.

Joey shrugged and shook his head. "None of my drivers are vouching for you, you're shit out of luck, rich kid. Go sit on the sidelines and watch how the big boys—er, and girls—do it."

There was a small scuffle behind me, but I didn't bother turning around. I knew what I'd find. Some sort of testosterone fueled standoff between Beck and Dante.

That shit was getting real old, real fast.

"Let's roll," Rabbit said with a wicked grin, throwing me a wink. "Ready to get knocked off that throne, Riles? This is my year, I can *feel* it."

I scoffed a laugh, shaking my head as I sidestepped both Beck and Jasper and made my way back to the Mustang. I was just opening my door when he caught up to me. I knew he would.

His hand closed over my bare upper arm, and I shivered—except this time it wasn't from the cold.

"Don't do this, Riley," Beck demanded, his voice rough. "I've heard about this race. People have *died* in this fucking thing."

"No shit, Beck." I laughed with bitterness. "It's called Widowmaker for a reason." I spun around to face him, jerking my arm out of his grip. I shoved him sharply in the chest, forcing him back a step and creating some space between us. "The next time you touch me without permission, I'll make you regret it."

I slid into the Mustang before he could say anything more, but as I slammed the door shut I couldn't help catching his murmured response.

"I already do."

Despite my anger toward him, that small comment felt like it had just cracked my heart in two. Clenching my jaw, I swallowed past the tears that threatened in the face of Beck's *regret* and revved my engine.

"See you at the finish line," I snapped, giving Beck one last glare before taking my car over to join the other racers at the starting point.

LUCKY FOR ME, THE RACERS and spectators at Widowmaker were anything but impressed by Beck and Jasper and their flashy cars. I had no idea where Evan and Dylan had ended up, but they were probably warned not to bother coming by.

This place did not like Delta heirs.

The thought made me snicker as I shifted gears and slammed my foot down a bit harder to increase the gap between me and Rabbit. He hadn't been joking about those NOS upgrades, but all the power in the world was useless if you were a shitty driver.

Not that Rabbit was shit, but he didn't have a patch on me, and he knew it.

The two of us flew over the finish line with a car length between us. We eased off the gas and let our cars slow down gently before circling back to where the cheering spectators waited. Rabbit pulled his car up beside me and rolled down his window as we crawled back toward the crowd, and I did the same.

"Still got it, eh, Butterfly?" He was just teasing, but that nickname had taken on a whole life of its own and I gritted my teeth.

"Never lost it, Rabbit," I replied with a grim smile. "Clean race this time, or what I saw of it."

He jerked his head in a nod. "Joe is drinking, so can't have been any crashes." He nodded ahead where the race organizer had an arm slung around a petite blonde, and a can of something in his other hand.

Rabbit and I had reached the cleared area for parking, and we cut our engines.

"Time to celebrate." He grinned at me, then hopped out of his car and caught the little redhead who practically threw herself at him.

I unclicked my seatbelt and reached for the handle, but before I could grab it the door flew out of my grip and I was snatched out of the vehicle. Arms like steel pinned me between a hard body and the side of the Mustang, and I let out a small squeak of shock and protest.

"I swear to fuck, I want to lock you in a damn cage and never let you out," Beck muttered into the side of my neck where his face was pressed. "Jasper is right, you drive like a fucking wet-dream, but you could have fucking died, Butterfly."

The shock cleared a little and I struggled in his embrace, trying to free myself. All he did was tighten his grip further, and my anger flared. Shifting my weight, I crossed my fingers that my aim was true and brought my knee up. Hard.

Bullseye.

Beck immediately released me, groaning and clutching his junk as I sidestepped out of reach.

"What did I fucking tell you about touching me, Beck?" I snarled at him. "And no chick wants to be locked in a cage, you deranged psychopath."

With a disgusted sneer, I left him cradling his family jewels while I snatched my jacket out of the Mustang and stalked across the abandoned lot to where Dante waited ... with Jasper.

"What the fuck is *he* doing here?" I snapped at Dante, barely sparing a cursory glance at Jasper. My winning mood was officially soured.

Dante heaved a sigh and exchanged a look with Jasper. Since when the fuck did Dante and Jasper know each other well enough to share looks?

"Riles, babe, I think—" Whatever Dante was about to say, I didn't want to hear it.

"Nope." I threw up a hand to cut off his words and shook my head. "You're on my side or theirs. No middle ground." Dante opened his mouth, and I knew he was going to argue, just based on the set of his jaw, so I glared at him harder. "Them or me, Dante."

He held my gaze for a long time, like he was checking if I was serious or not.

"You, obviously," he finally said on a long sigh. "Always you, Riles. But—"

My sharpened death glare made him think twice about whatever he was going to say, and he just shook his head instead.

"Can I say something?" Jasper asked, putting his hand in the air like we were in elementary school or some shit.

"No," I snapped, grabbing Dante's hand and stalking back toward the Mustang.

Beck was limping in our direction, his face drawn, but I breezed past him like he didn't even exist.

"So much for a fun night out," I snapped when Dante joined me in the car and I revved the engine. I could see that the other racers who'd just finished looked confused that I was leaving, but fuck them. I had zero desires to hang around those lying, traitorous bastards a second longer.

We drove in silence for a long time before Dante shifted in his seat to stare at me.

"What pissed you off more?" he asked. "The fact that they played you?

Or that you fell in love with that asshole?"

My jaw dropped, and I shot Dante a glare. "I did *not* fall in love with him," I spluttered my denial, but my cheeks heated and my stomach churned.

"Uh huh," Dante murmured, then cranked the stereo and wound down his window. Apparently that's all the conversation he was in the mood for.

Fucking fine by me. The last thing I wanted to do, was examine whether I was more pissed off at Beck for forcing me to kill a man, or the fact that he made me ... care.

Chapter 5

Dante dropped me off at Jefferson the next morning, and I waited until the very last minute to get out at Ducis Academy. A uniform, makeup and hair shit, had been delivered to Dante's last night, so I was dressed the part. Even if I was all broken inside.

"See you later, Riles," he called through the window. "Call me if you need anything."

I nodded and blew him a kiss. "I will. Drive carefully back to Jersey."

He had shit to do this week and couldn't hang around to babysit me. Which was fine. I was planning on keeping my head down, ignoring Delta, and moving into my new apartment. One promise Catherine was going to keep.

"Go away," I growled as Evan fell into step beside me on my way to class.

"Would if I could," he muttered on a sigh, but it was his irritated tone that had me pausing in the empty hallway and scowling at him.

"What the fuck does that mean?" I demanded. "I didn't ask you to stalk me, so just *go away*."

Evan rolled his eyes, scrubbing a hand through his brown and blond streaked hair. "Cut the shit, Riles. It's Beck you're pissed at so quit taking it out on the rest of us."

Outrage choked me for a moment, and I stared at him like he'd just grown three heads. "Ex-*cuse* me? I'm not pissed at *you*? Oh, I guess I just imagined that happy family bullshit at breakfast just *hours* before masked goons kidnapped me *naked* and then I got forced to *shoot someone*." I was trying really fucking hard to keep my voice down, but hot pulses of anger had me on the edge of losing control.

Evan darted his gaze around to make sure no one was listening before glaring at me. "You know it's not safe to talk about that shit here, Riley." His voice was pitched low and full of ... what? Regret? Doubtful. "But it's not an option to leave you alone. Things ... shit has happened while you've been gone and it's important that people know you're still one of us."

I scoffed a humorless laugh. "I've fallen for this cloak and dagger bullshit one too many times, Evan. Why should I believe a damn word out of your mouth?"

He didn't reply, his jaw tight and his fists curled by his side as he looked down the hallway, like he was waiting for...

"Of course," I sneered. "You were nothing but a glorified stalling tactic."

Beck stormed toward us with long strides, and I shook my head. I couldn't face him again so soon. Not after how rattled he'd left me after the race. Despite my tough bitch act, and my strong words to Dante, when we'd gotten home I'd spent the whole night crying. It was only through the grace of makeup that the evidence didn't show today in my puffy eyes.

"I'm late," I muttered, hurrying toward my class and slipping inside mere moments before Beck reached us.

I was totally unsurprised to see Evan stroll casually into the class about five minutes later, despite the fact that he was a fucking senior in the university part of Ducis. Apparently the teachers didn't see an issue with it either as Mr. Greensmith barely batted an eyelid at Evan's presence. Money talks, I guess.

Since the incident where I was forced to kill a man, the real world had faded away, and I'd been living in a weird suspended reality. So it was no surprise that I'd completely forgotten my class was calculus. And being in calculus meant…

"Riley!" Eddy's familiar voice hurt almost as much as Beck's.

I slowly lifted my eyes and met her wide, worried ones. "Yes," I said without inflection.

She blinked at me, and my chest ached at the wounded expression on her face.

"I've been so worried about you," she said softly. "Jasper wouldn't tell me anything, you weren't answering your phone, and you haven't been in school for over a week."

I shot Evan the quickest side eye ever, and he gave a brief shake of his head.

She doesn't know.

The worst fucking shit of my life had happened in the past week, and my best friend didn't know. Of course she didn't. This was all about the fucking *heirs* of Delta. But … she was still part of them, of this world that I was determined to cut out of my life as much as possible.

She took a shaky step closer. "Did I do something?"

My eyes burned as I lurched to my feet. Pushing past her, I sprinted from the room, slamming open the door of the nearest bathroom and hauling ass inside.

My breathing was so fast that I felt light headed, and I wondered if maybe I was hyperventilating or something, because I couldn't seem to catch my breath. Bracing myself against the sinks, I stared at my reflection. Despite my skill with makeup, I'd barely managed to hide the dark circles under my eyes. Even if I hadn't had Beck angst keeping me awake, nightmares were a constant lately. I'd been having them ever since I found myself in this world, only now I could add a gunshot and blood spatter across walls to the fucked up visions.

The door opened again, and I knew it was Eddy without even turning my head.

"Girl, seriously. We are not leaving this fucking room until you talk to me."

Straightening, I turned to her, relieved that my breathing had returned to normal. The tightness in my chest remained though. "There's nothing to talk about. I can't trust anyone involved with Delta."

Eddy's face fell. "I don't understand. You were fitting in really well, all of the guys consider you one of them. The first chick, at least since they were adults, that they've ever truly cared about. What happened to screw it all up?"

They fucking happened!

I wanted to scream, at the top of my lungs. "They betrayed me," I said. "I trusted them, and they let me walk right into a fucked up situation."

Eddy threw her hands up, exasperation creasing her face. "You know that Delta controls them. They have to play the game, otherwise shit gets really messed up. You have to ignore the bad stuff and remember the times that were real … remember how they made you feel when everything was on the line."

Anger washed away my sadness. "If I hear the word *game* one more goddamn time, I'm gonna lose my mind."

Some of my anger was forced because I was trying really hard not to think about her other words. I did remember lots of times those fuckers had been there for me. Starting with the plane crash—they'd saved my life. The training. The family breakfast. How Dylan had told me to remember that moment when we were all together. Beck had said that this was the only real thing they had. Something worth more than money.

So why hadn't they stepped up for me this time? How could they let me walk into something like murder without a fucking heads-up? How could they hurt my best and oldest friend? Threaten to kill him?

"What about me?" Eddy demanded. "I didn't betray you. I'm your best friend and that's not going to change, no matter what our fucked up parents and their heirs do."

She wore her stubborn expression, arms crossed over her chest, but the hurt was still there in her eyes.

A long sigh left me. "I love you, Eddy. You're the first chick I've bonded with in a really long time. But right now, I need some time. I'm angry and hurt, and I know it's shitty of me because you don't have a clue what actually went down, but please try and understand, right now I can't be around you. You remind me too much of what I've lost."

Needing to escape from the pain in my chest—indirectly related to the girl across from me— I pushed past her toward the door.

She stopped me with softly spoken words. "Have you even given them a chance to explain? Not everything is black and white in our world. It might have looked like betrayal from the outside, but maybe they were still working for you. For the five of you."

I didn't turn back or answer, but again, those words hit a soft spot inside of me. I hadn't given them a chance to explain, even though they had tried a million times. I couldn't imagine a single thing they could have said to justify their actions, but…

I left, unable to deal with Eddy or my thoughts a moment longer. Evan was in the hallway waiting for me, and he wasn't alone. Clearly he'd had to call in the reinforcements to deal with me.

Beck, Jasper, and Dylan stepped forward the moment I walked out. I scowled, stopping them in their tracks. Smoothing my face into something neutral, I looked across the group. My eyes resting on each perfect, gorgeous face. Despite my best efforts, I did care about these assholes, and I wondered if it would ever stop hurting to be around them.

"Why are you here?" I asked shortly.

"We need to tell you something," Jasper said, his eyes doing that pleading thing that he was so good at. "The school is not safe grounds any longer. We've just learned that Huntley has enrolled a student here. We don't have any other information yet, but for now, we need to appear as a strong, united team. We cannot allow them to see any weakness in our ranks."

Fear and panic pushed through my apathy. "You're lying."

This had to be some sort of ploy to get me to fall back in line with them. It had to be, because this was their territory, and they still had all the power. Right?

Beck shook his head. "It's the truth. There is a lot you don't know. A vote coming up that could change the structure of our council, and this is the start of Huntley's play for power. Showing a united front amongst Delta's successors has never been so critical."

"No," I said without giving it another thought. "I won't be pushed around by you like this. If this hasn't come from the ones controlling my strings, then you can all go fuck yourselves. I do official Delta business only."

Beck's eyes were blazing when they met mine, and the darkness in them was a warning. A warning that I was pushing him past the point of comfort. That he was going to figure out a way to punish me for making life difficult.

Bring it on. He'd crushed me so hard that I was basically half a foot shorter, in spirit at least, so they better bring their best.

"If you don't join us, Butterfly," Beck said softly, his tone causing every hair on my arms to rise, "then we'll have no choice but to make it very clear that the rejection was caused by us. We need to show strength and unity. An heir choosing to leave us, especially a new, female one, is a weakness in our ranks. But if it looks like it's us hazing you, pushing you out to prove your worth. That isn't the same."

I snorted. "What the fuck can you do? Gonna beat me up and stuff me in a locker?"

They didn't answer, and then one by one, they turned their backs on me, and walked away.

"Remember that we warned you, Riles," Jasper said, over his shoulder.

"Whenever you want back into the fold, you know where to find us," Evan added.

Beck and Dylan didn't say anything, but the looks they leveled on me before they exited the hall had so much *emotion* in them, that for a beat, I couldn't catch my breath.

Eddy, who must have been standing nearby, even though I hadn't noticed her the entire time, stepped up to my side. "What the hell just happened?" I asked her, confused as fuck.

She turned a pale face and wide eyes on me. "They're publicly rejecting you, Riles. Whatever you're mad about, you need to get over it right now."

My middle name might as well have been stubborn. "Hell no! They're the ones who fucked up. They betrayed me. There is no way I'm going to just forgive it all now because they've forced me into some sort of shitty position."

She shook her head, movements fast and jerky. "No! You don't understand. Seriously. They rule this school. Every girl wants to fuck them, every guy wants to be them. You've been under their protection almost from the first moment you walked in here. If that protection disappears ... worse, if it's clear that you're not one of them now, then the vultures will tear you to fucking pieces. You've been where all of them want to be, and they're going to punish you for that."

Seriously?

"I think you're overreacting. Despite their opinions on the matter, they're not actually gods. And no one cares about me. I'll just be forgotten."

Eddy shook her head, making a small disparaging sound. "Trust me. You were in the inner circle and everyone was jealous of you. You should have heard the chicks bitch about how you didn't deserve what you had, and the guys all guessed what an awesome fuck you must be. Bottom line, now that you're on the outs, they'll make your life hell. You said the guys aren't gods, but in this school, they might as well be."

I couldn't believe her, because if I did, then I'd be right where those assholes wanted me: needing their help and protection. With a shake of my head, I strode back to calculus, entering the room without knocking or offering any apology or explanation. That was how it usually worked when I was with the guys, but this time Mr. Greensmith leveled a glare on me.

"I'm not sure how your old school worked, Ms. Jameson, but here in Ducis, we do not just run in and out of classrooms like we own the place. See me after class."

"Uh, sorry," I said, stumbling back to my desk and sank down into the chair.

That was the first time I'd been reprimanded in this school, and the teacher had a point: I had been treating this place like I owned it. But no one had an issue until now … Eddy's words ran through my head.

Could it really be happening already? Was it possible that people cared this much about the opinions of the Delta heirs? I tried to discreetly look around the room, and more than one set of eyes were on me. But … that didn't mean anything. I mean, people had been curious about me since day one. I was a Deboise by birth but not by name; I was part of their elite crowd, but never actually claimed in any way. Beck and I had a relationship of some sort, but almost no one knew about that.

I was an enigma. That was the only reason they were looking at me. It had to be.

Focusing on the teacher for the rest of the lesson, I managed to take one page of notes and gain zero understanding of what we were learning. When the bell rang and the students filed out, I slowly made my way to his desk.

"I really am sorry," I started, as soon as we were alone.

He didn't seem to care about an apology though, already writing something on a green piece of paper, his lips pursed, making his wrinkles a little more defined. "Detention slip," he said, handing it out to me. "Next time you're late. Or you leave without permission, it'll be two. See you this afternoon."

With a low, almost inaudible groan, I reached out and took the slip before I tucked it into my folder. "It won't happen again," I told him, and then spun to rush from the room. No way in hell was I going to be late for my next class.

The guys might have won the first battle, but I was going to win the war. I was determined.

Chapter 6

By the time the lunch break bell chimed, I was more than ready for the detention. At least there—hopefully—I would be left alone.

News of the Delta boys "rejecting" me had traveled like fucking wildfire, and by the time I'd left calculus every eye in the school was on me. For several classes, I was just stared at, but come lunchtime—when I quite deliberately chose to sit as far away from the boys as possible—it was like the floodgates opened. Some bitch tried to trip me before I even got to my table, and it was only thanks to Eddy's shouted warning that I didn't end up wearing my massive, overflowing plate of roast chicken, vegetables, and gravy.

In my defense, while I despised almost everything about Militant Delta and their dodgy, shadowed world … the food wasn't one of those things. The food was something I'd actively missed, and I would have been pissed if that bitch had made me waste it.

"You sure you want to sit here?" I asked Eddy with an arched brow as I placed my tray down and sat. "In case you didn't get the memo, I'm public enemy number one now."

Eddy snorted a laugh. "Oh, girl. No one missed *that* memo, trust me."

I glared at her, and she just rolled her eyes and shrugged. "I'm still a Langham, even if I'm not a successor. The boys withdrew their protection from you, not me."

I glared harder. "Gee, thanks."

"It's entirely within your power to stop it, Riles. I don't understand what they did to get you so worked up, anyway?" It was posed as a question, her head tilted slightly to the side and for a moment I just wanted to tell her everything. But that would mean admitting to murder.

My breath escaped in a heavy sigh, and I poked at my food. "I can't tell you."

Eddy nodded, her eyes downcast. It was clear she was hurt. She'd spent her whole life around the secrets of Militant Delta and now here I was, her best friend, keeping secrets from her.

"I'm sorry—" I started, but she shook her head.

"I get it," she said with just a touch of bitterness. "I just think you're being stupid. Or stubborn. Whatever, same thing in this situation."

I groaned and scrubbed my face with my hands. I'd only been back at school for half a day and it already felt like a fucking lifetime.

"Change the subject," I muttered, trying to find a topic of conversation that didn't make me want to rip my head off. "Uh … wanna come look at real estate with me this afternoon?"

My heart wasn't in the offer. I was still leery as fuck of all things even remotely Delta related—Eddy included—but knowing that the entire school planned on hazing me, a friend in my court surely wasn't the worst idea. So, fake it till you make it. Right?

Eddy's brows shot up, a forkful of lettuce halfway to her mouth. "Real estate? For what?"

My lips curled up in a half grin. "I'm getting my own place. Debitch and I came to an agreement."

Eddy's jaw dropped. "Uh, does Beck know?" She answered before I had a chance. "I'm going to guess no."

I shrugged. "Doubtful. Unless Catherine told him? What does it matter?"

My friend's eyes cut across the lunch room to where I *knew* Beck was watching us. I could practically feel his eyes burning holes in my back. "We all live within the Delta compound for a reason, babe. There have been like, loads of assassination attempts on the guys ... not to mention Oscar." Her voice dropped to a whisper as fear decorated her face. "I just think Beck is going to have an issue with it. Especially now."

I laughed a bitter, humorless sound. "Beck has issues with a lot of things right now. Doesn't mean I should give two shits what he thinks."

Just as I finished saying that, something wet hit me on the cheek ... and stuck there. Horrified, I raised my hand and swiped the gob of saliva soaked napkin paper from my skin and turned my death glare in the direction of where it'd come from. A pack of cackling students congratulated one of the boys for his superior aim, and a blonde girl I'd never seen before smirked at me like she'd just won some sort of competition.

"Who the fuck is that?" I muttered, gritting my teeth and turning my back on the table of snickering cretins. I wasn't prepared to take on the whole school. Not yet, anyway.

Eddy wrinkled her nose in distaste, sneering in blondie's direction. "*That is why the guys are going into major freak out mode. Katelyn Huntley.*"

I spluttered the sip of water I'd just taken. "Sorry, fucking *what?*"

"They didn't tell you? Seems a bit stupid," Eddy was muttering, and I snapped my fingers at her to bring the focus back.

"They told me there was a spy, but they didn't say it was an actual fucking Huntley heir. I thought Delta owned this school?" I was trying to keep my volume down, so my words were coming out in a harsh whisper. "How is this possible?"

She shrugged. "Beats me, no one tells me anything, remember? I only know who she is because I hacked into her school records just before lunch. She's enrolled under Katelyn French, but her birth certificate has her surname as Huntley. She's the youngest daughter of Graeme Huntley, CEO of Huntley Tech. Oh, and his wife, Cunt— Christie Huntley."

It was very clear that Eddy was not a fan of the wife. If she was anything like the daughter—my one minute impression of her anyway—then I wasn't surprised.

A dull ache was forming behind my right eyeball and I rubbed at my forehead. *A Huntley heir.* Fucking typical of the boys to leave that minor detail out.

"She looks like a bitch," I commented, casting another look in the new girl's direction. She'd moved fast, already surrounding herself with fawning acolytes who appeared to be pandering to her every whim—including shooting a spitball at me.

Eddy snorted. "She's that and more. Worse yet? She's spending a lot of time hanging off Beck, which is both weird and screwed up. They're enemies."

Jealousy and primal possessiveness flared up inside me, and I had to swallow it back with conscious effort. "Good for her," I said, keeping my tone as neutral as possible. "They'd make a lovely couple." The words were like acid on my tongue, and suddenly I'd totally lost my appetite.

My friend started laughing, grinning at me like a hyena. "You're a sucky liar, Riley Jameson." She nudged my tray. "Are you done with that? You should probably get going to the gym before the bell rings. I can only imagine what these bitches will have cooked up over the lunch break." She shuddered, and I groaned.

"Fuck it." I sighed as I followed Eddy to put our trays away. "No amount of high school bullying can make me forgive Beck for what he did." She made a noise, and I realized what I'd said. "Or any of them."

Eddy gave me a quick hug, like she was wishing me luck in my next class, then headed off in the direction of her own, leaving me with my gloomy thoughts.

Fucking Beck. Yes, I was the most pissed off at him, and rightly fucking so! None of the other boys had lured me into their bed. None of the others had made me care. Made me think *they* cared.

Pain rippled through me as I acknowledged the falsity in that line of thought. I *had* thought they cared. All of them.

But not like Beck.

WHEN THE REST OF THE girls in my class entered the gym and saw me sitting there already in my sports clothes, their scowls could have stripped paint. Eddy was right. They'd been planning something.

Even so, they satisfied themselves throughout the class by tripping me, throwing balls at my face—which I managed to dodge—and shoulder checking me way more than a game of volleyball called for.

The whole thing was baffling. They acted like they would get some kind of prize for being bitches toward me. Maybe they thought they would? In the form of Beck's dick down their throat in a dirty supply closet.

The thought should have made me roll my eyes with contempt and disgust, but all my body could conjure up was burning jealousy. Goddamn Sebastian Roman fucking Beckett was still under my skin.

After the class finished I hung around as long as humanly possible before entering the locker rooms. As badly as I wanted to skip the whole showering and changing situation, I smelled. Bad. The amount of effort it had taken to evade the worst of the attacks during volleyball had left me sweating and exhausted.

"Hello?" I called out cautiously as I peered around the seemingly empty locker room. "Anyone in here?"

No sound came back to me except the dripping of the showers. I'd managed to kill a solid twenty minutes *slowly* packing up the volleyball equipment and it was already well into the next class period so I'd have been surprised if anyone else was still here. Still, it didn't hurt to check.

Quickly as I could, I checked all cubicles to verify that I was indeed alone, then grabbed my stuff and locked myself into a shower. Only once the little bolt clicked over did I let out the breath I was holding.

"Fuck me," I muttered under my breath as I stripped off my sweaty sports clothes and hung them on the back of the door. "This social outcast shit is exhausting."

I took my time in the shower because, screw it. I was already so late for my next class that I may as well take my time. It wasn't until I'd dried off and pulled on my underwear that I noticed.

"Fuck," I cursed, holding up my uniform. Someone had taken to it with a pair of scissors or a knife or something, because my skirt was shredded into ribbons and my shirt was full of holes. I hadn't noticed when I'd grabbed it from my locker because it'd been tucked into the top of my bag where I'd left it.

A rustle of fabric was all the warning I got, a split second before a hand darted over the top of my shower door and snatched my sweaty sports uniform—leaving me with nothing to wear.

"Hey!" I yelled, slamming the door open and racing out to try and catch the clothing thief. "Of course it's you," I sneered, spotting Brittley—Beck's fake girlfriend and all around town bicycle—standing by the door, holding my clothes up like a trophy.

"I knew this day would come," she crowed, her eyes gleaming in triumph.

I arched a brow, propping my hands on my hips and giving her a withering glare. "What day? Seeing me in my underwear? I had no idea you were so into chicks, Butters."

Her cheeks heated and a small scowl formed between her brows. "It's Brittley, you fucking weirdo. And I meant I was waiting for the day Beck and his boys retracted their protection of you. You're fair fucking game now."

I couldn't help it. I laughed.

Brittley's face boiled with rage. "You think this is funny?" she screeched. "I'm not joking around. I'm going to destroy you and there's nothing you can do about it!"

"You really think so?" I challenged her, not able to wipe the smirk from my face. "Try it. I guarantee it's not going to work out how you think it will."

A brief moment of indecision crossed her face before she tilted her chin up in ignorant stubbornness. "You think I'm bluffing? I'll show you." She spat the words at me like a curse, then stepped backward out of the locker rooms—taking my clothes with her.

I heaved a sigh and mentally cursed myself out. I just had to push her. Why couldn't I have kept my trap shut and lured her closer until I could grab my clothes back? Now I was going to have to face the whole school in nothing but my French lace panties and bra. At least it was a cute set.

Chewing my lip, I debated wrapping back up in my towel, then quickly dismissed it. Brittley and her crew were seeking to humiliate me, so I couldn't show them even the slightest bit of embarrassment.

Rolling my shoulders, I sucked in a deep breath, pulled up my metaphorical big girl panties, and barged out of the locker room. Right into the middle of the crowd gathered around Brittley—who kept sneaking glances at Katelyn Huntley like she was seeking validation from the new girl.

Somehow in my exchange with Brittley, I'd missed the fact that the end of class bell had rung and more people were gathering by the second.

Cat calls and jeering almost deafened me, but I still caught it when Katelyn made a bitchy comment about my supposed promiscuity. Same old narrative from high school bullies, it was almost boring in its predictability.

I rolled my eyes and folded my arms under my breasts, totally unconcerned with being in my underwear. Why should I be? My swimsuit covered less skin, and that didn't stop me wearing it in public during the summer months.

"Hilarious," I remarked in a tone dryer than the Sahara. "Now give my clothes back, Britters."

A cruel, slightly deranged smile played across her face, but she made no move to hand my sports uniform back. In fact, she handed it to Katelyn, who grinned at me as she poured her soda all over it.

My jaw clenched, and I fought back the urge to march over there and punch this blonde bitch right in her perfect nose. I could break it, Dylan had taught me how.

Just as I was giving in to the impulse, I felt the heavy weight of eyes on me. Beck.

Turning slightly, I met his gaze from behind a group of younger jocks taking pictures with their mobiles. His eyes were blazing with fury and his whole body radiated tension, but to everyone else, he looked totally blank. Uncaring.

Narrowing my eyes at him, I changed my trajectory. Brittley and her new BFF were forgotten as I shoved the amateur photographers aside and confronted Beck and the guys.

"You asked for this," Beck said so softly I was sure no one else would have heard him. It only infuriated me further, though, and I let that anger show in my glare for a tense moment before breaking our eye contact and looking to his side.

"Jasper," I said in a neutral tone, "Give me your sweatshirt."

Jaspers eyes widened and he ran a hand through his platinum blond hair. "Riles," he groaned, flicking his gaze at Beck and shaking his head reluctantly. "You know I can't."

His words, like Beck's, were quiet. The students around us had all backed up, giving us a wide berth as they waited eagerly for the Delta Elite to give me some sort of verbal slap down.

"Let me rephrase," I snapped, narrowing my eyes at him. "Give me your sweatshirt and I'll forgive you." His jaw dropped slightly, and he looked torn. "Prove to me that you didn't fake our friendship for your own gain, Jasper."

He held my gaze, and I recognized all the guilt and regret within his. He only hesitated a second longer before unzipping his hoodie and tugging it off. "Sorry, bro," he muttered to Beck, ducking his head to avoid the rage filled death glare that Beck was aiming at the both of us.

Jasper wrapped his body-warmed hoodie over my shoulders, and I wasted no time stuffing my arms in and zipping it closed. I wasn't embarrassed or humiliated to be in my underwear—like those bitches had hoped—but it was only early spring and I was fucking freezing.

My shorter stature thankfully meant Jasper's hoodie covered my ass, but I was still cold as shit so the rest of the school day could kiss my ass. I was getting out of there. I'd deal with the detention and missed classes later.

Jasper grabbed my hand and started leading me out to the student parking lot, but I couldn't help myself. I turned over my shoulder and gave Beck a smirk and the middle finger.

"You're going to be the death of me, Riles," Jasper complained as I hurried across the freezing parking lot behind him. "Do you have any idea how badly I'm going to get chewed out for taking your side over Beck's? He's going to kill me. Oh my god, I just committed suicide for a chick with nice tits."

He was fast deteriorating into melodrama, and I couldn't help laughing a little at his expense. "Oh stop it, drama queen," I teased him, "Beck isn't actually going to do anything to you. His ego is just a little bruised, and if you ask me, it's about damn time. Now, can I drive?"

We'd just reached his canary yellow Lambo and Jasper threw his hands up, mouthing words at the sky like he was cursing out a god for landing me in his life.

"Sure," he finally said on a heavy sigh, tossing me the keys. "Only cuz you drive like a wet dream and I need to enjoy my final moments on this earth."

I snorted a laugh but happily slid behind the wheel of his sports car. Maybe I should thank Brittley ... this was a much better use of my afternoon than sitting in detention.

Chapter 7

BECK

"This is getting out of hand," Dylan told me, totally unnecessarily. As if I didn't fucking know. As if that scene in the hallway hadn't made me almost totally lose my control and throw Riley's lush ass over my shoulder like a caveman.

Fucking hell.

"No shit," I snapped back, staring after Jasper's obnoxious yellow Lambo as it peeled out of the Ducis Academy parking lot, carrying my girl away. "I want every fucking phone in this school wiped of all photos. Not one image of Riley in her underwear had better hit the internet or I will break some faces."

"I'm on it," Evan replied, whipping out his own phone and scrolling for the right contact. As tempted as I was to physically snatch all those phones and stomp all over them, Delta had more subtle ways of getting it done.

From the corner of my eye, I saw him pause before hitting dial.

"Is there a problem?" I demanded, glaring at him.

Evan's jaw clenched, and he darted a sharp look around us—probably checking that none of the other students were within earshot—before replying.

"Yeah, Beck," he said quietly, "I have a problem with all of this. I hate leaving Riley at their mercy. They're fucking animals when they smell fresh game, and we all know it."

"I agree," Dylan muttered, "This doesn't sit right."

I snorted a sarcastic laugh, unable to help myself. "Of course you don't like it, Dylan. If you had your way, Riley would be playing the part of your girlfriend."

I wasn't being dramatic. When we'd discussed how to best handle Riley's safety at school, Dylan had offered to be her "fake" boyfriend to keep the haters away and divert attention away from my clear weakness where she was concerned.

Not that Riley would have ever gone for it, given how pissed she was at all of us. But I shot that suggestion down pretty fast. I hadn't expected her to take this angle, though. The whole threat of publicly denouncing her had been nothing but bluster and bullshit. But one of Katelyn's little bitches had been spying on us and we'd been forced into a corner.

Fucking appearances.

"She'll come around," I told them both, but really I was trying to convince myself. "She's not stupid, and Jasper will talk her down. It'll be fine."

Dylan grunted a disagreeing noise. "She's not stupid, but she's damn stubborn. I think she'll put up with a whole lot more than a bit of public nudity before we're forgiven." He eyed me up with pity. "You especially."

I clenched my teeth hard to prevent punching my best friend in the face. "I'm aware that I fucked up. That we fucked up. But she will get over it, in time."

This time it was Evan who sighed and gave me a skeptical look. "Whatever you say, boss."

"In the meantime," I continued like they hadn't just been questioning my judgment, "we need to keep an eye on her, from a distance. As much as possible, just try to keep her in sight. Delta won't let us remove Katelyn until they know what Huntley is up to, but I don't trust her near Riley."

Both of my friends nodded their agreement then headed out. Dylan was no doubt going to tail Riley because it was fast turning into his favorite pastime, while Evan was dealing with getting the pictures erased from every phone in Ducis Academy.

"Quite the show your little throwaway put on for the school," a sultry, sarcastic voice commented, and I didn't need to look to know who'd just slinked up.

"Fuck off, Katelyn," I snapped.

She made a sound of indignation and batted her overly mascaraed eyelashes at me. "Such hostility, Sebastian. I thought our generation was meant to forge alliances, not continue the warring ways of our parents."

"Don't call me that," I told her with a growl underscoring my words. "We are not friends, and I have no interest in forging any sort of alliance with a common high school bully like you."

She laughed a fake laugh, and the sound grated on my ears. "You act like I had something to do with your little tramp's striptease. I promise, I was just as shocked as everyone else." She paused, grinning like a shark. "Besides, isn't poor orphan Riley on the outs with you all now? So why do you care who pulls innocent little pranks on her?"

She cocked her head to the side, and I had to resist the urge not to kill her on the spot. "We don't. But you're acting childish and Delta has no use for children, so cut it out."

This actually seemed to offend her, and she raised her chin as though to argue the subject with me further.

"I have more important places to be," I told her in a bored voice. "Go torture someone else with your whining."

Without waiting for her response, I headed across the parking lot and slid into my car. Our attendance at Ducis was becoming a bit of a joke since Riley had started, but we'd all graduate regardless.

Katelyn was proving a bigger problem than I'd first given her credit for … which meant she needed to be dealt with. If only Delta council would let us handle her.

I hesitated a moment before starting my car, my head filled with images of Riley's determined, beautiful face as she cut her deal with Jasper.

Fucking Judas. Not that I blamed him… I'd rather she forgive him than stay mad at all of us. She needed some people in her camp to get her through all the shitty crap that came with Delta, and if it couldn't be me, then I was glad it was Jasper.

Unable to stop myself, I opened my phone and tapped out a message to her, hitting send before I could talk myself out of it.

Me: Riles, baby, are you okay? Where the fuck did you go?

It made me sound like a pussy whipped prick, and I didn't even care.

Chapter 8

We'd barely even left the academy when Eddy started blowing up my phone. I'd changed my mind *again* about keeping her at arm's length for multiple reasons, but high on that list was her own safety, so I rejected all her calls and ignored her messages. Catherine's threat to break Eddy's fingers still echoed around my head, and it made me nauseous to think she might actually be hurt to force my compliance.

Still, it was a moot point when Jasper immediately took her call and told her where we were.

"Really?" I muttered, glaring at him when he hung up.

He frowned in confusion, tilting his head to the side. "What? Why are you pissy at Eddy? She didn't know anything about … uh … you know."

My glare flattened out further. "About the four of you playing me so I'd trust you enough that I wouldn't see the corner you were backing me into until it was too late? I never thought she did. *Eddy* wasn't faking our friendship." My voice was dry and harsh, not bothering to hide my residual anger.

Jasper's mouth tightened, and he dropped his gaze from mine in a clear sign of guilt. "We weren't faking it, Riles," he murmured with a sigh. "Not totally. Or ... not at the end."

Ignoring that statement, I pulled up in front of a very impressive apartment complex, and I got out of the car to find Stewart already waiting for me on the sidewalk.

"Miss Riley," he said, his eyes twinkling as he took a step closer.

I reached out and hugged him, because we were kindred spirits. Both trapped and working for Catherine Debitch. Stew cleared his throat as he stepped back before he held a bag out to me. "I brought clothes as requested, and the rest of your wardrobe is being packed up as we speak. You'll be ready to move the moment you find an apartment."

Not a moment too soon. I slipped back into Jasper's car, and ruffled through my bag, finding jeans to slip on under Jasper's hoodie. There were shoes as well, which I pulled on, and then I was good to apartment hunt.

The one I was after was on the third floor, which was also the top floor, and we had to go past a doorman, who asked for identification before we could access the elevator. The agent was waiting for us inside, and after a quick greeting, I moved straight to the huge bay windows that were a centerpiece of the main living area.

"It's a million dollar view," the agent gushed, moving in next to me. "Not to mention the hardwood floors, fireplace, and top notch security."

I didn't bother to join her in the over enthusiastic speech, I just nodded. "We'll take it," I said with a tight smile. The apartment was gorgeous, but even more importantly, it wasn't near Catherine. "Stew, can you do the paperwork stuff?" I looked to where the silver haired, well suited gentleman was standing politely near the door.

He gave me a small nod then turned a charming smile on the agent. "Shall we?" He indicated for her to join him at the dining table to sign the necessary papers. "I believe Miss Riley would like to move in immediately, so we had best get going on these papers."

The agent spluttered something about bank transfers and keys, but I tuned them out as I turned my attention back to the view. Stewart had assured me that if I liked something, he'd use the force of Delta to ensure I'd move in on the same day. Money talked.

"So this is the one, huh?" Jasper commented, joining me as I wandered out to the balcony and leaned on the railing. I nodded, and he gave me a lopsided smile. "Nice."

I shrugged. "It's only temporary. Despite the lengths you've all gone to lock me down, I'm not just rolling over and accepting my fate."

His grin spread wider. "I never thought you would."

My phone vibrated in my pocket—again—and I sighed. It was probably Eddy, and seeing as Jasper already told her where to meet us it was pointless to ignore her. I slipped the phone out and clicked the side button to light up the screen then grimaced.

Not Eddy.

"Fuck off," I muttered to my phone, swiping my thumb over the screen to delete the message from Beck.

Jasper made a noise that sounded suspiciously like a laugh, and I glared death at him. "Don't start with me," I warned, and he held his hands up in surrender.

"Wouldn't dream of it," he replied with a grin. "I'm back in your good graces and that's all that matters to me. Beck can clean his own shit up."

I laughed. At least he was honest about *that*. "Some messes can't be cleaned, no matter how much scrubbing you do."

My cynical comment wiped the smile from Jasper's face, and he shifted uncomfortably, diverting his gaze back inside the apartment that Catherine had just bought for me. "Hey, it looks like Stew might be a while on this paperwork. Want to meet Eddy down the road at that burger joint?"

"Sure," I agreed. My phone buzzed again in my pocket, and I ignored it, pretty confident that it was Beck again. "Just make sure she's alone. I won't be held responsible for my actions if anyone else tags along."

Jasper gave me a small frown, like he wasn't totally sure if I was serious or not, then quickly tapped out a message on his phone. "All good, let's go."

WE CHOSE A TABLE NEAR the back, where it was darker and we had more privacy. Eddy burst in about ten minutes after us, still dressed in her Ducis uniform.

"Riley!" she exclaimed, sinking into the booth next to me, her arms wrapping me up in a hug. "Are you okay?"

I shrugged. "Yeah, nothing like a bit of public nudity to give you an awesome reputation."

Eddy grimaced, her lips pressed tightly together. "Don't worry about it. I mentioned it to Dad, and he has Delta tech people wiping it from social media. It'll creep up again, but they'll stay on top of it until the interest dies down."

Crossing my arms, I dropped my head onto them. "This day sucks," I said softly. I still wasn't embarrassed, I just didn't get this thing with teenagers posting every fucking thing they did and saw onto social media. I mean, why? Who cared if I was wearing underwear in school. I hadn't actually been naked.

"Are you ready to order?" The waiter made his appearance, looking nervous as he stared at Jasper. The pen was shaking slightly in his hand.

"Yep," Jasper said, confident as always. He rattled off his order, and Eddy followed, and I just picked the first burger and fries that looked appealing.

The guys hurried off then, and I snorted. "You four do not deserve your reputation."

Jasper looked affronted. "You take that back! We worked fucking hard for our reputation."

Eddy laughed out loud, and I joined her, because Jasper was only partly kidding. The Delta successors loved their power and privilege. If only all the bad shit didn't go with it.

Jasper leaned back in his chair, arms spread out on either side of him. "Everything will be okay now. Riles will come back into the fold, the bullshit at school will stop, and we'll make sure Katelyn Huntley gets the fuck out of our territory."

"Nope," I said stubbornly, crossing my arms. "Riley will not be coming back into any fold. None. End of story."

Jasper and Eddy exchanged a glance before they leaned in closer to me. "Riles, do you understand what you're saying?" Eddy started softly. "Today was only the beginning. It will get worse. They're animals at that school, and now they have a new zoo keeper to stir them up."

Jasper nodded, for once serious. "Katelyn is bad news. She's definitely causing trouble behind the scenes, and I can't protect you at school. What happened today ... that's a one off, unless you crawl back to us. I have to keep a united front there..." His eyes went really wide. "Even though you know I'm on your side here."

I clenched my fists together, anger, my old friend, giving me the strength to say, "I will never crawl back, not even to keep myself safe at school. I know this is some sort of bullshit scheme to make me reliant on you. To throw me back into your world. I won't do it, Jasper. You and I are okay now, and I don't expect you to weaken Delta anymore to hang out with me in school, but don't ask me to be part of you again. I won't."

He opened his mouth to argue more; I could already see the stubborn light in his eyes, but our food arrived before he spoke, and I grabbed at the distraction. For the rest of the afternoon we talked about my new apartment, and things happening at school, but Beck and Delta were not mentioned again. I think Eddy and Jasper both knew I would ditch both of their asses if they continued to push me. I had so little power left to me—they controlled and owned and dictated so much of my life—that I was holding on to my small independence.

As we were getting up to leave, my phone buzzed again, and I pulled it out to find an incoming call from Stewart.

"Hello," I said when I answered.

"Miss Riley, your apartment is all ready to go. I've had your clothes and personal belongings transferred, and your keys are waiting at the front desk. Along with a credit card from Mr. Deboise. He advised me that Catherine can still see everything you purchase, but that you are free to use it for food and any other extras you need to make your apartment a home."

I smiled. "That was nice of him. Could you please thank him?"

"Of course," Stewart said. "I'll text you his number as well, just in case of emergencies."

The thought of old Stew texting was a humorous one, but I was so glad I'd befriended him.

Eddy and Jasper stared as I got off the phone, and I smiled. "My apartment's ready!"

"I'll drop you off and check it out," Jasper said, keys in his hand. "Make sure everything is safe before I leave you for the night."

Not one to turn down a free ride, I didn't argue. After we arrived, Eddy raved about my apartment before she wistfully stared out the window. "Do you think Dad would let me move out?" she asked. "I'd like some space from Delta too, if I'm being perfectly honest."

Jasper snorted derisively, having just done a walk through, checking out the bedroom, bathroom, and living area thoroughly. It was not a huge apartment, but I didn't need anything bigger. "You'd have a better chance of winning the lotto that you never buy tickets in," Jasper told her.

Eddy pouted, but she got to her feet and followed her brother to the front door.

"Call us if anything happens," Jasper warned me. "Remember, you're out of the compound, and you'll be vulnerable here."

"Are you going to tell Beck?" I asked, remembering Eddy's warning about Beck losing his shit.

Jasper shook his head. "No, I'm staying out of this as much as I can, but he's no doubt already heard. He's the oldest heir, and you already know that gives him more power than the rest of us."

That would explain the dozens of text messages I'd been silencing from him all night.

Eddy and Jasper left me with a hug, and I made sure to lock and bolt my door before sliding a chair over to prop under the handle. It wouldn't stop someone that really wanted to get in, but I'd have a little more notice.

Standing in the middle of my new apartment, in a living area with couches I didn't choose, in clothes that were only half mine, I wondered how the fuck my life could just keep getting weirder.

Chapter 9

Stewart hadn't lied about my clothing being unpacked, but since this place had a much smaller closet, a lot of it was still in boxes. But they'd gotten out all of my uniforms, my underwear and pajamas, and basic jeans and shirts, so I had everything I needed for now. After a shower, I crawled into bed before plugging my phone into the charger next to me.

It flashed its stupid light over and over, and I reached out before dropping it again. *No.* Fuck. I could not let him draw me in like that. I should have just deleted all of his messages, but I apparently loved to torture myself, and instead just silenced Beck.

If only I could silence him from my brain just as easily. Closing my eyes, I tried to force myself to sleep, but all I got was flashing images in my head. Blood spatter. Death. This was the first night I'd slept alone since it happened. Fuck, it was one of the few nights I'd slept alone in weeks.

Before the betrayal, I'd had Beck keeping my nightmares at bay. I had new nightmares now, and Dante had done an okay job of holding me together, but now I had no choice but to face them.

So much darkness, it felt like it had seeped into my blood and was tainting it. Turning me slowly from someone I used to know into a Riley that I barely recognized.

"Argh!" I screamed, bashing my hands on either side of me into the soft bed. Over and over I slammed my hands down, my throat aching as I tried not to scream again. Last thing I needed was the police being called my first night in my new place.

But fuck. How was any of this fair?

Pulling myself up to sit, I tried to take deeper breaths, counting as I inhaled and then exhaled, attempting to calm my brain and pulse.

The light blinked at me again, and I was too weak to resist him any longer. Settling back against my pillows, my hands trembled as I slid my thumb across my phone.

Beck: Riles, baby, are you okay? Where the fuck did you go?

My heart started to pitter patter in a frantic beat inside my chest. He hadn't called me baby much, and every time it got me. Even when I was so angry at him.

Message two had a little more attitude about it.

Beck: Stop fighting me…

Then the third.

Beck: Betrayal is part of our life. You have to learn to live with the hits, and get back up. We're on the same side, Riley. You and I are on the same fucking side. Always.

Anger cut through my heartache, and I wanted to smash my phone into the wall. It wasn't its fault Beck was an arrogant asshole though. *Betrayal is part of life.* Not my fucking life, dude.

Beck: I won't give up, Riley Jameson. I will fucking find you, and when I do, I'm going to smack that perfect ass of yours until you scream my name.

Jesus. My body was apparently not as angry at Beck as the rest of me, because it was turned on and ready to run right into Beck's arms.

There was something a little darker and more out of control in his next few messages, until the final one was just: *Beck: See you soon.*

I had no idea why that was so ominous, but Beck still scared me, deep deep down where I'd never admit it to anyone but myself.

For some reason, after I allowed myself to read his messages, I could finally drift off into a restless, nightmare filled sleep. Apparently, I was going to relive my first murder forever, each night as I closed my eyes.

The next morning I dressed for school slowly, not at all enthusiastic about going back. But I had no choice. My deal with Catherine required me to keep up appearances and not let my grades fall. Of course, I'd skipped out on half my classes yesterday and missed a detention, so no doubt it was going to be a shit show today when I got there.

Eddy picked me up, and she ran her gaze over me when I hopped in. "What?" I said, wondering about her curious stare.

"Just checking you survived the night in one piece." She spun her wheels as she took off along my new street, heading toward Ducis.

"Tired but alive," I said, dropping my head back on the headrest.

She shot me a side-eye. "No Beck?"

I shook my head, and her forehead crinkled. "I thought for sure he'd have smashed your door down the moment he found out you didn't live in the compound."

I sat a little straighter. "He actually didn't mention it in his text messages. Maybe he doesn't know."

I realized then I'd all but admitted to reading his messages, but Eddy thankfully didn't push me on it. Driving faster than was legally allowed got us to school early-ish for a change. When Eddy pulled up in a spot near the front door, the Delta spots were empty, none of the guys here yet, which was the best news I'd gotten all day.

"I probably need to head into the office," I said with a sigh, opening my door. "I skipped out on classes and a detention yesterday."

Eddy shrugged. "Nah, I told Jasper and he got it all taken care of. There are some things they can still deal with, even if you're iced in public."

I shot her a glare, and she held both hands up. "I'm not saying the guys don't deserve it. I've been around the five … four of them long enough to know that they can be the worst kind of assholes. I just…" she cut off for a beat. "Just don't get yourself killed over stubborn pride, you know. Sometimes the enemy you know is better than the one you don't."

She got out then, and I followed a moment later, her words running through my head. Was I just being a prideful dick about this? I mean, I'd never been a fan of the whole cutting your nose off to spite your face thing, but this had been a real betrayal. Crawling back to them for my own safety was exactly what they wanted from me, and I wouldn't give them the satisfaction. Not after what they did.

Eddy left me near the front entrance, and I headed toward my first class. It was at the end of this building, and thankfully the hall was almost empty, so I didn't even have to deal with the dirty looks and cough*whore*cough situations. Just when I was almost at my room, the door swung open on a supply closet next to the science lab, and a strong hand wrapped around mine, yanking me inside.

I choked back a scream as I was plastered against a rock hard body, familiar heat and scent wrapping around me as my head spun.

"Riley," Beck growled softly, his chest heaving as he held me prisoner.

I swallowed hard. "Your car…"

His car hadn't been here. Fuck. I'd been led into a false sense of security.

Beck's eyes were the stormiest gray, boring down into me as he held me, not allowing an inch of space between us. "How did you get to school this morning?" he asked softly.

I tilted my chin up, meeting his gaze unflinchingly—on the outside anyway. Inside I was a quivering mess of emotions. "How did *you* get to school this morning?" I countered. "Your car wasn't in the lot."

The corners of his mouth lifted in a small, smug smile. "You were looking for me."

"No, I—" Damn him. I had been, but only so I *didn't* have to run into him. Not that his arrogant ass would believe any excuses I made, so I just folded my arms over my chest and took a step back so we weren't so intimately positioned. "What do you want, Beck?"

His smile slipped, and he traced a rough thumb down my face. I flinched away from his touch, and his eyes hardened. "You ignored my messages last night."

It wasn't phrased as a question, so I said nothing, just let my flat glare speak for itself.

Beck's eyes narrowed, and he let out a frustrated sigh. "You can't just ignore me forever, Riley. I'm still the leader of our team, whether you like it or not."

"Not," I snapped, channeling my best petulant child routine. "Is that all you dragged me in here to say? That you're top dog and I better roll over like a good little bitch before you punish me?"

His hands clasped my waist—tightly—and he pulled me back closer to him. "You probably don't want to start me on punishments while we're alone in a closet, Butterfly," he practically purred into my ear. His warm breath teased at my neck, and I couldn't fight the shiver of arousal that traveled through me. It was a purely physical response though, and my brain wasn't falling for it.

"Take your hands off me, Beck," I said, steel in my voice.

He leaned back just far enough to meet my gaze, and when he saw the conviction in my eyes he carefully lifted his hands from my waist. "You moved out of the Delta compound." Again, not a question. "It's not safe to do that, Riley. You need to move back."

I barked a sharp, sarcastic laugh. "Not happening. Is that all? I don't want to be late for class. No doubt there will be glue on my chair or some shit."

His jaw tightened and a quick glance down told me his fists were clenched tightly at his sides. "This isn't a fucking game, Riley. It's bigger than us."

"Us?" I curled my lip in a sneer. "Don't pretend there is anything between *us* other than betrayal and lies. I'm not your fucking monkey, and I won't dance to your tune. Unless the orders come from the actual Delta council, don't bother me again." Using my shoulder, I shoved him back just far enough that I could squeeze back out of the closet and into the slightly less than empty hallway. Great. Knowing my luck, there would be rumors about what I'd been doing with Beck in the closet circulating by the end of first period.

Fuck it. What did I care what a bunch of spoiled rich kids thought of me?

I'd only taken a couple of steps away from the closet when I heard it open and close again behind me, and a kid in a sports uniform gawped at me.

"Take a picture, it lasts longer," I snapped at him, stalking down the hall to my class with my ridiculous high heels clicking on the marble floor.

By the time I took my assigned seat in my class, I was in a sour mood, something that wasn't helped by the fact that someone had actually shortened one of the legs on my chair.

Not even joking.

They'd somehow managed to cut about half an inch from one of the chair legs so for the entire class I bobbled back and forth without being able to rest comfortably. I had to hand it to those snickering assholes ... they were creative.

Eddy was appropriately stunned when I told her about it at lunchtime. The chair thing, combined with the convenient drip right over my desk in the next period sort of made them evil geniuses. If I hadn't been the target of their maliciousness, I might have been impressed.

"Girl, that's like ... military level torture techniques," Eddy muttered as we gathered our food and headed for our usual seat. Or what was our new usual seat, since I'd turned my back on the Delta boys. As we crossed the dining hall, Jasper gave me a small nod of support but the other three wore unreadable masks as they blankly stared past me.

"You know he cares about you, right?" Eddy blurted out as we sat down, then clapped a hand over her mouth like she couldn't believe she'd said it out loud. "Sorry," she squeaked from behind her hand. "It slipped out."

I rolled my eyes and stabbed a piece of pasta on my plate. It was chicken, sundried tomato and pesto and was fast becoming one of my favorite lunches at Ducis. "I'm not discussing that douchecanoe and his flawless ability to manipulate everyone around him to achieve his own twisted end game. Sorry, but no."

"Uh huh." Eddy filled her own mouth up in a clear sign she didn't particularly want to discuss it either. "So. What do you think Katelyn and her crew have planned for you this afternoon? Bit of hair pulling? Some rotten food in your locker? Maybe she'll go full *Carrie* and dump pig's blood on you!"

I grimaced and glanced in the direction of the shining blonde Huntley daughter. "Don't give her suggestions," I muttered to Eddy. "What do you think she's here for anyway? Doesn't it seem super suspicious that Huntley suddenly manages to enroll a student here? Like, doesn't Delta own this freaking school?"

My friend just shrugged, tucking some short blonde hair behind her ear. "You know they don't include me on company business. How would I know?"

I leveled a flat stare at her. "Uh, coz you're way sneakier than you let on, and I don't believe for a second you haven't been listening at doors you weren't supposed to."

"Hmm," she hummed, a wicked smile teasing her lips. "Still, I have no idea. I heard Dad ranting about it to Mom last week but it was along the lines of 'how the hell did this happen' rather than 'these are all the answers Edith is hoping to hear,' you know?"

"Yeah, that would have been awfully convenient," I murmured. "Yet another mystery to unravel."

"Hey." Eddy tapped the table to get my attention back from my conspiracy theories. "More important topics. Are we having a house warming at your sweet new pad?"

She was beaming with excitement, and I couldn't help laughing. "And invite who? Did you forget you're my only friend, aside from Dante?"

Her expression turned cagey, and I knew it was because of their brief romance. "How is he? Jasper mentioned something about him being in a fight?"

My mood soured significantly and I scowled in Jasper's direction. "Something like that," I agreed. "He's okay, though. Just ... steering clear of all this shit for a bit."

I'd texted him between classes and told him about my new place. He badly wanted to come by and check it out, but I wanted him nowhere near any of the Delta bullshit. Look where it had landed him last time.

"Come on," I said, stuffing the last mouthful of pasta in my mouth. "Let's get out of here before I catch a plate of spaghetti on my head or something terribly clichéd like that."

She laughed, following me to drop our dirty trays. "There wasn't even any spaghetti on the menu today, so that'd be impressive!"

"There are resourceful bullies at the rich kid academy."

Apparently, I was dabbling in foresight because the afternoon was just as irritating—and creative—as the morning had been. As hard as it was, I kept my mouth shut and my hands to myself throughout all of it. Lashing out at silly high school bullies wouldn't solve shit. My issues were with Beck, and they weren't going to magically solve themselves overnight. So in the meantime I would simply ignore, ignore, ignore until—hopefully—the bullies got bored.

Chapter 10

After school I rushed straight home. I needed to, in order to shower off the chocolate sauce *and* feathers crusted into my hair. At least it hadn't been something totally gross like fish guts or dog shit. Still, the expensive sort of chocolate sauce they'd used had hardened into clumps, and even as I ran my shower to warm the water up, I was cringing at the thought of picking it all out. Maybe I could just crank the heat up and let it melt out?

My phone buzzed on the vanity, and I gave it a death glare. Considering Eddy had *just* dropped me off and Dante had said he was "doing shit" tonight, it could only be Beck. I mean, sure, it could have been Jasper or any of the other guys but my Spidey sense screamed Beck. Especially when it buzzed again a scarce thirty seconds later. Then again. And again.

"Fuck off." I groaned, ignoring the vibrating device and stepping into the massive double shower.

I took my sweet ass time in the shower, opting for the melt-it-out technique, so by the time I got out, my fingers were pruned and the bathroom was thick with steam.

"Woops, forgot the fan," I murmured to myself, feeling just a tiny stab of guilt that this was technically my apartment that I was potentially water damaging. It probably wasn't something rich people ever noticed but my Mom had been a stickler for using the fan when we showered. Mold and buckling from moisture were expenses we couldn't afford.

My phone flashed its annoying little light at me while I towel dried my hair, and I glared at it. I should just change my number. That was the sane thing to do, right? When you got played by a sociopathic nutcase who now won't leave you alone, you changed your number. It was only smart.

And yet, my fingers were itching to check those damn messages.

"Nope, no moments of weakness for this chick," I scolded myself, quickly picking my phone up and rapidly swiping all of the unread messages into the trash. It was safer than leaving them there begging to be read when I couldn't sleep later.

I dried off and dressed in my comfiest pajamas, then ordered my very first pizza to my very own apartment. Okay, technically it was Richard Deboise on the deed, but he'd made it clear that he was putting my name into some clause that would see it transfer to me on my eighteenth birthday ... only three weeks away.

When I'd eaten half my body weight in pizza and dusted off a full family sized bottle of coke, I dragged my bloated self through to the bedroom. Not that I was going to be able to sleep, but at least I could say I tried.

A shadow appeared in my bedroom as I stepped in the door, and I let out an ear-shattering scream, already bringing my hands up to defend myself.

"It's just me," Beck said quickly, stepping forward, and wrapping his hands around my biceps.

I sucked in some deep breaths, in and out, trying to calm myself. "Jesus fucking Christ. How did you get in here?"

His eyes darted to the double glass doors of my bedroom which led out onto the balcony, and I blinked at him. We were three stories up ... could Beck have seriously climbed up the side of the building like Spiderfuckingman?

"What are you doing here?" I asked now that we'd both established he was insane and liked to pretend he wore tights in his spare time. "I thought I made it pretty clear that I didn't want to talk to you."

Beck narrowed his eyes, taking a step back so he could look me over closely. My hair was still damp, the ends curling across my white tank top. I wore no makeup, my pajamas were not that fancy, and I was out of fucks to give.

"Have you checked your messages?" he asked.

My phone was sitting in plain view on my bedside table. Flashing its obnoxious light at me. "No," I said what we both already knew. "I haven't had time."

Beck's chest rumbled, and I knew I was pushing him too far, but I still was on the no-fucks-to-give thing, and I wasn't about to start worrying about Beck's temper now.

"You're in danger, Riley," he said.

I scoffed. "Right, and what could possibly be more dangerous than your crazy ass scaling three stories to stalk me in person?"

"How about a direct threat delivered today to the Deboise estate?" he said, voice like ice. "A threat that detailed how they were going to kidnap you.

Torture you. Rape and murder you."

I choked on my next words, fear slicing my body like cuts from an actual blade. The mental images his blunt words evoked were strong and soul shattering, and I found myself almost stumbling forward. "Are—" I cleared my throat. "Are you serious?"

There was murder in Beck's eyes, and now that I was no longer looking at him with my own anger, I could finally see—and feel— his fury. Beck was absolutely vibrating with it, and that's when I knew that the threat was very real. That someone had managed to make it into the Delta compound, and they had managed to deliver their threat.

"Why me?" I whispered, hugging myself to try and ward off my own fear.

Beck made a low, angry growl. "You've given them an easy target. The sole female heir. Living out here on her own. Outside of our protection, without our training, and publicly rejected by all of us so that you appear even more vulnerable."

Fuck. I tried to think it through. In my desperate attempt to distance myself, to not rely on anyone, I had done exactly what Beck said. On the other hand, running back like a scared little bitch, would send the wrong message too.

"Do you have my gun?" I asked.

Beck stepped into me so suddenly that I didn't even have time to register it before his arms were around me and he had me back, pressed against the wall, my feet dangling as he held me off the floor. He didn't say anything, just let his heavy, angry breath wash over me as his eyes flared with storm clouds. The moment that delicious, spicy scent of Beck hit my nostrils, I fought my body's urge to wrap my legs around him and bring him closer to my aching pussy. Fuck. Fuck him and fuck me for being so goddamn weak.

"Put me down," I said, using anger to hide my arousal.

"Stop. Fucking. Pushing me. Butterfly," Beck bit out, his jaw solid as he clenched it.

I jerked my head up, anger and stubbornness fighting within me. "I'm fine, Beck. I don't need Delta. I don't want Delta. Just give me my gun and I'll defend myself."

I gulped at the small tic high in his jaw as he continued to hold me like I weighed nothing. What would happen if I pushed him over the edge? A tiny, stupid part of me kind of wanted to see. The much smarter, larger parts knew, though, that I might not survive it. At least not with my heart intact.

He dropped me suddenly, and I felt light headed at the loss of his warmth and scent. "I'll take the couch," he said, storming from the room in a few long legged strides.

What? I mean ... what?

I hurried out to find he'd already started to rearrange my couch, throwing all the cushions off and dropping a pillow and throw over the way-too-small for him piece of furniture. "You can't stay here," I said breathlessly and half hysterical. "I refuse to let you. This is my apartment. My sanctuary. I will call the police."

He laughed dryly, and his mask was back in place now. That arrogant, I don't give a fuck look he wore so well. "Do it, Butterfly. I probably owe them a timely reminder of who owns this town and pays for their service."

My fists clenched as I fought back a scream. He couldn't do this! Fuck!

Throwing my hands in the air, I swung around and stormed into my room, cursing that there was no door. I hadn't expected I would need one in my own apartment. After triple checking my locks on the glass doors—they were all secured—I climbed into the bed and noisily punched my pillows. Huffing a few more times, I settled back into the bed and closed my eyes, more than a little aware that Beck was only a few feet away from me.

I could hear him ditch his jeans and shirt. Use my bathroom. Slide in under the throw. Muthafucker.

Making himself at home like he was the one who owned this place. I angrily rolled over, and then back again, over and over, tossing and turning as I fumed. All the while fighting the hot burn of tears that were choking me. I would not give him the satisfaction. I'd already cried too many tears over that asshole; he deserved no more.

Eventually, I must have fallen asleep, somewhere mid-angry memory, and the next thing, I was locked in my nightmare world. *Everything was grayscale, the only color the splash of red whenever blood spattered across the scene. My hands trembled as I held a gun, and this time, the one in the chair was Beck. He watched me without expression, his eyes locked on mine like I was the only thing in the world he would ever see.*

Like I was the last thing in the world he would ever see.

"I trust you, Butterfly," he said, and I sobbed loudly, tears blurring my eyes. "Pull the trigger."

"No," dream me screamed. "No, Beck. I can't."

He showed no fear, and it felt like my hands lost all feeling, as I no longer had control over them. Just like a puppet being controlled by the puppeteer, I lost the ability to stop the tragedy from unfolding. My finger squeezed down on the trigger, and I screamed out loud, but it was the same as always. The same as the half a dozen times I'd had this dream since I'd killed the Huntley operative. The crack of *the bullet, the heat from the gun, the recoil as my hand jerked, and the thud as the bullet pierced Beck's skull, wiping the light from his eyes.*

I screamed and cried and thrashed as I fought against my puppetmaster.

"Butterfly!"

The soft voice started to penetrate my pain, and I slowed my fight, even though hot tears still seeped out from under my closed eyes.

"Butterfly, please. You need to wake up now, because you're killing me. I will fucking destroy your new place, because if my anger doesn't go somewhere..."

"Beck?" I whispered hoarsely, the fact that it was only a dream finally registering. My heart still pounded like it had been real, but the warmth of the man wrapped around me, brought me back to reality much faster than usual.

I pried my eyes open to find Beck's face mere inches from mine as he held me against his chest. In those first few moments of being awake, I was frantic, my hands running over his face, confirming that I hadn't blown it to pieces with a perfectly placed head shot.

Beck just held me and didn't even ask what the hell I was doing.

Eventually I realized it had been a dream, and I remembered that I was angry with him, and I removed my hands from his skin, and swallowed roughly.

"I'm fine," I said, hoping he would let me go. "It was just a nightmare."

Beck didn't take my hint. His body remained flush against mine, and I was having a hard time remembering why the fuck I'd kicked him out of my life in the first place.

Dante. Betrayal. You killed a fucking man and that's why you're having these nightmares!

Some timely reminders was all it took, I was back to being furious, thrusting myself away from him, and almost tumbling to the floor.

"What are you doing in my bed?" I demanded, letting my anger and fear flow out of me. "Who the fuck do you think you are? Touching me without my permission. Fuck you, Beck."

He looked confused for about a second as he stared up at me, and then suddenly he was the angry one, off the bed and stalking around to my side.

"Who the fuck do I think I am?" he bit out, his tone soft, but the fury behind it very clear. "I'm the one comforting your ass when you cry out in your sleep. I'm the one who didn't just throw a fucking glass of water on you and tell you to shut up."

I wanted to scream. "I'm only having nightmares because of you! You did this to me!" I slapped my hand on my chest, trying desperately not to cry. I would not give him the satisfaction.

I pointed toward the couch. "Get out. Please. And don't come back unless I'm being murdered."

His eyes were glittering jewels in the half-light, watching me with the sort of intensity all predators carried. I expected he would argue with me, but he didn't. Maybe he noticed that I was hanging onto my sanity by a thread, or maybe he'd had enough of my shit for the night as well, because he just stalked his big body off to the couch, and I crawled back into bed.

BY THE TIME I WOKE the next morning, thankfully without any more nightmares, he was gone. I did my best not to think about last night, about how it felt to have his arms around me again, about the nightmare which would just not leave me alone, no matter how much I wanted it to. I was associating the killing and Beck, and somehow the two formed that horrible scenario.

One more thing to be mad at him for.

"You look like shit," Eddy said when she pulled up in front of my building.

"Feel like it too," I mumbled, so tired I could barely keep my eyes open. "Had a nightmare last night." Two if you counted Beck breaking in and refusing to leave. "And I didn't get much sleep."

She nodded and started to drive, her eyes darting around almost frantically. "Everything okay?" I asked, wondering why she was acting so suspect.

"Did you hear about the threat?" she asked, flying through an intersection without even looking for another car.

I nodded. "Yeah, I heard. Someone delivered a death threat."

She jerked her head toward me, eyes wide. "Why the fuck don't you look more worried?"

I shrugged. "I mean, I'm not happy about it or anything, but I really don't see what the big deal is. Delta have death threats issued to their members all the time. This one's for me; it had to eventually be my turn."

Eddy cursed as she sped into the school, slamming her car to a halt near the front door. "Yeah, but the difference is that you're unprotected. I mean, Dad said they had security on your apartment, but you're not in the compound. I don't like it, Riles."

"There is security on my condo?" I asked, pissed off I wasn't consulted. It really shouldn't have surprised me at this point. I probably should phone Richard at least once a week and get all the news off him. I still felt like my bio-dad was an ally I wasn't utilizing.

Eddy opened her door and jumped out. "Well, yeah, that's what Dad said anyway. He said Beck was dealing with it and he had security on you."

It clicked then, and I scowled inwardly. Beck was my fucking security detail. I guessed I could do worse, and even though I wanted to kick him in the balls, again, I would prefer someone I knew versus complete strangers on my couch.

I followed Eddy into the school, my satchel tucked close to my side and my senses on high alert. I never knew where the assholes would come from, and I had to be ready.

Lockers slammed around me as the bell rang, and I waved goodbye to Eddy as I hurried toward my class. I needed to get there first.

"See you at lunch," Eddy called after me.

I waved but didn't look back. I was on a mission.

Only two students were in the room when I slid inside, and I hurried straight to the back, and settled into the seat in the far corner. This was the safest place to be because no one was behind me for spitballs, gum in my hair, or an icy drink down my back.

The room started to fill, and I ignored the mocking smiles sent in my direction, pretending to read ahead in the text. I should be actually reading ahead—all of my drama lately had me falling a little behind in class, but I was sure I could catch up. If I just had a few days without bullshit.

The teacher entered the room, and I let out a low breath. I was slightly safer in the presence of a teacher. Slightly.

Not that it made any impact on the newest form of stereotypical bullying. Not five minutes into the class and a few beeps and distinctive vibrations sounded through the class as everyone—*everyone*—got an email at the same time. Including me.

I didn't immediately check my phone, but the snickers and pointed looks from the rest of the class clued me in pretty quickly that this was today's first attack. Using technology seemed almost too advanced for some of the morons who'd jumped on the bully-Riley wagon, but they constantly surprised me.

With a heavy sigh, I pulled my own phone out and tapped into the mass recipient email. There weren't any prizes for guessing what I was about to find—the teacher had already lost control of the class with several girls calling me names like *dirty slut* and *whore*. A few boys were taking it further by suggesting I meet them in the bathrooms and show them my "skills," so I was totally unsurprised to find an image of "me" in the midst of a very graphic four-way sex scene. I had to hand it to whoever had orchestrated this one, the photoshopping was impressive.

With a shrug, I powered off my phone and slid it back into my bag, then faced the front of the class with my very best poker face in place. Hanging out with the Delta boys had taught me a few things in the art of a blank expression, and I could tell my sheer lack of *any* reaction was confusing the ever loving shit out of my classmates.

"Miss Deboise?" the teacher asked with a small hesitation over my name. "Is everything okay?" Her gaze was serious, encouraging me to fess up and report the bullying. But I wasn't stupid. The teachers held considerably less power in this academy than most. Saying anything would only result in more bullying for me and probably a loss of job for her.

The rest of the class went by uneventfully. I hadn't really reacted to their big reveal, which left them all a little shocked, from what I could tell. Not that it stopped the *slutwhoreslut* comments or the catcalls from the guys when I left the classroom.

I'd been the last one out, which was pure survival instinct, but they were waiting for me at the door.

I lurched back as a bag of trash was thrown at me. It tumbled to the floor and then there were condoms everywhere. Like hundreds of them, some even looked used.

"We gathered this from your last whore-session," a chick said, laughing at me as I stared down with disgust.

"Hope you're getting well compensated," another called out, and I shook my head, ready to fight my way through this crowd.

"Get the fuck out of my way," I said without inflection. It was a game now, refusing to let them see me break. They were not going to break me.

A familiar face came into view, and our eyes locked. Hers were glittering with mirth and evil intent, the smallest of an asshole smile on her face. Katelyn Huntley did not participate in the bullying, but she was there, watching, and enjoying it all.

I had a sneaking suspicion that she was the one orchestrating this all behind the scenes. But to what end? What was this bitch doing in Delta's school? Was it just about making sure the five heirs were divided? Or was there something even more sinister in her plan?

Her smile grew, and she winked before pushing her way through the crowd and out of my line of sight.

Shit! She was definitely up to no good.

I had no time to worry about that though, I had to get the fuck out of this group of dickbags that were trying to get a rise out of me. Just as I raised my fists, ready to make good on my promise, the crowd stepped aside, finally allowing me to exit the classroom. I ground to a halt when I realized that they hadn't moved for me. Beck, Dylan, Jasper, and Evan stood in a row, their faces completely unreadable, but I knew the four of them well enough by now to see the fire in their eyes. That slight rigidness to their jaws. The cut of muscles in Beck's arms that said he was about to lose his shit.

The memory of his arms around me last night slammed into my mind, and I actually shook my head to try and dispel the thought. I had to stay strong. I could deal with this. I did not need to run back to the guys who had betrayed me.

Jasper took a step forward before he halted and squeezed his eyes shut for the briefest of seconds.

He was remembering that he couldn't help me here. That none of them could protect me.

It was my choice, and I needed to live with it.

"Hey, assholes," I said as I strolled past. "Here to join the revelry? Apparently I do a four for one in my whore sessions now."

There were more beeps across all the phones around us then, and with trepidation, I pulled mine out and tried to mentally prepare myself for whatever was about to happen now.

Only it was blank. As was the previous email that was still sitting in my inbox. Someone had gone through and wiped all of the emails, somehow. That would have taken some high tech hacking to achieve such a feat.

Beck gave me the briefest nod that I knew no one else caught, and then he turned and left, his friends at his side.

Fuck. My chest ached, his actions slicing away at the shield I wore around my heart. The memories, my anger, all fading under the smallest of actions from the Delta guys. Fuck.

Chapter 11

I made it through the rest of the day without too much trouble. Which only made me suspicious for what they had planned next. That night Beck showed up silently, and before I could even say a word, he strode across and climbed into my bed.

"Uh, what are you doing?" I demanded, trying to figure out if I was seeing him correctly. "Get the fuck out of my bed."

He shook his head before he reached over and grabbed the back of his Henley, slowly pulling it up over his head. I swallowed hard as his body was revealed, piece by delicious piece. "You don't have nightmares when I hold you," he said after he'd finished tormenting me. "Let's just cut out the middle man here, and start the night how it's going to end."

I spluttered and glared and stomped around the room, but I knew I wouldn't be able to move his stubborn ass, and I sure as fuck was not sleeping on the couch in my own home, so I dressed in my most revealing pajamas—because if I had to suffer, so did he—and I strolled across the room, as slowly and sexily as I could.

I felt a little like a baby giraffe trying to walk for the first time as I swung my hips, but Beck didn't seem to mind. His eyes dark and glittering as he watched me cross the room. I wore just a tiny pair of boy shorts and a cropped top that revealed my stomach and most of my boobs.

When I crawled into my side of the bed, I swung around and pointed a finger at Beck. "If you touch me, I will rip your dick off. Got it?"

His smile grew, but he didn't make any promises, and I wondered how the hell I would sleep with this fluttering brush of butterflies all through my body. Being near him was like being near a live wire. I could feel the energy, the buzz, and the danger.

So much fucking danger. Why the hell couldn't I stay away? Because I was kidding myself to think it was just one sided. I fought him, but not as hard as I should have been. In some masochistic way, I liked torturing myself as long as he was close.

And we were back to needing therapy.

Somehow I slept, and not a single dream came along to bother me. Which did fucking bother me, because Beck was the reason for my nightmares, and I hated that he was the one who also kept them at bay. At least he was gone when I got up, and I tried not to think about how much my pillow smelled like Beck, indicating we'd spent the night wrapped up together, as always.

Dressing for school felt a little like dressing for a funeral. I was depressed as I pulled on the stupid uniform and slid my feet into my Converse. Fuck wearing heels today. I didn't even care if I got detention.

My phone beeped when Eddy was out front, and she hugged me hard when I got in. "How are you doing today?" she asked seriously.

I snorted. "Well ... they haven't broken me yet."

She laughed, but it was strained. "I'm not going to ask you to reconsider again, because I'm starting to realize that you might just be the most stubborn of the heirs, but ... let me know if anything bad happens. I have some pull still, and I will not fucking hesitate to cut a bitch. You hear me?"

I shot her a grateful smile. Even after everything, including me trying my best to push her out of my life—out of self-preservation from anything Delta related, and also fear that Catherine would make good on her threat to hurt her—Eddy had been loyal and steadfast. She'd stayed by my side. Accepted my many flaws, and never gave up.

"I love you, girl," I said, staring out the window because I wasn't the best with the emotional shit.

"Love you too," Eddy said. "Even if you are an idiot."

Couldn't argue with that.

We were late to school today, and I should have been on high alert with so many students around, but I really couldn't find the energy to give a fuck. Maybe it was emotional overload, but I was starting to feel a blank sort of acceptance of my current situation. It was depressing, and it hurt worst because I missed my parents more every fucking day. It hurt so badly that I still could barely even think about them.

"See you in chem," Eddy said when she left me at the door and headed off in the opposite direction.

I nodded, still caught up in my own head. In my own pain.

Maybe if I'd been paying attention I would have noticed the looks.

The gathering of students in odd positions, groups that were blocking off doorways and stopping people getting through. Maybe I would have noticed Katelyn, with her evil smirk, standing at the head of the hall, watching me as I stumbled along. Maybe I would have noticed and protected myself before the first fist swung out and slammed into the side of my head.

I stumbled into the crowd on the opposite side as something hit me again. I had to blink for a second as my brain shorted out. What the fuck had just happened? I was shoved again, and then slapped, all of it happening so fast that my brain was struggling to catch up with it all.

"What the fuck," I growled. Dropping my bag, I tried to face the next threat.

The faces around me were dark and creased in evil intent, and one thing was strongly clear: they wanted to hurt me badly enough that I would be forced to leave.

"You don't belong here, slut," a girl shouted as she slapped at me again.

I managed to slam my fist into her nose before she got another word out, but there were too many for me to fight them all. Hands pulled at me, slamming me into a wall of lockers, and then I was pressed against it by a huge body. I managed to turn my head to see him, squinting at the guy. I didn't recognize him immediately, as he jammed the hard lines of his body right into my ass.

"Stuck up bitch," he whispered in my ear, dry breath and spit somehow landing on me at the same time. "You'll give it up for everyone else in this school, but not for me?"

It was then I remembered exactly who he was. That dirty blond hair and watery blue eyes. He was the one who had grabbed me at my first party here, the one who didn't like to take no for an answer.

Throwing myself back, I kicked and struggled as hard as I could to dislodge him, but he was so much stronger and bigger than me, that I had almost no leverage to move. He continued to press his dick into me, his hands roughly gripping my boobs, squeezing them to the point of pain.

"Let me go!" I screamed before a hand came up to wrap across my mouth. It wasn't his hand; he had friends helping him out. Someone else wrapped their hand in my hair, yanking my head painfully back, and I screamed against the palm holding me.

Everything in my head went dark and scary, and I fought against the panic because that would get me nowhere. I needed a level head if I wanted a chance to get out of this situation relatively unharmed.

I mean, he wouldn't rape me right here in the hallway, right? In front of everyone?

Before that thought could even settle in my head, I was being lifted, multiple hands preventing my kicking and fighting limbs from connecting to anyone, and then we were in a classroom. Just like the other day with Beck, I was dragged into a space that I didn't want to be in, but unlike with Beck, I was absolutely fucking terrified right now.

"Hold her down," one of the guys said quickly, and I tried to bite the hand over my mouth so I could scream again. There were too many of them. At least six guys that I could roughly see from where they held me and all of them bigger and stronger than me.

"We need to hurry before a teacher investigates," another one of them said. "There's bound to be more than one snitch out there."

I was slammed into the ground, and the hand over my mouth slipped, and I let loose with a bloodcurdling scream, knowing that it might be my one shot at getting help. Something hard crashed into the side of my head, and everything went dark for a minute. I couldn't pass out yet, I had to fight more, so I forced myself to focus.

I tried to buck off the heavy body pressing me down. The hand was removed from my mouth again, and just as I went to scream, a rough, bruising sort of kiss pressed against my lips. I bit at the tongue that was trying to invade my mouth, all the while trying not to vomit at the perverse invasion of my body that was about to happen.

These guys were not kidding around. They were dead fucking serious in their attempt to rape and demean me, to reduce me to nothing more than a body they could fuck, without a single consideration for the person I was. The bullying had been escalating the last few days, but this was an entirely new level. We had moved past high school pranks. This was real life fucked up, and I was about to lose whatever innocence had survived the death of my parents and me being forced to kill a man. There had been a small sliver there. But it would be no more. I'd truly be broken.

Even as my reality flashed through my mind, I was still fighting. To the bitter end, I would never stop.

"Hurry up," one of the guys muttered. "We're getting paid good fucking money to make sure she never comes back here again."

Another one chuckled. "Oh, she is gonna come. All over my dick."

Bile rose in my throat. A scream followed it, and I wondered if I'd choke on my own vomit before they even got my clothes off. They were using most of their body weight to hold me down now, and I wondered if my right elbow was dislocated, they had it at such an angle.

One lifted my skirt and hooked fingers in my underwear. I screamed again, muffled by the hand over my mouth, and despite my determination not to show them how they affected me, tears leaked from the corners of my eyes.

I was helpless. So fucking helpless.

My shirt tore as a frenzy entered the faces I could see, and then my bra was being pulled at the same time as my panties. Spots danced in front of my vision, and just when I was about to close my eyes so I wouldn't have to see their faces, there was a huge bang. From where I was being held down, I couldn't see what had caused it, but for a moment I hoped it was the door. That someone had come for me.

Knowing my luck though, it was more likely another fucking rapists wanting to join in.

For a fraction of a second, there was silence, and I heaved for breath.

Then all hell broke loose.

Limbs flew everywhere, and I caught just the briefest glimpse of Beck's terrifying, furious face before some asshole's shoe caught me in the temple and the world went fuzzy. Unlike the damage inflicted on me up until then, I was pretty sure that one was an accident and most of the boys who'd been involved in my near-rape were desperately trying to get out of the classroom before Beck killed them all.

Or, that's what I could make out from the noises, shouts, and blurry shapes moving around as I tried to both clear my vision and cover myself up.

A warm pair of hands brushed against mine as I tried to fix my clothing, and I screamed.

"Shh, Spare, it's just me," Evan murmured in a low, soothing tone like he was dealing with a frightened animal. Fuck, he *was*. "I've got you, little bug, take a breath."

His arms wrapped around me as my vision started to return, but my head pounded like I was being hit with a battering ram so I squeezed my eyes shut and let Evan half carry, half drag me over to the side of the room.

"What's going on, Evan?" I asked, trying and failing to button my torn shirt with shaking hands and slitted eyelids. "Is Beck...?"

"About to be expelled from a school we fucking own?" Evan finished for me. "Yeah, pretty much. Are you okay if I go stop him from killing that kid?"

I pried my eyes open a fraction more, peering across the classroom to find Beck punching the shit out of one of my attacker's faces. Like, seriously laying into him. Blood sprayed with every hit, and the kid's whole body was limp in unconsciousness. A deep shudder of revulsion ran through me, knowing what those boys had intended to do to me, and for a moment I considered letting Beck kill him. What would one more body matter? Beck's hands were already stained beyond repair.

But ... was I really that person?

"Go," I told Evan, giving him a small push. I clutched at the jacket he'd draped over me and watched in numb silence as Evan smoothly intervened before Beck's blood coated fist could land again. I stared at them, unblinking, while Evan spoke in low tones. Beck's jaw was taut, his whole body coiled as tight as a bow string and his gaze ... his gaze was locked firmly on me from across the room. I stared back at him as he abruptly released my unconscious assailant from his grip, dropping him to the hard floor with a painful sounding thud. Still, he stared, even as Evan continued speaking, handing him a rag from fuck knew where to clean off his hands.

Beck stalked across the room to me, and I swallowed back the terror threatening to pour out of my throat in a scream. Logically, I knew he'd just *saved* me. In my heart, I knew he'd never hurt me. Not really, not physically, and not intentionally. But that primal, instinctive part of me saw his iced expression, those eyes that held murderous fury, and the hulking strength of his body… and wanted to flee.

He paused when he reached me, crouching down until he was on my level, all the while maintaining that unwavering eye contact. My whole body was trembling in uncontrollable shivers, my teeth chattering, and my fingers turning numb, yet I couldn't look away.

"Butterfly," he breathed, reaching out a copper scented finger and stroking a tangled snarl of my dark hair off my face. I flinched. I didn't mean to, but I was no longer in control of my own reactions. Fear had driven all semblance of logic and reason out of my body, and my arms tightened around my knees, tucking me into a tight, quivering ball.

Beck's face tightened further—if that was even possible—and he gusted out a long sigh. "I won't hurt you, Butterfly. I'd never…" He trailed off with a grimace and we both knew why he couldn't finish that statement. Sure, he'd never hit me. But that didn't save me from how badly I'd been hurt by his betrayals when it came to Delta.

"Riley," he tried again, voice a graveled mess as he shifted slightly closer on his knees. "Please, baby, let me hold you?"

I still trembled violently and my instincts screamed at me not to trust him, but I couldn't give a fuck. I needed Beck to erase the fear, just like he'd done every night since the plane crash. All it took was a tiny nod, and he gathered me up into his arms, sweeping us up off that dirty, blood splattered classroom floor.

Deep shudders of relief rolled through me, and I buried my face in his chest to hide the tears streaming down my cheeks. Reality was smashing my state of numb fear to pieces.

I'd almost been raped.

Gang raped. By boys at my *school*.

And for what? Money? One of them mentioned a pay off, so I could only imagine Katelyn—or whoever had set this up—had offered a serious monetary reward for defiling me. Given how rich the students of Ducis Academy already were, it had to have been an astronomical amount too.

"Hey," Evan called out as Beck carried me out of the school in long, purposeful strides, "This is going to require Delta intervention, Beck. I've called our paramedics but…" I could hear the pained groan in his voice that suggested some of Beck's victims—my attackers—weren't faring too well.

Beck's grip tightened around me, and his chest rumbled with a sort of growling, angry sound. "I'm not leaving Riley alone," he snapped back. "Go grab Dylan, he can deal with Delta."

Evan muttered something I didn't quite catch, and Beck stopped abruptly, spinning us around—I presumed to face Evan. "I said *no*. Get Dylan. I'm taking Riley to my house."

"No," I protested, pushing back slightly from his chest to frown up at him. "No, take me home. I want to be in my own room."

Beck's jaw clenched, and I could see how badly he wanted to argue with me, but clearly thought better of it when he nodded sharply and continued across the grass to where his car was parked in its usual spot.

He placed me gently in the passenger seat and buckled my seatbelt when my hands shook too much to grasp the clicker. When he was seated behind the wheel, he leaned over and clasped my face between his hands gently, and I noticed the slightest tremble in his arms as he met my gaze. "I won't let them touch you again, Butterfly," he said softly. "Never again."

Tears ran unchecked down my cheeks, and I didn't care. Beck had seen me at my worst anyway. "Please take me home," I managed to get out, my body shaking. "I need to burn these clothes, and shower."

Beck's jaw tightened, but he just nodded and released me, starting the car up and leaving the parking lot. He drove slower than I expected, but he should have known better than to baby me like that.

"Faster," I said, and that one word had his head snapping to the side, eyes running over me. He must have seen it in my expression, the desperate clawing need.

The Bugatti surged forward and Beck ignored all the road rules, running red lights and through intersections, so that he never had to ease up on the accelerator. He pushed the car to her limits, and as the familiar, throaty roar of the engine filled me, the screaming void of pain inside my head started to ease. Just a little. Enough that I was no longer digging my nails into my thighs, desperate to tear these clothes off.

When we pulled up at my place, Beck was out and at my door before I could even get my seatbelt unclicked. He helped me out, and I knew he was about to carry me again, so I shook my head. "I can walk," I said.

Those bastards did not break me.

Beck's dark gaze never left mine, and I would have been worried about the simmering fury still buried deep in those storm cloud eyes, but I knew it was not directed at me for a change.

"Did you kill them?" I asked while we waited for the elevator.

"I hope so," he said without inflection.

When I was finally inside, I ran for my bathroom, unable to stand the clothes touching my body any longer. I wasn't gentle as I tore off the uniform and my underwear, nails scraping along my skin at the same time.

Gentle hands stopped me. "Butterfly! Riles!" Beck said, getting my attention. "Let me help you," he pleaded.

Memories were pressing in on me again. Their fucked up faces filled with anger and desire. The laughter. The helplessness I'd felt when they'd pinned me.

A keening sound fell from my mouth, and I gulped to try and stop it. To try and fill my lungs with air. But I couldn't. I couldn't breathe. I couldn't stop the memories.

Hot water splashed over me, jolting me back to the present, and I realized that Beck had stepped into the shower with me, holding me, while the water beat down on us. I was naked. He was fully clothed. Both of us fucked up messes.

I screamed, beating my hands on his chest as my tears mixed with the falling water, stealing them down the drain. Beck let me hit him, never moving or flinching. He took the punishment, even though in this second, I was not angry with him.

Sure, I could have blamed Beck for this—the actions of Delta put me in this situation—but that wouldn't be fair. It wasn't his fault.

He'd saved me.

Some of the thoughts scratching in my head eased, and I was finally able to allow rationality to enter. I let my hands fall and slumped forward. As I stared down, I finally noticed the red streaked water, and it took me a moment to realize that was from Beck. He had been covered in blood. Blood that he'd earned protecting me.

"I'm sorry," I whispered against his chest. "You saved me. I'm sorry."

"Never fucking apologize to me," Beck growled, and wanting to see his face, I tilted my head back. "I don't deserve it."

That was true. To some extent. But on the other hand, I'd seen real evil today, and it wasn't the guys from Delta. Needing something to do, I reached for my body wash and loofah, and for the next five minutes, I scrubbed at my skin like I could remove memories if I removed layers.

Beck remained in the shower with me, his eyes locked on my face, arms crossed and expression hard. Finally he reached out and stopped me. "I think that's enough, Riles," he said. "You're starting to bleed."

His gentle caress brushed over the top of my thighs, where I'd been scrubbing, and I finally felt the slight burn I'd left from almost rubbing my skin raw.

With another sob, I dropped everything, letting it clatter to the floor. Beck took over again, shutting off the shower, wrapping me up in a towel, and gently placing me on my bed. He disappeared for a beat, and I heard him throw his clothes into the dryer before he entered my bedroom with a towel around his waist as well.

My limbs were still shaking and I felt bone-deep cold as I slipped under the covers, pulling them tightly around myself, trying to hold my shit together. Beck crawled in next to me, but he stayed on top the covers, wrapping me up in his arms. For once, I didn't fight my natural instinct. Lately I'd had to push Beck away out of anger, but my body had hated it every single time I did it. Today I could just let myself be with him. Feel his comfort. Today, I could have Beck back.

"Thank you for saving me," I said, realizing I hadn't told him that yet.

His lips pressed against my forehead, and I closed my eyes, pretending that everything was okay between us. "I should have gotten there sooner," he said in a deathly cold voice. "The bastards had it well planned. Dylan and Jasper are with their parents this morning, and Evan's front tires were slashed in the parking lot. I was helping him change them when it happened."

Those fuckers had been planning this for a while. "How did you get to me in time then?"

He brushed a hand over my head, gently stroking back the long wet strands of my hair. "Not everyone in that crowd was okay with it," he said. "Someone told us that we'd better get in there."

"It was all setup by Katelyn," I whispered. "It had to be. She's the only one with the money and resources to know that Dylan and Jasper were out for the morning, and to pay enough people to make all of that happen. When I walked into the school, about twenty of them were waiting for me."

Beck's chest heaved as I told him the rest, but he didn't interrupt me.

I didn't leave any of it out, not even the part where those assholes mentioned being paid to rape me. To chase me from this school, or maybe even kill me. I had no idea what they planned to do when they were done with me.

"If I didn't fucking kill them, I'm going to now," Beck finally said, his body as hard as a rock. "Delta will not let this stand. I will not let this stand. Huntley is going to pay, I just have to figure out the best way to do it."

Now that some of my pain and shock was fading, a fury more potent than anything I'd felt before, simmered in my chest. "Whatever you're planning, I want in."

Before he could reply, a phone rang, and Beck got up to retrieve it from the bathroom. "Talk to me, Evan," he said, coming back to sit on the side of the bed. He started to brush my hair back again, and I let my eyes flutter closed at the soothing motion. I was exhausted.

"No," Beck bit out, and I opened my eyes again, wondering what Evan was saying.

Beck grumbled. "Fuck. Fine. Okay. You need to come and sit with Riley while I'm gone, and bring me some clothes. Mine got wet."

His face was expressionless, but it was always his stormy eyes that gave him away. "I have to go and give my report to Delta. They're trying to clean the mess up, but it was very public this time, and I need to help them navigate it."

I nodded, pulling myself up. "Do you want me to come as well?"

It was about the last thing I wanted to do, spill my pain to those old bastards, but I would do it if it meant Beck was not in trouble.

He shook his head. "No. Fuck no. I don't want you to have to be around them anymore than necessary. They'll use any weakness against you. But you do have to get dressed…"

Because Evan was coming, and he didn't want me naked.

Beck helped me up, and I shuffled into my closet, grabbing out underwear and my comfiest pajamas. They were warm and fluffy, and left almost no skin showing. I couldn't stand to look at my bare skin right now.

I didn't get back into bed, instead choosing to wait for Evan on the couch. Beck sat beside me, and we didn't speak, but he held my hand in his, and it was enough.

Beck

LEAVING RILEY WITH EVAN AFTER what I'd just witnessed, was about the hardest fucking thing I had ever done. My butterfly... They had come very close to breaking her. Just the fucked up memory of their faces. That gleam in their eyes as they held her down...

I slammed my fist into the wall outside her building. I wanted to do that over and over until some of the rage inside died down. Breaking a ton of bones, their bones, hadn't even nearly sated my bloodlust. I wanted them dead. It was only the thought that I might end up in jail, unable to protect Riley, that stayed my hand. I'd always had a fucked up anger issue, and Riley brought out the worst ... and the best in me.

I couldn't face Delta like this though. Going in there with my emotions clearly on my face, was a good way to get us all screwed.

"Hey, Beck," someone called as they passed me in the street.

I didn't bother to respond, and the look on my face was enough for them to hurry the fuck along. Safest thing for anyone around me today.

You got there in time.

We had, but it was almost too fucking late. That wasn't good enough. Not for Riley.

She didn't know it yet, but whatever distance she'd tried to maintain between us was done. Fucking done.

Chapter 12

"**W**hat's happening, Evan?" I asked him. "He's not going there alone, right?"

Beck had just left, and now it was Evan and me, waiting to hear what punishment Beck was going to face. Evan looked far less relaxed than usual; his hair was a mess, like he'd run his hands through it a bunch of times, eyes bloodshot, and there were even some very light spatters of blood on his shirt. He reached out and pulled me into him, and for a second my body froze, until I remembered it was Evan. I sank into his embrace.

"Fuck," he murmured against my shoulder. "You took ten years off my life, Spare."

"You should have been in my position," I joked weakly.

He led me to the couch, and I found comfort in having him here. Not the same as Beck, but it was still comfort. "Dylan and Jasper are with him against Delta," Evan said as we sat. "I'd be there too, but we can't leave you alone. You're our priority too."

"Isn't that a bit dangerous?" I asked, shifting around until I was comfortably snuggled up against his side. "Letting them know you guys care about me?" Even as I said it, I knew it was true. They did care, despite their betrayal. I'd been so mad about it all, about how they tricked me into trusting them and then forced me into shooting a man, that I hadn't wanted to see things from their point of view. But deep down, I knew they did care. It hadn't all been bullshit.

"Too bad," Evan huffed, reaching over and grabbing the TV remote to click the screen on. "We won't play their games if it puts you in any real danger, and today was way over that line. Way over. They could have..." He trailed off with a pained sound, staring straight at the TV and not meeting my gaze. "Spare, they weren't going to stop."

A deep shudder ran through me, thinking what would have happened if Beck and Evan hadn't intervened. "I know." My voice was quiet and thick with fear.

"No, you don't know," Evan replied with a shake of his head. "That guy, Todd, he has a bit of a history. Only reason he isn't locked up somewhere is that the girls who report him all mysteriously retract their statements and inevitably change schools not long after the fact."

This made me sit up straighter and stare at Evan in shock. "A 'history?' What, you mean he's raped other girls at Ducis?"

Evan shrugged and started surfing Netflix. "We think so. He's also suspected of slipping drugs into girl's drinks at parties. There were also rumors that he physically abused his ex-girlfriend. She disappeared at the beginning of the school year and no one seems to know what happened to her."

"What?" I squeaked, placing my hand against his chest as I went rigid with shock. "Do you think he did something to her? Like... did he kill her?"

Finally, Evan turned away from the TV and met my eyes with a heavy sigh. "One thing I've learned, growing up in a Delta family, is that people are capable of much worse than you'd ever expect. All they need is the means to get away with it and all bets are off."

"That's..." I shook my head in stunned disbelief. Then again, given what had just happened to me *at school* of all places, I could understand where he was coming from. "That's so fucked up," I whispered, sagging back into the couch and letting Evan tug me close. "This whole world you live in, it's totally fucked up."

"We," he corrected. "As shit as it is, you're a part of this world now too."

He was right, and for the first time in a long time, that thought didn't make me want to grab those fake IDs in Richard's office and run for my damn life. Katelyn's orchestrated attack had shown me the stark reality of human nature. Blackmail, bribery, violence, death... These things weren't exclusive to Delta and Huntley. They were everywhere, and maybe Delta was my best chance of surviving it all.

Or maybe it would see me killed.

I decided to drop the subject. I'd done enough falling to pieces with Beck, and now I just wanted Evan to distract me and comfort me. Reaching over, I grabbed the remote from his hand and took over the movie search.

"Taken?" he suggested when I flicked past the Liam Neeson classic. I turned a horrified look at him, and he grinned sheepishly. "Kidding," he offered weakly. "You choose."

Giving him a side-eye, like he was fucking insane, I quickly selected a cheesy comedy. The absolute last thing I wanted to watch was a goddamn action film about sex trafficking.

Chapter 13

BECK

It took all my years on years of practice in self-control to keep from punching my fist through a wall as I left the Delta office in Jefferson. My dad had been too busy to even call in and participate, and Langham had been in New York so I'd been left to face Dylan and Evan's asshole fathers, and *Catherine*.

And to think, I'd just agreed to owe them a *favor*. That promise sat uncomfortably across my shoulders, making my skin itch and crawl with sick premonition.

Fuck, I hated that bitch.

How the hell she'd managed to pull the wool over Richard's eyes all those years ago, I had no idea. In my eyes, she was a snake just waiting to strike. But for what end game? For all accounts she seemed to despise her family more than anything. Was she trying to use Delta's power to take Huntley down? If so, she should be more up front. We'd happily help, especially if it gave me a shot at punishing Katelyn for this revolting attack on Riley.

Almost as if my thoughts had summoned him, my phone buzzed with an incoming call.

Beckett Sr. flashed across my screen and my thumb hovered over the "decline" button for a moment before my better judgement—or years of brainwashing—set in and I answered the call.

"Sir?" I snapped, putting the phone to my ear as I crossed the road to where my Bugatti—Riley's dream car—was parked. I'd always loved this car, but knowing it turned her on so hard gave it a whole new lease on life in my garage.

"Heard you have been making waves, Son," my father stated, his voice cold and devoid of emotions. "I taught you better discretion than this."

It wasn't a question by any stretch, but I knew when to reply, and when to keep my mouth shut. This was the former.

"Yes, sir. You did."

My father grunted an annoyed sound. "This girl, the Deboise throwaway. She's causing too much trouble."

Ice formed down my spine and bile churned at the deeper meaning of his casual statement. Rome Beckett didn't tolerate trouble, and he was a hundred times more trigger happy than I was. Growing up, I'd seen more bloodshed than most retired war vets saw their entire careers. If Beckett Sr. perceived someone to be interfering with business, he would have them killed or do it himself.

"She had nothing to do with it," I forced myself to say with careful neutrality.

My father barked a harsh laugh. "Oh no? You didn't publicly put a slew of kids—from influential families, I might add—in the ICU to save her getting a solid fucking? What, you can't share your toys any more, Sebby? I remember a time—"

"It was nothing to do with her," I barked, cutting off his disgusting reminiscing. "She was just a pawn that Katelyn Huntley chose to get at me."

There was a long pause, then my father made a thoughtful sound. "Huntley, eh? You're sure this was one of their stunts?"

I hesitated in my answer just a second. Riley had been confident this was Katelyn's doing, and I agreed. "Yes, without doubt."

"That still begs the question how they knew you'd react so violently at this little attack on that Deboise slut." His insult of Riley made me want to throttle him, but I settled for strangling my steering wheel instead. "You've clearly got something going on there, Son."

Threats underscored his seemingly innocent words, and I knew Riley's fate hung on how I reacted … but I couldn't do it. Ignoring her at school the past week had damn near killed me and then to find those fuckers all over her, trying to defile her … nope. No more.

"You listen carefully, old man," I told my father in a deathly quiet voice. "You lay one finger on Riley, you make one more thinly veiled threat against her, and I will personally see to you getting skinned alive. After all, you know I have *that* skill, don't you, Dad?"

Tension lay thick in the long silence after I delivered my threat, and I scarcely dared to breathe. I had never, *never* threatened my father.

Fuck. I've just signed Riley's death certificate. I need to get her to run… hide…

The explosive laughter down the phone shocked me back to reality, and I pulled the phone away from my ear for a second, double checking it was still Rome Beckett on the other end.

Eventually, my father stopped laughing long enough to speak. "I see how it is, Son," he chuckled, sounding like he hadn't laughed that hard in a long time. Hell, *I'd* never heard him laugh like that. "Sounds like this little girl has more under the surface than we saw from the pathetic creature who cried while shooting that Huntley scum. I'll be keeping an eye on this interesting development."

The line clicked and went dead before I could respond, and I smashed my fist into the steering wheel.

"Fuck!" I yelled, thankful for the privacy of my heavily tinted windows so passersby couldn't see my loss of control. "Fuck, fuck, *fuck!*"

I threw my phone onto the passenger's seat—Riley's seat—and it bounced onto the floor.

Shit.

My reckless threat had an even worse result than I'd first feared. My father no longer wanted to kill Riley … he was *curious* about her. This was much worse.

I drummed my fingertips on the leather of my steering wheel, staring out the windscreen and debating my next moves. Take Riley and run? I knew Richard had fake IDs made up for her, I'd found them when snooping his office one night. Knowing Richard, they'd be immaculate forgeries … but he was still Delta. And Delta—right now—was firmly under Rome Beckett's thumb.

Not for long, though.

My father was becoming less and less interested in Delta day to day, to the point where he was already handing over part of his responsibilities to me. I wasn't dumb enough to think he was just prepping me to take my seat in a few months when I turned twenty-one. He was up to something.

A flash of blonde hair grabbed my attention, and anger boiled inside me.

I slammed my car door open, stepping out onto the sidewalk and grabbing the arrogant Huntley bitch by the throat. Ignoring her strangled squeals of protest, and the shocked gasps of her friends, I hauled her into an alleyway and slammed her into the dirty brick wall. An overflowing dumpster sat just feet away, and its pungent smell reflected the human trash in front of me.

"Sebastian," Katelyn purred, a suggestive smile curving her lips despite the firm grip I had around her throat. "I wondered when you'd come to your senses."

Her body curved into mine like a cat in heat, her hands snaking around my waist like a lover's embrace. Was she totally oblivious to the danger here? Or just reckless as shit?

"Katelyn, I swear to fucking God," I growled, barely containing my fury, "it is only through the grace of our family feud that you're not getting your neck snapped right now. Fuck it, maybe I should do it anyway and just deal with the consequences later. It might be worth it to rid the world of you."

Her smile widened, totally ignoring the choke hold I had on her as she smirked. "So what are you waiting for, Sebastian? Kill me now. Or are you scared what my daddy will do to you?"

My temper flared and my hand tightened, causing a strangled sound of protest from the Huntley bitch. "Don't fucking call me that, Katelyn."

She stared back at me for a long moment, and finally I found a flash of fear in her gaze. Finally, she seemed to be getting it.

"You make one more move against Riley, and even Graeme Huntley won't be able to keep you safe. Understood?"

"What's your fascination with her anyway?" she demanded, her face twisting in ugly anger. "She's a dirty, slutty tramp who probably would have had a good time this morning if you hadn't interrupted. She's not one of us."

This time, instead of being driven into a wild rage at Katelyn's hateful words, I started laughing. She was so painfully insecure, so threatened by Riley ... I almost felt sorry for her.

Almost.

"Touch her again and I'll make you wish you'd never been born," I promised her in a dangerously quiet whisper, then released her with a shove and started to stalk out of the alleyway.

"You can't protect her forever!" Katelyn yelled after me, her voice an ugly mix of fear and hate. "You can't be everywhere!"

I turned my head just enough to catch her rubbing at what would undoubtedly be some bad bruising on her throat soon. "Try me, bitch."

As I left her there in the dirty alley and returned to my car, two things became painfully clear in my mind.

Riley was still in danger, and I was done with giving her space.

As soon as I got the rest of this shit under control today, which required heading to the hospital with Dylan and Jasper to assess injuries and deal with paperwork, I would be at Riley's side.

And I wouldn't be leaving her unprotected again.

Chapter 14

My afternoon with Evan turned out to be surprisingly pleasant. A Delta medic—sent by Beck—had stopped by and made a huge fuss about checking me for injuries, applying bruise balms and making sure I wasn't concussed from the kick I'd taken to my head. To my relief, Evan shooed her out as soon as it was clear that nothing was broken and I wasn't about to slip into a coma. Not that she wasn't lovely, I just hated being touched by anyone I didn't trust.

She stuck around long enough to call Beck in front of us, giving her report and informing him that we were asking her to leave. After she was gone, we simply avoided all topics related to my almost-rape, the man I'd been forced to kill, the blade that Delta held over all our necks, and definitely anything associated to Sebastian Roman Beckett. In the void created by those off-limits subjects, I actually got to know Evan a whole lot better.

I learned that his dad was a serious piece of shit who Evan suspected was abusing his mom, but she was too brainwashed by the lifestyle that Delta gave her to say anything. He had an older sister who'd been sent away to finishing school—which I understood was a rich person version of reform school—when she was fourteen and Evan hadn't seen her since.

All in all, I felt sorry for him. His home life sounded tense and unhappy, which sort of explained why he was the most withdrawn in the Delta heirs group. He put up a front of being a playboy, but I'd never seen him follow through like Jasper. He acted like the smooth, arrogant powerful heir, but didn't hold a fraction of the natural respect and fear that Beck demanded. He had a quiet and dangerous, mysterious vibe but it lacked the scary depths of Dylan's haunted eyes. He was a chameleon, adopting little bits of all his friends but never revealing the real Evan.

But I saw glimpses of it today, just sneak peeks, and it made me want to get to know him better. I wanted to strip away the layers of Evan, and find out who he was. Deep down.

"*Dragon Ball Z* is without a doubt the best Japanese anime on the market," he said, arguing with me. We'd been binging on the first season.

I shook my head. "I'm not disagreeing with you, but I would be a liar if I didn't say that at times, having to watch one more full episode of them 'powering up' makes me want to rip my fucking hair out."

He shrugged. "Drawing out the suspense." He nudged me. "I'm definitely Vegeta."

I snorted. "Beck is Vegeta. The hot headed asshole, who has 'grown quite fond of us.'" That made me snort out more laughter just thinking about how those two assholes were the same. "And none of you are Goku—he's just too nice and dumb, even if he is mega powerful. Dylan is probably Piccolo, the wise badass one." I eyed Evan. "You can be Trunks if you want. Vegeta's son is more your attitude."

Evan pissed himself laughing. "I cannot believe you watch Japanese anime. What the fuck? Now you're even hotter."

I nudged him. "Shut up. What's your next favorite?"

Evan was suddenly very serious. "*Kenichi*, of course."

I stilled. "What is this Kenichi you speak of? I don't know *Kenichi*."

Evan's face lit up and he snatched the remote up from the table. "Oh, fuck, Rile. Hold on to your designer underwear. You're in for a treat."

HOURS LATER, WHILE OPENING THE pizza boxes, I smiled at him. "Thanks for staying with me today. I needed to ... not be alone, I guess."

He nodded, and didn't say anything back for a few minutes while he chewed the massive amount of supreme pizza he'd just crammed into his mouth.

"I get that." His comment came some moments later and didn't invite any further discussion so I let it drop.

We continued watching anime—*Kenichi* was fucking amazing—and eating pizza until it was late, and we really couldn't ignore the fact that Beck still wasn't back.

"Do you think he's okay?" I finally asked Evan, after catching myself staring at my front door for about the millionth time. "What would Delta do to him?"

Evan frowned and scratched at the back of his neck. "Honestly, I thought they'd be done by now. I haven't heard from Dylan or Jasper either so they must still be in chambers with the board."

I nodded slowly, chewing my lip and staring at the door.

"You've forgiven him then?" Evan asked gently, and I didn't play dumb pretending I didn't know what he was talking about.

Shaking my head, I looked to my hands and my ratty, chewed nails. "No. Not even close."

"Good," he replied, surprising me into looking up at him. "We all betrayed your trust, Spare. We all pretended you were one of us, when all along we knew Delta would pull something like what they did. But Beck…" he broke off with a grimace, running a hand through his hair. "He went too far. He shouldn't have gotten in so deep with you, not when there were so many secrets between you both."

I gave a sarcastic sort of laugh. "Never thought I'd see the day one of you disagreed with his actions. You all seem to worship the ground he walks on."

He shook his head and flicked the TV off. "We're loyal to the death, but it doesn't mean we're sheep. He fucked up, and he knows it, but if it makes any difference I've never seen him like this before."

The whole subject was making me uncomfortable. No, I hadn't forgiven Beck. It was sort of his fault I'd become a killer, for fuck's sake. But in the same vein, he'd saved me this morning and possibly killed at least one of my attackers. Now he was facing Delta's wrath over it so … yeah. Uncomfortable.

Complicated.

"I should go to bed," I muttered, pushing up from the couch and tossing my empty pizza box on the table. "Do you mind staying?"

Evan gave me a quick smile and grabbed a throw blanket from the back of the couch. "Totally fine. I'll stay until the boys get back, but I'm sure it won't be long."

"Cool." I rubbed at my arms as I made my way toward my bedroom, but paused when he called out my name.

"He probably doesn't deserve you, Riley," Evan said quietly. "But you're exactly what he needs."

If that wasn't the kick in the gut I didn't need right before I tried to get some sleep.

I just shook my head without answering, because what could I say. Beck and I were two disasters constantly drawn together through some fucked up attraction. But it wasn't like the disaster in us canceled each other out when we got close. Instead it intensified and created a fucking hell of a storm. We knew it. But we still couldn't walk away.

After peeing and then brushing my teeth, I crawled into bed and pulled the covers tightly around me. Today had been up there with one of the worst of my life, although it hadn't made the top two, which spoke of how fucked up the last three months had been.

Shit. It was my eighteenth birthday next week. The point where I thought I would be able to run away and forget Catherine Debitch and this shitshow she had dragged me into.

What a naive fool I'd been.

They had me. I was going nowhere.

"Go to sleep, Spare!" Evan yelled from the couch. "I can hear you thinking from over here."

"Fuck you, Evan," I shouted back, rolling to my side and pulling the pillow over my head.

He chuckled but was smart enough not to make the sort of remark

Jasper would.

I tried my best to empty my mind. To forget everything and get the sleep my shook up body needed, but I couldn't shut it down. Mostly I was worried about Beck.

After two hours of tossing and turning, I finally reached for my phone.

Me: *Are you okay?*

I desperately wanted to call him. To hear his voice and judge for myself; it was so easy to lie over text. But I also didn't want him to think that I cared too much.

The phone was clutched in both hands as I stared down with desperation. I never even noticed Evan perched in the doorway, not until my phone buzzed and he wandered closer, leaning over to read the text.

Beck: *I'm fine, baby. I'll be back in ten minutes.*

My heart squeezed in my chest. It actually hurt, and I almost coughed to try and relieve the pain. My fingers were moving before my brain caught up.

Me: *Don't call me that. Please. Just don't. I just needed to know you were not going to get into trouble for me. Don't come back here. Evan can stay, or I'll be on my own.*

My finger hovered over the button to send it, when Evan cleared his throat. "That won't stop him, you know. If anything, you're just waving a red flag at a bull by pushing him away so hard."

I paused, my eyes lifting to meet his. "What are you saying? I should stop trying to reject him? You think Beck just likes the chase?"

Evan shook his head. "Fuck no. If you were any other chick, your attitude would have fucked him off long ago, and he would have lost your number in a split second. But like I said, I've never seen Beck like this. Not ever. I think you might be the first thing he's ever wanted to fight for, Riles. He's not scared off by challenges. Your anger does not scare him either."

I threw my hands up and the phone went flying off the side of the bed. "What can I do then? I'm not playing around. I'm so fucking angry and broken up by what he did. What you all did, but most of the blame is with Beck. He fucked me knowing that he was going to betray me. The rest of you don't have to wear that."

Evan almost preened. "I knew you couldn't stay mad at me for long. No one could hate Trunks." His gaze turned thoughtful. "I am a little pissed that Jasper won the bet, though."

I narrowed my eyes. "What bet?"

Without an ounce of contrition, he grinned. "We were betting which one of us you forgave first. To be honest, I chose Dylan. You seemed to be closest to him behind Beck."

Another twinge in my chest. Not as strong as the one Beck caused, but it was still there.

"We were close," I said softly. "And that's why I'm still fucking furious with him. Not to mention, he hasn't even tried to fix it."

Evan cleared his throat, and I stood suddenly because that was a suspicious sound. Bending down to grab my phone, I narrowed my eyes on him. "Spit it out…"

He looked uncomfortable. "He'll kill me for telling you this, and trust me, Dylan knows how to kill a person in like eighty-four brutal ways, but he's been really broken up. He fought with Beck, and it was fucking insane. They almost brought down a damn building. If I didn't know better, I might have guessed that you and Dylan had something going on as well…"

He trailed off, leaving that little fact dangling there, like he thought I was going to fall to my knees and confess. "I have been a busy little Delta whore, haven't I?" I said sarcastically.

Evan laughed. "Ah, if only that was the case. But for real, you should talk to Dylan. Before he accidentally kills all three of us in anger. The dude doesn't have much in the way of family life, just like the rest of us, and to lose someone he cares about. He's not doing okay."

I almost felt bad then. Almost.

My phone beeped again and I looked down to realize that the message from before had been sent, somehow. Must have knocked it when I dropped the phone.

Beck: You know that's not going to happen. You belong to me, Riley Jameson.

My resolve wavered again. Damn him.

Evan caught the message, and a shit-eating grin lifted his lips. "Don't fucking say it," I warned him.

He didn't speak, but the grin remained firmly in place.

A knock on the door startled us, and I almost dropped my phone again. Evan's entire demeanor changed, and he shifted into what I like to call "stealth mode." He crossed to where his jacket was, and I blinked as he lifted a gun from one of the pockets.

Fuck. He'd had that with him the entire time and I hadn't even known.

He lifted the peephole so he could see who it was, holding the gun out to the side, like he could be back in a defensive position in a moment if needed. "We need to get you a security camera here," he muttered, but then relaxed, lowering the gun.

He pulled the door open and Beck, Jasper, and Dylan were waiting on the other side. Stone faced. Dressed in dark jackets with windswept hair. The weather was wild out there. Their eyes were almost the same. Fierce and untamed.

They filed in silently, and as Evan closed and bolted the door again, I was swept off my feet. Dylan held me tightly, his arms trembling slightly as he lifted me. He'd moved so fast that I hadn't seen a thing until I was in his arms.

"I'm so sorry, Riles," he murmured close to my ear, sounding broken up. Evan's words hit me then, I remembered everything he'd said, and I allowed myself to relax against Dylan. Even going so far as to wrap my arms around him and hug him back.

"It's okay. I'm okay," I said over and over, like I was trying to convince us both.

When he finally set me down, his face looked as devastated as his voice had sounded. "I can't believe we let them touch you," he growled in that graveled tone. "Fuck. I wish I was there to kill them all."

Evan snorted. "Yeah, trust me, Beck needed no help."

My gaze was drawn to Beck. Everything about me was drawn to Beck, and I fought the natural urge to go closer. Jasper distracted me when he swept me into a hug. "I'm so glad you're okay," he told me, pulling back so he could see my face. "No more separation at school." He was dead serious. "I don't care what's going on in our personal lives. If you still hate us, that's fucking fine, but you will not be separated from all of us again."

He set me on my feet, and I swallowed some of my angry pride and nodded. "Agreed. We will present a united front, because that Katelyn is definitely here to fuck shit up. To separate us. To create chaos. I don't know exactly what Huntley's end game is, but I'm determined to destroy them first. And to do that, I need you all. I need Delta."

"You have us," Dylan said quickly. "We have your back."

Jasper whipped out his phone then in a rush. He was dialing as he lifted it to his ear. "Yeah," he said when they answered. "I need you to buy a couple of apartments." He then rattled off the address and name of this building.

I opened my mouth, slammed it closed, before opening it again. But I didn't protest. I'd agreed to this outward showing of unity, and I would still have my own place here. A little protection around me was not something to complain about.

"Kick them out," Jasper replied to whatever the other person had said. "Or offer them double what they're worth. I don't care how you do it, just get us a few apartments on Riley's floor."

He hung up.

Beck shook his head. "If you'd asked me, I would have told you that I've already arranged to buy out this floor. Even if Riley didn't want us to move in here, I still preferred she have no neighbors that could be easily manipulated into betraying her."

I closed my eyes, searching for some inner peace. These spoiled, arrogant assholes, were so used to ramrodding their way into everything. Always getting their own way. I was kind of glad I'd made it a little hard for them. At least for a while.

"It's time for you all to go now," I said. "I'm tired. We have to be at school tomorrow, and I don't need to keep up appearances until then."

Jasper, Evan, and Dylan didn't argue with me. They just hugged me tightly, and one by one filed out the door. I always knew Beck was going to be the most difficult to reason with. He was a fucking immovable rock.

"You can go too," I said to him when we were alone in the living room.

He responded by dropping his ass on the couch.

"Beck..." I said warningly. "I'm grateful you saved me. I really am. But I don't forgive you. We are not friends. You don't get to spend the night in my home with me. I need the space. I need you to fuck off, just for a while."

He shook his head, picking up the remote. "I let you out of my sight today, and you almost got raped. Gang fucking raped. Don't push me on this, Butterfly. Not tonight."

All of my fury and fear and pain rose up in me then. Tonight was my breaking point, and suddenly words were spewing from me with a ferocity that was almost scary.

"I hate you, Beck!" I snarled. "I fucking hate you! Don't push you? You fucking pushed me right off a goddamn cliff. How could you betray me like that?"

I curved forward as if to protect myself, but I was really holding my chest so that my heart didn't burst from it. Something that might have been impossible, but the pain I was experiencing made it feel like it could happen. A sob escaped.

This fight was a long time coming. I'd tried icing him out, but that hadn't done anything. So now he could see my fury. My agony.

He was on his feet again, paying no attention to the television. "I told you, Butterfly," his soft voice about killed me, "this is a game. If you don't play the game, you lose. Losing is not something that I'm interested in."

I shook my head violently, straightening. "No. No fucking games any longer. That's just an excuse you all use to do fucked up shit. This was real life. This was a real choice that you made. You hurt my best friend. You hurt Dante."

Beck's face darkened, shadows crossing it and turning perfect, handsome lines into something that scared the ever loving shit out of me. "Trust me, Dante deserved everything that was coming to him." He was very close now. I could have reached out and touched him. "Not to mention, it was Dante or you."

I had not expected those words to come out of his mouth, and I gasped a few times as I tried to comprehend what he was saying ... or more accurately, implying.

"What did Dante do? Why was it Dante or me? What does that even mean?"

Beck moved with that stealthy speed that was almost inhuman, and his spicy scent hit me. I forced myself not to step into him. Not to touch him.

"Our parents are not good people," he said without much inflection. "You must already have seen that. They will stop at nothing to get what they want. To force our hand. If they knew that you meant more to any of us than just the fifth seat of Delta, they would use you against us." His hands twisted in the hair at the base of my neck, pulling me to him. "They would hurt you, Butterfly. Break those perfect wings. Destroy your fighting spirit."

I couldn't breathe, my hands somehow against the hard planes of his chest as he continued. "I would take Dante a hundred times, and beat him a hundred times more to make sure it's not you."

A gasp choked from me, and I frantically tried to suck more oxygen in before I passed out. "No!" I cried, finding my anger again and shoving him as hard as I could.

He let me go, because there was no way I could have forced him, and I pressed myself against the wall. "I don't believe you. You're just telling me what I want to hear. You're a fucking brilliant liar; you had me completely fooled."

Beck scrubbed his hands through his hair, sending the thick dark strands into more disarray. "I don't fucking lie, Butterfly. I've never lied to you."

Lies of omission were still lies.

His face softened, and it was such a weird expression on Beck's features that it had me pausing.

"You're scared," he said softly.

Fuck yes I was. My life was in shambles, and I'd lost the one safe anchor I thought I'd had.

"You don't want to believe my words, because then you'll be vulnerable again. You're scared to trust us again because then we'll have the power to hurt you again."

My temper made itself well known. "Can you fucking blame me?" I was close to screaming. "You fucking assholes almost destroyed me the last time I played happy freaking families with you. I've learned my lesson."

"We are a family," Beck said, his calm fading. "You're just delaying the inevitable. The five of us, that is meant to fucking be."

Today we were both a storm, mingling together to form a hurricane that would destroy everything.

And leave no survivors.

"Please just go, Beck," I said hoarsely. The moment his nickname left my lips, sadness crossed his face, and for a moment my resolve wavered. I'd called him Sebastian most of our time together. Something he had loved. But right now, I needed the distance. So Beck it was. "I'm not ready to forgive you. I don't know if I'll ever be ready. You can come in here with your pretty excuses and perfect lines, but in the end, you could have warned me. You could have done things differently. There's always a choice."

His gaze devoured me. It was like being burned from the inside out, the heat in my center flowing like lava through my veins. The longer he stared at me, the more my resolve faltered.

I missed him so much.

"Go to bed, Riley," he murmured. "There will be no solution to this issue tonight. Tonight we just need to survive."

More angry words were on the tip of my tongue. More accusations and pains I wanted to slash him with, but all of a sudden, I was tired. Not even just tired. Exhausted. Weary. Broken.

For the second time tonight, I crawled back into bed, and closed my eyes. I had no idea what Beck was doing, I didn't even bother to look again. I just wanted to escape.

Chapter 15

The next morning I woke in Beck's arms, and for a split second, right before reality crashed into me, I snuggled closer. Letting my face rest against his chest, enjoying the safety I felt being cradled against him like this. I breathed in deep, absorbing his sexy, masculine scent before the haze of sleep faded and it all came back to me.

Delta. The man I'd killed. The rape attempt.

As carefully as I could given how sore I was, I extracted myself from his embrace and slid out of the bed. Beck was still asleep—possibly the first time he'd ever slept longer than me—and I allowed myself an indulgent moment admiring his sculpted chest and broad, strong shoulders. Of course the devil was beautiful, how else did he lure you into evil?

"You can always come back to bed, Butterfly," Beck's sleepy voice murmured, his eyes still closed. It was the dose of reality I needed, though, and I scampered my ass into the bathroom to take a long shower. My whole body ached from the attack, my muscles all locked up and screaming at me, so the hot water was sheer heaven.

Showing up at school today was so far down my list of things I wanted to do, but I'd be damned if I'd let Katelyn think she had won for even a second. So I took my time to wash and blow dry my hair into a silken sheet, then carefully applied makeup to ensure all the small marks—fingertip bruises along my jaw—were covered. My uniform would cover the rest of the damage from kicks and punches and really, I'd survived worse after the plane crash. This damage was mental, and to my frustration that wasn't something I could cover with concealer.

When I finally emerged from my bedroom, in full uniform with heels and all, Beck gave me a slow once over then nodded his approval.

"Say the word at any point, we can turn around and come home. Ducis Academy doesn't rule us, we just let them pretend for the sake of appearances." His words were intended to comfort me, but I just shivered with the weight of my new life. How the fuck was I going to survive this cut throat world?

"You've got this, Riley," Beck said softly, clearly seeing my hesitation. "You're the strongest person I know."

I snorted a laugh. "Don't lie to me, Beck. I've met Dylan." I rolled my eyes and bit back a wince of pain as I brushed past him to grab my school satchel—Prada, of course. Avoiding his questioning gaze, I simply held the door for Beck to exit my apartment. "I guess you're driving me?"

He nodded, waiting for me to lock up, then made as if to take my hand before thinking better of it. "Yes, I brought your favorite car. A peace offering."

I pursed my lips and decided not to acknowledge that comment. Yes, we had aired some of our issues last night, but things were far from okay. This was real life. Real, bloody, painful, heartbreaking life. People don't just magically forgive and forget overnight.

We drove to school in near silence, neither one of us really knowing how to handle this diplomatic truce, so it was a relief when we pulled into the parking lot and spotted Eddy waiting with Jasper.

"Holy fucking shit, girl," she exclaimed, tackling me into a huge hug when I stepped out of Beck's Bugatti. "I'm so, so, so, so sorry. I can't believe they did that. What could have happened if Beck and Evan—"

Her rambling was cut off by Jasper's hand over her mouth, and she released me in her surprise.

"Eddy, shut up," Jasper hissed to his sister, "Just. Shut. Up."

My bestie looked confused for a second, then her face flushed with red as she realized how uncomfortable I was. "Crap. Sorry, girl. You don't wanna talk about it. Totally understand." She mimed zipping her lips and throwing away the key.

"It's fine," I said with a weak smile, digging my fingernails into my bag strap. "But yeah if we could just … not talk about it. That'd be great."

"Absolutely." She nodded her agreement. "Anything you want."

Eddy grabbed my hand and started walking with me toward the main school building, but Beck pushed between us and claimed my hand with his own.

"What do you think you're doing?" I demanded, stopping in the middle of the path and staring pointedly at the hand which Eddy was holding a second ago.

Beck glared. "United front, remember?"

My eyes narrowed at him. "United, yes. Dating, no." Using my other hand, I peeled his fingers off and took a deliberate step back. "Besides, don't you have a degree you're supposed to study for? This is the high school building." I waved my hand in the direction of the building in front of us—in case he wasn't aware.

Beck's jaw tightened and his eyes flared with anger at my defiance. I knew how messed up it made me, and it was certainly something to discuss with my future therapist, but *fuck me* if my belly didn't flutter with desire at his pissed off face.

"We're not leaving you alone, Riley. Not today. Not. Ever." His words were quiet, his teeth still clenched and his fists tight at his side. Such a control freak.

"Okay well, one of the guys can come. But you've spent too much time tailing me and not studying. You probably need all the degrees you can get if we're going to change the world."

He stepped closer to me, tipping his face down to meet mine as I looked up. "Is that what we're going to do, Butterfly?" he breathed. "Change the world?"

Tilting my chin higher, I met his gaze just inches away. "You're damn right we are. Starting with this corrupt company we're about to inherit."

A small smile touched his lips as he studied my face, and I was powerless to look away. Damn him.

"You're incredible," he murmured, then planted a quick kiss on my cheek before I could step away. And by my cheek, I meant way too close to my mouth for it to be anything *but* sexual.

"We're not okay, Beck," I snapped, stepping back a safe distance from him and his sinful lips. "Don't mistake this truce as forgiveness."

He just winked at me. That smug fuck *winked* at me then shouted for

Evan to accompany me to class and disappeared toward the college side of Ducis with Dylan and Jasper.

The first step into the school was much fucking harder than I'd ever admit to. There were students everywhere, and immediately I had a flashback to yesterday. To the crowds that pushed and kicked at me. To their faces, all cut from the same angry, disgruntled, evil cloth.

My breathing intensified, and for a moment, I wasn't sure I could actually make it inside. My feet didn't seem to want to move.

"Riles?" Eddy said softly, pressing closer to me. "Are you okay?"

I shook my head minutely, unable to speak. What was happening to me?

"You're having a panic attack," Evan growled, low and close to my ear.

His heat surrounded me as he pulled me closer into his arms, pressing my face to his chest. From the outside, it probably looked like we were just hugging, but from where I stood, it was exactly what I needed to snap myself out of the panicked state.

Evan smelled fresh, like clean laundry and the newly turned spring air. It washed away some of the school scents that had immediately assaulted me. Rubber from shoes. Unwashed teenagers. Stale cigarettes from whichever teacher or student was sneaking out for a smoke.

"You okay?" Evan asked, his hand rubbing gentle across my back, in a soothing circular motion.

I nodded, pulling back finally. My breathing and heart rate had calmed, and I felt much more ready to get my game face on.

Lots of faces were watching us, and I wasted no time in shooting Evan a wink. "Thanks for that, babe," I said sweetly. "You always know just the right thing to do."

Whispers started, and I smirked. Evan, catching on quickly, slung his arm around me, and walked me down the hall to my first class. Eddy peeled off about halfway along the hall, giving me one final hug before she disappeared into her classroom.

"Everyone is watching us," I muttered from between my clenched-teeth smile.

Evan chuckled. "Don't worry yourself, Spare. They're looking at me."

I shot him a disparaging look before shaking my head. I had Evan's number now, and he was nowhere near as confident as he portrayed to those outside of his inner circle.

Classes passed in slow motion. I barely paid attention, too frazzled to give a fuck about the lessons. Evan remained by my side in every class, mostly playing with his phone, or occasionally nudging my leg with his when all of the staring got too much.

Their fucking eyes were on me at all times. Basically everyone in the school had either heard about the incident yesterday, or they were trying to figure out why I was back in the Delta inner circle. Either way, I was sick of their staring faces.

As I left English lit, a chick a few inches shorter than me, kind of blocked the doorway.

"Seriously," I snarled. "Can't you stare from a distance?"

Her alabaster skin pinked across the cheekbones, and she shook her head. "No, sorry, I just wanted to say that I am appalled by what happened here yesterday. My father is a lawyer. A very rich, very powerful lawyer in New York. Let me know if you ever want to take legal action against those assholes."

I felt the tiniest bit bad then, because she clearly wasn't like the rest of the animals in this school.

"Uh, thank you," I said softly. "I appreciate you reaching out."

She shrugged. "In this fucked up world, women need to stick together." She brushed back her long blonde curls. "I'm Sami. Just holla if you want to take it further."

Sami left then, and I blinked at Evan. "What do you know, some rich people do have souls."

Evan snorted. "Yeah, for now. It never lasts."

Wasn't that a sad, screwed up truth.

It was time for lunch, and I dumped all my crap in my locker. Maybe now it'd all actually be safe there. Everyone was already waiting for us, and I grabbed a plate full of food—teriyaki chicken with hokkien noodles—before sliding in next to Eddy. Beck, Dylan, and Jasper were on the other side, right across from me, and all three of them checked me out like they were searching for new injuries.

"No troubles?" Beck asked. The intensity he was throwing off had me all off balance.

I shook my head. "Nope. Except for a lot of staring, it was uneventful."

Eddy leaned in closer. "Have you heard what happened to the guys? The ones who dragged you into that classroom."

Jasper groaned. "For fuck's sake, sister. Can you seriously not keep your mouth shut for five minutes?"

Eddy looked contrite, but she had piqued my curiosity. "Did any of them die?"

We were whispering, and I could sense the tables around us leaning closer, trying to hear our conversation. That was until Beck lifted his furious gaze, and they all backed right the hell up.

"All of them are still in the hospital," Dylan said, his tone somber. "Most of them with serious injuries. Beck broke two jaws, four arms, twenty ribs, and about eighteen teeth between the six of them."

Something hot and primal stirred in my gut, and I should have been scared that he was capable of that much carnage, but I really wasn't.

"Will we be pressing charges?" Eddy asked, louder and more pissed off. "Those fuckers should be in jail. Or dead."

She didn't sound like she was kidding, and I remembered exactly why we were best friends.

"Delta is cleaning up the mess," Beck said, sounding like he was over this conversation. "All six of them will be shipped out of the country, forced into the sort of reform school that makes the army look like an amusement park, and their parents are leaving Jefferson for good. In all the ways that counts, they're dead to Delta. Dead to our companies."

I shook my head. "And you're not going to get into trouble at all?" I checked with him. I hadn't really asked him last night, and I realized now that was kind of an asshole move on my part. I'd just been so overwhelmed with everything.

He shook his head, leaning back, relaxed. "Nah. The council asked for a favor from me, and for that, they'll make sure that this all disappears."

Unease twisted in my chest. "A favor? What sort of favor."

Delta leaders were evil little snots. I wouldn't trust them as far as I could throw them. "I find out tomorrow," Beck said shortly. "Actually, we will all find out. They've requested a full meeting again. In the New York offices.

Apparently, this favor is going to require all of us."

I paused. "Even me?"

He nodded. "Yep, it's an all heirs request. Pack a bag, Butterfly, you're going to New York."

Chapter 16

My official summons came later that night, when Beck had illegally entered my apartment, refused to leave, and was now watching me pace as he sat on the couch.

"Catherine is such a fucking bitch," I snarled, trying to walk off my anger. "This is her message."

I held the phone up and scrolled across to the text.

Debitch: You will be in our offices in New York tomorrow by 9am. Or I will burn your apartment to the ground.

Another angry sound left my mouth. "Who the fuck says things like that? And the worst part, she actually means it. Goddamn psychopath."

Beck's eyes were amused, even though he was smart enough not to actually laugh at me. "You should take that message as a positive sign."

I stopped walking and narrowed my eyes on him. "Say what now?"

He shrugged. "She's scared by how little she can control you. I mean, these are no small, idle threats. She has her work cut out for her trying to keep you in line."

My head was starting to ache. "I just want her to leave me alone. But since that doesn't appear to be an option, I'm hoping to talk to Richard and see if we can get her booted from Delta. Somehow. She's not an heir. She's nothing. He needs to fuck her right off."

Beck looked more interested now, standing and moving closer to me. "You have a plan?"

I nodded. "Yes. I need some sort of evidence that Catherine is not loyal to Delta. I mean, she's Huntley blood. She's always in the midst of the drama and fuckups. I know there is something there, I just have to find it before I confront Richard."

Beck tilted his head, like he was considering my words. "Richard has always had a blind spot when it comes to Catherine. My father briefly contemplated having her killed a few years ago because she constantly has her nose in everything, but he refrained out of respect to Richard."

That didn't surprise me at all about Beck's father. The killing part anyway. Him respecting someone other than himself was actually a bit of a shock.

"Richard doesn't seem quite as enamored by her these days," I said slowly. "We might have a chance."

It was on the tip of my tongue to tell Beck about my insurance policy in Richard's office, but for some reason, I held back again. *We are not friends.* I had to keep reminding myself of that. Beck might be bulldozing himself into my life, but I could not trust him. I could not fall back into that same life and pattern as before. That naïveté allowed me to be completely blindsided.

I woke the next morning wrapped in Beck's arms, and I allowed myself the briefest of seconds of peace before I pulled away and got ready for the day. It took me longer than usual, given how sore and stiff I still was from fighting off my attackers, but it was nothing I couldn't handle with gritted teeth and a couple of aspirin.

We were taking one car to New York City, and it turned out to be a huge Escalade, black on black, and all the fancy shit. Jasper was driving, his eyes covered by reflective glasses. "Morning, Riles," he said when I climbed inside, throwing my duffle bag over the backseat. "You ready for the road trip?"

I shook my head, glad that it would only be a couple of hours. "Why did we need to pack a bag?" I asked. "Surely we can have the meeting and make it home tonight?"

Beck slid in next to me, Dylan on the other side, and suddenly I was sandwiched between two of the hottest, scariest dudes in existence.

Some days, I swear fate hated me.

Or loved me. Depending on what way you looked at it.

Jasper started the car and "Humble" by Kendrick Lamar blared through the sound system.

"We should grab some food when we get there," Evan said, turning from the front seat. "I love that little deli right near Delta."

"Fuck yes," Dylan groaned, and I couldn't help but smile at him.

"Sounds like some deli," I commented, looking at all of their faces.

"You should taste their subs," Jasper said, spinning the wheel and getting us started. "Out of this world."

My stomach grumbled at the mention of subs, and I licked my lips in anticipation. "Meatball?" I asked Jasper, my eyes wide with excitement.

He grinned at me in the mirror. "With cheese."

Moaning, I sunk back into my seat. "Fuck yes, I'm so on board for that. What a shame we have to deal with our tyrannical parents first."

"About that," Beck said, scratching at his stubbled cheek. "This favor ... it usually ends up being one thing. They have a job for us, and this time I can't even argue about it." He looked annoyed but resigned to this fate. "Everyone's been a bit on edge at headquarters lately..." He looked like he was going to say more, but stopped himself and clenched his jaw.

"Hey." I jabbed him in the ribs. "No more secrets."

"Delta council falls into a whole other category, Riles," Dylan answered for him. "With Beck about to take his seat on the board, he's privy to information that we aren't. We don't need to like it, but we do have to respect it."

Beck sucked in a deep breath and released it in a heavy sigh. "Do we, though?"

A tense silence fell across the car, and both Dylan and Evan leaned to stare at Beck.

"Say what?" Evan blurted.

"Beck," Dylan said in a carefully soft voice. "Are you suggesting going against Delta?"

Beck said nothing, just stared out the window, drumming his fingertips on the arm rest.

"You can't," Jasper spoke up.

"Why not?" I asked, looking between them all. "I feel like I'm missing something here."

Beck shrugged. "Riley said something yesterday about how we need to change things. Change Delta. She has a damn good point."

"No, Jasper's right," Dylan agreed, "Even if it weren't for all the shit they have on us in the vaults, you signed an ironclad NDA. We need to play by their rules for another three years."

Beck said nothing, just kept staring out the window for a long while then ran a hand through his dark hair as he sighed again. "Let's just get through whatever bullshit they've cooked up for us this weekend."

No one really seemed to know what to say back, so Jasper cranked the stereo, and I slipped my sunglasses back over my eyes. It was a long drive, and I was not a morning person on the best of days. Maybe I could catch a few extra minutes sleep.

When I woke up again, my face was snuggled into Beck's neck while my feet were tucked up in Dylan's lap. Despite the fact we were squished up in the backseat of a car, I was stupidly comfortable and I didn't want to move. Not ever.

"So, you guys talked things through?" Evan's question was quiet enough that I knew they must've thought I was still asleep.

Beck hummed a low sound, and I fought not to snuggle my face deeper into his warm skin. "Sort of. Yes. Not really."

Dylan chuckled, his hands lightly massaging my feet in his lap. Where my shoes had gone, I had no idea, but that boy knew how to give a fucking excellent foot rub.

"Never heard you all twisted up like this over a girl, Beck." Dylan's hands paused for a moment on my feet, like he was anxious to hear his best friend's response, despite his light, teasing tone.

Fuck knew I was!

"She's not just any girl, and you all know it," Beck growled. "We talked.

Or… we fought. But fighting with her is like…" he trailed off, and I held my breath waiting for his sentence to finish. "Like fucking electricity. It makes me feel alive like I never have before. I'll take fighting with Riley over her silence any damn day."

Butterflies erupted inside me, and it was everything I could do to maintain my breath and keep my body relaxed. I was enjoying the little insight into boy-chat and was in no hurry to end it by "waking up."

"I don't think any of us are going to disagree with you there," Jasper commented with a dry laugh.

"Shh, shut up," Evan hissed, and I heard the distinctive sound of him whacking Jasper. "You'll wake her up with your snickering."

"Ow, no I won't," Jasper grumbled. "Girl sleeps like the dead. When she's not having a nightmare."

There was an extended silence, like they all knew they were somewhat to blame for the nightmares in my life.

While I did want to hear more of Beck's feelings, I also didn't, because it was crumbling my resolve like it was made of cheese instead of steel.

I shuffled around and started to mumble a few sounds, like I was just waking up. A fingertip traced across my cheek, and I knew from the angle that it had to be Beck, and I let my eyelashes flutter before I opened my eyes and sleepily met his steely gaze.

"Hey," I said clearing my throat. "Sorry, I didn't mean to fall asleep on you."

I pulled myself up, settling back into the seat. To my relief, the ache in my muscles was easing, and I was feeling a bit less like I'd been thrown through a meat grinder. Yawning, I rubbed a hand over my face. "What did I miss?"

They all started talking at once, each saying something different, and I couldn't help but smile.

"That much, huh?"

Jasper laughed loudly. "You missed the start of the city," he said, and I leaned forward to see the New York City skyline which was now proudly in view.

"Whoa," I murmured. I'd never been here before, despite living reasonably close. The city was not for my family; my mom hated the bustle and crowds and traffic. Dad never had an opinion one way or another, but he did mention once or twice that the city was no place for a simple steel worker.

I'd told him that he was too good for New York, not the other way around.

For a brief moment, grief knocked me so hard that I almost sobbed. It just came out of nowhere, and it hit me until I couldn't breathe. There were still moments that I wished I'd died in the crash with them.

Save ever feeling this pain.

Beck shifted beside me, and like he could feel the grief pouring off me in waves, he reached out and took my hand. Dylan took my other hand. Neither of them said a word, they just held onto me. And somehow, between the two of them, they stopped me from splintering into a million pieces and drifting away in the breeze.

A single tear escaped and trailed down my cheek, and I let it fall, until I could taste the saltiness on my lips.

Until I could taste my pain.

Thankfully we were distracted by the surge of traffic around us, and I managed to get all of that sadness back into its box. Locked down.

Jasper maneuvered the huge car surprisingly easy through the city. It was clearly not their first time driving here, and despite the slow movement of cars around us, we managed to make it to the Delta offices in good time. "Which tower is Delta's?" I asked, looking at the four huge towers, each shiny and intimidating. I couldn't see names on any of them, but I assumed one was the Delta headquarters.

Jasper pulled into an underground parking lot, and we waited for the gates to open.

"All of them," Beck said.

I paused. "All four?"

"Eight," Evan corrected me. "We own the full block here."

I sank back into my chair, slamming my mouth shut. Well, fuck. I mean, I was aware that Delta was rich and powerful. I knew they basically controlled half the world. But the real estate alone here, in the center of New York City, arguably one of the most powerful and expensive cities in the world, would be worth a billion dollars.

The underground lot was massive, and the cars in there made me drool a little as we passed them. Jasper pulled into a spot right by the elevators, and we all filed out.

The guys were changing again, adopting their "Delta personalities" as I liked to call them. Game faces on. When we got into the elevator, it powered us up to the first floor, where we had to get out and cross by the huge front desk. There were four ladies there, greeting people, assigning security badges, and basically running the show.

There were people everywhere. The noise was insane, and everyone was dressed in what I was dubbing business chic. Of course, I looked like the teenager I was, dressed in jeans and converse.

"Should we be in suits?" I asked the guys as they surrounded me when we stepped further into the chaos.

Beck snorted. "Well, our parents would like that, but we live to piss them off in whatever way we can. They might be able to dictate a lot, but for now, we still dress ourselves."

All four of them were dressed in their version of rich playboy. Designer clothes, but still jeans and Henleys, boots and white high-tops. Nothing that suggested they were businessmen. Not today, anyway.

"Excuse me," one of the desk chicks called out when we strolled past, heading for the second bank of elevators behind them. "Everyone needs to sign in."

Jasper and Evan laughed, both of them shaking their heads as they continued forward.

"You need to sign in!" she shouted again before she turned and hollered for security. Two huge buff dudes hurried over but got no more than ten steps in our direction when Beck lifted his hand and gave them both a two fingered salute. "Hey, Paul. John," he said.

Both dudes relaxed then, shaking their heads before strolling back to their posts by the metal detectors at the doors.

"Name is Sebastian Beckett," Beck said to the chick who had her mouth hanging open. "Best you learn who the fuck we are."

We strolled away then, and I shot her one last glance, not surprised to see her face was a splotchy red, despite the layered on makeup she was sporting. Poor girl was probably new or something and now she would be panicking about being fired.

"She was just doing her job," I said as I hurried to catch up. We waited for the next elevator to arrive, and filed inside.

"Everyone has the heirs' photos," Dylan told me, no sympathy in his voice. "She clearly didn't read her welcome package. No excuse for being bad at your job."

I shrugged then, not caring enough to argue any further.

When we were inside the elevator, Beck keyed in a code, and then he was able to hit the button for the top floor.

Everyone was silent for the ride, until the doors finally dinged open onto the top floor. We stepped out into a plush, expensive looking reception area where the middle aged, perfectly styled woman at the desk clearly knew who we all were. Or the guys, at least.

"Gentlemen," she cooed, standing in a smooth motion and running her hands down the front of her designer suit dress. "You're almost on time today. The board will be pleased." She stepped out from behind the desk and made a gesture for us to follow her as she sashayed on spiked heels down a corridor.

"Gentlemen?" I grumbled under my breath, "What am I, invisible?"

Normally I wouldn't have given a shit, but it was just plain wrong for a woman to belittle other women. What happened to female empowerment and girl power and all that shit? Clearly didn't exist in Delta's world. Even Catherine had to act like she had her own swinging dick to get any sort of say.

"Ignore her," Dylan murmured, walking so close to me that his arm brushed mine with every step. "She's totally brainwashed by our idiotic fathers."

Jasper was leading the way, allowing the woman who was old enough to be his mother to fawn all over him. As we paused in front of a set of impressive double doors, she was pawing at his chest and chortling like he'd just said the funniest thing she'd ever heard. Judging by the uncomfortable, slightly grossed-out look on Jasper's face, this was one pussy he wasn't down for.

"Thank you, Candace," Beck said in a cool, emotionless voice. "That will be all."

The woman cleared her throat and patted her hair self-consciously before nodding politely at Beck and swinging her ass back down the hall to her desk.

"Let's get this over with," Evan muttered, pushing open the double doors with a dramatic shove.

The heads of our five families—five of the richest, most powerful, dangerously corrupt bastards in the world—sat along the far side of a long conference table, and their conversation cut off abruptly when we entered.

"Oh look," Evan's silver haired father commented with heavy sarcasm, "Only thirty eight minutes late. This must be some kind of record for you four." His beady gaze turned to me and he corrected himself. "Five."

A gentle push to my lower back from Dylan encouraged me to take a seat when they all did, and I found myself sitting directly opposite my vile, conceited birth mother.

"It was late notice," Beck replied with that perfectly flat tone, betraying nothing. "And traffic was bad."

The disturbingly handsome older version of Beck sitting opposite him snorted a sound of disbelief as he shook his head.

"You insolent child," he spat at his son, "if I weren't bound by Delta traditions and seventeen hundred pages of legal documents, I'd be refusing your succession to this council."

A cold, cruel smile curved Beck's lips, and I needed to look away to stop from gasping.

"But you are," he replied to his father, "bound, that is. Now, what have you called us here for? I'm assuming something needs to be done that you old fucks lack the finesse to pull off on your own."

Catherine—nowhere near as practiced in "blank Delta face"—looked like she was about to shit an egg before Mr. Langham spoke over her.

"There is a charity gala this evening at City Hall. We've all been invited, as have Graeme and Christie. No doubt some of their spawn will be attending also." His lip curled a little in disgust as he said those names, and it took me a moment to click the pieces together.

Oh, shit. Graeme and Christie *Huntley* were invited?

This ought to be interesting.

Was it a bit twisted that I was curious to meet the bastards responsible for almost killing all of us in that plane crash? Not to mention the murderers they sent after us to make sure the job was done. Oh, and their daughter of course. She was a real delight.

I opened my mouth to say something on the matter, but Beck's hand closed over my knee under the table, silencing me.

"You called us in to attend a gala?" Beck asked, flat and skeptical.

"Bullshit," Jasper commented from his seat where he lazed like it was a beanbag. He was slouched low, his hands folded behind his head and his legs wide. I was pretty sure he was only a minute away from putting his feet up on the table.

"Appearances are important," Mr. Grant informed us. "Delta did not grow as large and as powerful as it has, without us always presenting a united front." This time his gaze landed on me. "I'm sure you've learned the importance of a united front now, Miss Deboise?"

My temper flared, and I needed to sink my fingernails into my leg to stop from screaming at these megalomaniac fruit loops. Was Dylan's dad seriously making casual mention about my attack at school like it was some kind of educational exercise? Fuck me, if I found out they had anything to do with it…

Beck firmly withdrew my fingers from my knee and wrapped my hand in his. We were hidden by the table, but still it sent a spike of panic through me that someone would see.

"But to answer your question, Son," Mr. Beckett continued, "No, that's not all. We have reason to believe Senator Green has been up to his old tricks again, but he's been using his office at City Hall rather than his home—which you know we have closely monitored. He's apparently created a hidden room behind one of the bookshelves, which is where he's storing all the video equipment along with the recordings. We need you to get in there during the gala and procure one of the tapes."

I was totally lost but was getting a vague idea that this Senator Green was a dodgy motherfucker.

"Of who?" Dylan asked.

"Natalia Petrova," Evan's dad replied. I was slowly figuring out which face belonged to which man, but I couldn't remember most of their names. I'd never really cared enough to ask. As far as I was concerned, they were all evil, old, and fucks. Nothing else was important to know.

Evan let out a low whistle and Jasper made a small sound of surprise.

"Konstantin Petrov's daughter? This senator either has shit for brains or balls of steel, I can't decide which." Jasper sounded genuinely impressed, and now I was even more confused.

"Konstantin Petrov is a Russian mob boss," Dylan whispered in my ear while the attention was on Jasper. "If this senator has a recording of himself fucking Petrov's daughter, it's invaluable blackmail material."

"Wait," I blurted, bringing all eyes on me, "You're telling me this senator fucks girls in his office and secretly films it? That's revolting, not to mention illegal."

Everyone just sort of stared at me for a moment, then Catherine snorted an ugly, condescending laugh, and Mr. Grant just rolled his eyes.

"Miss Deboise," Beck's dad drawled, "you have a lot to learn." Turning back to his son, he clasped his hands in front of him. "You have your mission. Don't fail."

"Appropriate evening wear will be delivered to your rooms. You're dismissed." This came from Catherine, and I had to resist the urge to reach across the table and smack her straight in the arrogant, Botox filled face. Not because I had anything against evening wear, just her in general.

The guys all stood without any further arguments so I followed their example.

None of us spoke again until we were inside the elevators, at which point I opened my mouth to ask a million and one questions, but Dylan gave me a sharp head shake.

"Not here," he told me, his Delta mask still in place. Looking around, all of them still had their Delta masks in place. Did that mean someone could be watching us?

Of course it did. This was Militant Delta, not some above the line *legal* company. Well, sure, their banking and investments looked above board, but they were so fucking deep in other illegal things, that they should spend the next 400 years in prison.

Once in the parking lot, we all piled back into the SUV and Jasper drove us out of the Delta Headquarters. It wasn't until we were out on the busy street in front of the towering skyscrapers that the tension slipped from the guys and their Delta faces melted away.

"Okay, Butterfly," Beck sighed, "Fire away."

I frowned. "What's that supposed to mean?"

He shifted slightly in his seat to face me and arched a brow. Fuck him for being so damn sexy. "You're practically vibrating with all your questions, and we're as safe as we're ever going to be in Jasper's car. So have at it. Ask away." His lush lips curved with a teasing sort of smile, totally capturing my attention.

My mouth opened, but suddenly all my questions fled my brain and just left an echoing void instead. A void which quickly filled with memories of Beck's hands on my naked flesh, his lips on mine, his…

"Fuck," I whispered, covering my face with my hands and breaking the intense stare off I'd somehow become locked in with my *former* fuck buddy.

"Riles? Are you okay?" Dylan's concerned voice was too close on my other side, and I jumped slightly, feeling my cheeks heat. What the fuck had just happened? I get told we have to break into a senator's office to steal a sex tape, and suddenly I couldn't form coherent thoughts without picturing Beck naked? Anyone would think his dick was made of cocaine and I was in withdrawals.

"Wait!" A thought finally resurfaced in my lust filled brain. "What does Delta want with this tape? I'm not believing for a second that it's just for a rainy day. What's the end game?"

Jasper grinned at me in the rear view mirror and Dylan nodded approvingly. "You're getting it now," Dylan commented. "I agree, and if I were to speculate ... I would wonder if this has something to do with a rumored arms deal with the Ukraine. Theoretically, this particular senator would have the power to cut some serious red tape on flight plans, customs inspections, all that fun stuff. He could be a real ace in the hole."

Evan and Jasper made noises of thoughtful agreement, but it was Beck's total silence that drew my curiosity.

"Is that what it is?" I asked him directly, then remembered the whole gag order bullshit that he'd signed. "Blink once if Dylan is right and twice if he's wrong," I suggested.

Beck turned his steely gaze back to me and held eye contact with me ... not blinking at all. Damn him.

Dylan chuckled, patting me on the knee. "Good try, Riles. Come on, we don't have time to stop at the deli, so let's order some room service before the wardrobe chicks arrive." He clicked his door open, and I peered out to see we'd arrived at some fancy hotel. A valet opened Jasper's door and took his keys, so I followed after Dylan and waited for my bag to be unloaded from the back.

"Come on, Spare," Evan said, slinging his arm over my shoulders and directing me to the main doors of the hotel. "Hotel staff bring bags, babe. Appearances, remember?"

"Appears like we're lazy as fuck," I muttered, but let him guide me through the opulent foyer and over to the elevators. We took them straight to the penthouse—of course—which required a thumb print access pad before the elevator would even move. I was coming to appreciate all the security, though.

"We own the whole penthouse," Jasper informed me, like I hadn't already guessed that. "We had it renovated a couple of years back so there were rooms for all of us, but uh…" He avoided looking at me and shifted awkwardly.

"But … I would need to sleep in Oscar's room?" I guessed what he was trying to say. "That's okay. I mean, it's a little weird, I guess? But I never met him, and it's probably a whole lot safer staying on the same floor as you all." I shrugged.

Beck made a small, rumbling noise of disagreement as the elevator dinged and the doors slid open on the top floor. "You're not sleeping in Oscar's room," he said in that quiet, don't-fucking-mess-with-me voice of his.

"Ooookay." I rolled my eyes, but who was I to argue. Oscar was my brother, but he was Beck's friend. Who was I to piss all over those memories? "I'll sleep on the couch. No big deal."

"No." Beck snatched my hand in his, tugging me along behind him as he strode through the *insane* penthouse suite. "You're staying with me."

I struggled in his grip—not super hard, but enough to say I put up a fight—before snapping at him. "Beck, just chill. We can argue about sleeping arrangements tonight, right now I want to hear more about this room service."

Beck reluctantly released my wrist—probably because I had a pretty good point about it not being remotely near sleep time—and took a seat on one of the soft leather couches. I barely got to glance around before he snaked an arm around my waist and dragged me into his lap.

Possessive bastard.

"Hey." I laid a hand on his chest and spoke as firmly as I could. "We talked, we're not okay. Quit acting like we are."

He stared up at me for a long moment, his eyes a puddle of angst and emotion, but nodded just the slightest bit and loosened his grip enough that I could stand up and move to another seat.

Jasper handed me a hotel menu. "Pick what you want. I suspect wardrobe will be bringing hair and makeup for you, so you'll need to eat quick. This is going to be an ... interesting night."

My brow wrinkled, but I opened the menu anyway. I was sick of constantly asking questions, so for once I'd just roll with it and take the night as it came.

Chapter 17

Cool air blew across my exposed back as I slipped out of my long coat and handed it over to coat check. A shiver ran through me, and I resisted the urge to hug my arms around myself. Appearances were going to be the death of me.

All my bruises were covered with movie quality concealer—the stuff they used to cover tattoos—but I could still feel the damn things.

"Have I mentioned how fucking sexy you look tonight?" Jasper grinned, falling into step beside me as we ascended the huge internal staircase, heading in the direction of music and chatter.

I grinned back. "Only seven or eight times. But keep going, my ego could do with the boost, right now. I feel like I'm playing dress up or something." Trying to cover my nerves with laughter, I smoothed my sweaty hands down the front of the scarlet silk evening gown. At least my makeup was so heavy I could almost pretend it was a mask. I sure as shit didn't look like me with the heavy dark lashes and blood red lipstick highlighting the paleness of my skin. I was like an anime version of myself.

"Back off," Beck snarled from behind Jasper. The blond playboy just gave me a cheeky wink and ducked out of the line of fire as Beck took my arm in his. "But he's right. You look stunning, Butterfly."

I huffed at the use of that nickname, despite my requests he not. But this wasn't the time or place for yet another argument with Beck, so I let it slide. Not to mention, seeing him—and all of the boys—decked out in black tie had me all frazzled. Like, they were super fucking hot. Do something stupid and regret it in the morning sort of hot.

"Are we going to meet the mysterious Graeme Huntley tonight?" I asked, needing a subject change. I peered around like he might just be standing close by.

"He's not all that mysterious," Evan commented from my other side as we entered the main party room. "Growing up like we did, you run in the same circles as other families of considerable wealth. Huntley being one of them."

"In saying that," Dylan added quietly, "None of us had ever met Katelyn before or any of her siblings."

Evan nodded. "Right. We've met Graeme and his wife at plenty of these functions but they pretty much keep their kids away from the business. Or the public side of business, anyway."

"Huh," I muttered. "I wonder why that is."

Dylan answered my non-question in a soft, low voice, barely moving his lips as he looked around the room. "The difference between Delta and Huntley, and the reason why Delta will always be more powerful, is that we came about from a union of five influential families working toward a common goal. Huntley is just the one family, trying to keep up. Despite all the current differences between the Delta board, it wasn't always like that. In prior generations, Delta used to actually be the united front they keep banging on about."

"So, what? Huntley has no such obligations to hand the family business over to the younger generation?" I was just trying to process all the information, but it seemed to keep conflicting. Then again, I'd been tossed in the deep end without a life jacket and everyone else had literally been born into their roles.

Beck gave a slight shrug of his broad shoulders. "I wouldn't be surprised if Graeme Huntley has no intention of handing his company over until he's on his deathbed. You think our fathers are bad? Just wait."

"Okay," I murmured, "Sounds fun. So, uh, what do we do now? I'm assuming we can't just march straight through here to do that thing that we need to do?"

A small, amused smile tugged at Beck's lips, and Jasper snickered aloud.

"Now, we get drinks and pretend we're here to party," Jasper informed me with an eyebrow waggle. "Care to join me at the bar, beautiful?"

I grinned and accepted the hand he was holding out. It meant dislodging Beck's grip from my other arm, but if I was being totally honest, I needed some space from him. There was only so much I could withstand and as previously noted, Sebastian Roman Beckett in a tuxedo was fast breaking down my anger and resentment.

"Champagne or martini?" Jasper asked as he escorted me through the designer clad party-goers. Most of them were our parents' age, but there were more than a few teenagers looking bored as all shit. Of course, none of them were here with a secret mission to steal a sex tape from a senator's office.

Biting my lip, I considered telling him to just get me a soda water. It hadn't been all that long since I'd totally sworn off letting alcohol influence my decision making ... but I was a walking ball of anxiety. My hands were shaking, and I could feel fine beads of sweat forming on my back where my gown dipped low.

"Martini," I ordered, impulsively. Hopefully a little vodka would take the edge off my nerves so I didn't totally fuck it all up by blurting our plans out to the senator himself.

"Yes, ma'am," Jasper replied with a grin and placed our orders with the bartender.

After we received our drinks, Jasper spent some time wandering around the room with me and pointing out people who I'd only ever seen in tabloids or on the internet before. Heirs to oil fortunes, actresses, artists, bored but rich housewives and their Wall Street finance husbands... everyone who was anyone in New York was in attendance it seemed.

"Who's that?" I asked, pointing to the handsome, mid-thirty-ish man who Catherine was batting her heavily mascaraed lashes at.

"That, my dear," Jasper said, "is Senator Green."

Our mark.

"Huh, okay. I get it."

I sensed his presence a second before he spoke. "What's that supposed to mean, Butterfly?"

Turning slightly, I peered up at Beck who was both way too close and not close enough. "Just that I can see how he's been luring all these women into his office. He's an attractive man. Here I was picturing someone like..." I looked around the room, then pointed to a white-haired man in his seventies "...like *that*."

"Gross," Evan whispered with a shudder, and I belatedly realized they'd all rejoined Jasper and me. "You picture old dudes fucking? You're messed up, Spare."

"What? No, that's not—" My protests were cut short by a middle aged man who looked vaguely familiar approaching us. In itself, it wouldn't have been anything alarming, but the fact that all the boys around me seemed to suddenly vibrate tension told me this was no casual party guest.

"Delta heirs," the man greeted my guys, his face carefully neutral. "You've all grown up so much since you last attended one of these shindigs. And this must be the missing Deboise heir." His gaze landed on me and I shivered. His eyes were ... dead. Cold, and cruel, like he took pleasure in hurting puppies in his spare time.

"Riley," I introduced myself, sticking my hand out for him to shake, "And you are?"

His eyes narrowed just a fraction at my clear insult, but it was quickly covered by a slick smile. "Graeme Huntley. Your uncle."

I sort of had a feeling that was who he was, but there was a certain level of victory in making him introduce himself to me. "My uncle?" I repeated with a frown, "You're ... Catherine's brother?"

Suddenly the familiar features made a whole lot more sense. He had the same dark hair, blue eyes and pale skin as Catherine ... and me.

His grin spread wider, seeing he'd surprised me. "Yes, dear. I was so shocked to learn my darling sister had another child whom she'd discarded. What a horrible thing for you to learn so soon after your parents' tragic passing." His voice dripped with insincerity, and I ground my teeth together to stop from cursing him out. Blah blah appearances.

Of all people, it was Catherine herself that came to my rescue.

"Graeme, dear, I told you I'd introduce you to Riley myself," she cooed, sliding her slim arm around her brother's waist to give him a hug.

Graeme gave me another calculating look before turning that fake smile on his sister—my birth mother. "Ah, but I spotted her over here and I just couldn't help myself." He leaned down and kissed Catherine on the cheek in a way that gave me the creeps. It was too intimate for a brotherly kiss, and I wrinkled my nose as I looked away.

"I'm sure you couldn't," Catherine muttered with a touch of sarcasm. "Come, Senator Green was just telling me all about a fascinating new bill that is about to be presented to Congress."

She made to lead Graeme away, but he paused and turned back to the five of us.

"Lovely to meet you, niece," he told me with that crocodile smile. "I look forward to seeing the five of you at the vote. It's about time some new voices were heard."

With that confusing gem, he let Catherine lead him away, and she shot us a pointed look over her shoulder. This was our opportunity. She—and the other Delta leaders—would be keeping both Senator Green and Graeme Huntley busy, so we could steal that sex tape.

"Show time," Evan whispered, and I bit my tongue on the questions Graeme had just raised. We had a task to perform, and I for one had no interest in seeing the consequences if we failed.

Chapter 18

It pretty quickly became clear why I'd been brought along on this mission, despite my severe lack of experience or training compared to the guys. As we made our way through the corridors of City Hall, the guys stopped to "show me a painting" every time we ran into another guest, or security. Apparently it was public knowledge that Catherine Deboise's long lost daughter had never attended a function like this before so I was their smoke screen for being outside of the main party area.

Playing tourist, so to speak.

Evan and Jasper peeled off from us at different points, lurking as the surveillance detail while Beck, Dylan and I continued on to the senator's office.

"Uh, isn't his office going to be locked?" I pointed out as the three of us hurried down a dark corridor. This area was strictly off limits to the party—we'd even had to step over a rope with a "no access" sign—so all the lights were turned off.

Beck shot me a half smile, and Dylan just pressed a finger to his lips, telling me to be quiet as he crouched in front of Senator Green's office door and pulled a folded leather pouch from his jacket pocket.

"Get out," I whispered. "You know how to pick locks? What is this, fucking *Ocean's Eleven?*"

Both boys just smirked at me, and I rolled my eyes as Dylan turned the door handle and held the door open for Beck and me to enter. Damn boys and their egos. They were probably already mentally deciding who was Clooney and who was Pitt.

"Okay, uh, anyone else seeing a problem here?" I hissed, peering around the dark room. "Your dads said the recordings were in a hidden room behind the bookshelf, right?"

"Ah," Beck grunted, seeing what I was talking about. "Yes. So very specific, as usual."

The office was huge, and three of the four walls were floor to ceiling bookcases. We could rule out the ones either side of the door, because it was just hallway behind those. But how in the hell would we find this fucking hidden room behind what must be thousands of books?

"Better move quick," Dylan suggested *so* helpfully. "These people have a flair for the dramatic, so it'll be a pull book entry. Start pulling books." He headed over to the shelves on the left and started tilting books out of the shelf and back again.

"Seriously?" I hissed to Beck, and he just shrugged.

"Got a better idea?" he asked. It was probably rhetorical, but I actually did have a better idea. Typical fucking males, not using their brains to work out the problem.

Looking around the dark room, I tried to work out where Senator Green would most likely do his fucking. Couch or desk? Desk was pretty clichéd and a quick glance over his meticulously neat papers and pens, I discarded that idea. He didn't seem like the type who would mess up his desk by mauling a chick all over it, so it had to be the couch.

I crossed the room to the couch in question and sat down on it—trying really hard not to think about whether he cleaned it often or not.

"Butterfly," Beck hissed. "What are you doing? We need all hands on deck here."

I rolled my eyes—not that he could see—and ignored him as I looked around the office. From where I sat, what would be the best camera angle? Well, for starters, it certainly wouldn't be on the side the couch was nearest.

"It's that side," I whispered to Dylan, who was working his way through the books beside the couch. He raised his brows at me, but quickly caught on and moved to Beck's side of the room.

I got up and went to join them, but didn't bother pulling books like they were. Instead, I was hunting for any sign of a camera.

"I can't see shit," I muttered as I ran my fingers over the spines of books, searching for something out of place. "Give me your phone." I held my hand out to Beck, and he handed over his iPhone. I ignored the fact that it was still warm from his pocket, and used the screen light to help see the bookshelves.

We searched for what felt like forever until Beck's phone light reflected off something above my head. "Fuck yes," I hissed, tucking Beck's phone into the front of my dress then reaching up and running my fingertip over a camera lens. "Found the camera," I told the guys. "Entry should be somewhere near here, right?"

I was all the way over, almost in the corner of the room and both Dylan and Beck rushed over from where they'd been searching. Between the three of us, it didn't take long to locate the entry-book. *Great Expectations.*

I snorted a laugh at the choice of title, but followed the guys through the tiny door and into the room behind. It was little more than a large closet that held shelves on shelves of whirring computer equipment.

"Sound proofed," Beck observed, "and a whole lot more than one camera, too." He traced the bunch of cords from a hole in the wall, back to a locked cupboard. Two seconds later, with the help of Dylan's lock picks, the cupboard was open and nine monitor screens showed us all angles of the office.

Dylan let out a low whistle. "Shit, he was really set up. I was expecting a nanny cam or some shit but this is..." he shrugged and shook his head.

"Professional?" I suggested. "Like maybe he's making these tapes for more than just personal use?"

"Exactly that," Beck murmured his agreement as he peered at the camera and monitor set up. "Let's find the Petrova recording and get out of here."

This part—the part where they hacked into Senator Green's dirty little sex server—I was of no help in. So I stayed out of the way and leaned my back on the open doorway, waiting patiently for them to do their thing.

A few moments later, Beck's phone vibrated against my boob. Then vibrated again. And again. "Beck, your phone is going nuts," I whispered, reaching into my dress to fish it out, but only managing to push it further down. There wasn't a whole lot of space to move in the tightly boned bodice and I'd somehow managed to push his phone down to the space *under* my boobs instead of pulling it out.

"Ugh, I can't get it out, either," I admitted when he frowned at me in confusion. "You need to unzip me, it's stuck here." I tapped his phone through my dress where it sat flat against my diaphragm.

"It'll be one of the boys," Dylan murmured, shooting Beck a sharp look. "Someone must be coming."

"Or Jasper is bored," Beck said back, looking indecisive. "We still don't have the recording."

"Keep going," Dylan urged him, "I'll retrieve your phone and check."

I almost laughed at Beck's look of horror, but we weren't really in a position to be arguing, so I turned my back to Dylan and swept my hair out of the way. "Quick," I hissed, "I'd really love not to end up in jail for breaking and entering if someone is coming."

Dylan didn't reply, just quickly slid my zipper down, and I needed to act fast to catch my dress against my breasts and prevent it from falling completely to the floor. His warm hand snaked around my waist, plucking Beck's phone from the waistline seam where it had gotten stuck, then deftly zipped me back up.

"Damn, Dylan," I chuckled. "Expert at undressing girls, huh?"

A warning sort of growl came from Beck, and Dylan just winked at me when I turned back around. His attention was on Beck's phone as he keyed in the passcode and opened the messages—then cursed.

"Yep, company. The senator is on his way with tonight's lucky victim."

Dylan reached past me and tugged the hidden door closed, shutting us inside the tight space, and I squeaked a sound of confusion.

"There's no time to get out without being seen," he explained to me, then indicated to Beck who was rapidly tapping at the little keyboard attached to the server. "Besides, we still don't have the recording we came for."

"So, we just ... wait it out?" I whispered back, a bit incredulous. "What if he finds us here?"

As I said this, one of the monitors showed the main door of the office open, and Senator Green enter with a pretty blonde on his arm. She held a glass of champagne in her hand, and was dressed in a cocktail length sequin dress.

"Wow." Her voice came through the speakers loud and clear to us, and I flinched in panic. "You have so many books."

"Don't stress," Beck murmured to me. "Sound proofed room, remember?"

I let out a sigh of relief. "Oh yeah. Sorry, I forgot we're living in a James Bond movie right now."

The inane conversation between Senator Green and his girl—who I was pretty sure I'd seen in a major motion picture recently—continued playing from the monitor's speakers, and I rolled my eyes at how airheaded this chick sounded. "Can we turn the sound off? Or down?"

Beck fiddled around with some switches then shrugged. "This one should be sound, but as you can see"—he demonstrated, turning the dial and the volume didn't change—"it doesn't seem to be working."

I groaned and slid to the floor with my back against the little door. "Let's hope she's not a screamer, then."

Beck shot me a wolfish grin, and I glared at him. The last thing I wanted to do, while getting front row seats to live action porn, was think about *him* making *me* scream.

Ignore, ignore, ignore.

"So what was that comment Graeme Huntley made about some vote?" I asked them, desperately seeking a change of subject as the sounds of conversation turned into breathy moans and the monitors displayed it all from every damn angle. Some were even zoomed.

Beck was the one to respond, as he plugged a thumb drive into the server and started a file transfer to it. "So, Dylan told you how Delta began as a combination of our five families? Well, technically Delta was meant to be six families. Balance and symmetry were big in those days, as well as the fact that the Langham ancestor had a wife who fancied herself a bit of a numerologist. She'd convinced him that six was the lucky number in business and Delta would only ever be completely powerful if there were six ruling parties." He paused, giving me a shrug. "People were superstitious back then."

"So what happened?" I asked, having to speak over the sounds of moaning as our friendly senator sucked on the actress's nipple. I wasn't even guessing, he'd positioned her in exactly the right place for the cameras to get *all* the action. "How come it was still only five?"

"The sixth family that was going to be involved was killed in a house fire," Dylan said, "and since they were all sentimental, the company decided to hold a sixth chair for them, to keep numbers even, but no new family would be added unless everyone votes and agreed on it."

"So every twenty years, a vote is held," Beck continued, leaving the file transfer running and joining Dylan and me on the floor. "And it's open for any other company to 'proposition' Delta for a seat on their board. A controlling vote. It requires a substantial buy in, of course, so that leaves very few in a position to even try. But Huntley has a lot of money."

"Until now they've never had any pull, but you only need two votes from Delta board members to have a shot," Dylan added.

"Fuck," I breathed out. "Catherine's one of those, right? That's her end game?"

Beck and Dylan exchanged a glance. "We don't know. She's done a very good job at distancing herself from Huntley; today was the friendliest I've ever seen her be with her brother. Usually it's sneers and harsh words."

That was probably the game, though. It had to be.

"Richard still has the Deboise vote, right?" I wanted to confirm. "Like, technically she's his proxy, but the vote is still really his."

They both nodded, but not with any sort of confidence.

"When is this vote?" I asked.

"In a bit over a month." Beck grimaced. "My father is going to allow me to step in as his proxy vote, since I'm so close to taking over my chair, and that's why we suspect the vote has something to do with Katelyn showing up at school." His face was harsh and pissed off. "And why Catherine was so desperate to hold onto her voting rights."

"What aren't you telling me?" I demanded, right as the senator's lover let out a loud moan followed by *"yes, oh my god, put your dick in me!"*

We all paused our conversation, instinctively looking up at the monitors just in time to get a close up of the actress's vagina, followed by the senators erect cock slapping her pubic bone.

"Wow," I muttered, tearing my eyes away from the screen before I could watch any further. "I think I need to bleach my eyes when we get out of here." The woman started this sort of yipping moan as Senator Green obliged her wishes. "And my ears."

Dylan snickered, still watching the screens. "It's not that bad, Riles. You've never watched porn before?"

My cheeks flamed, and I glared at him as I wrapped my arms around my knees and hugged them tight. I was defiantly ignoring the throbbing warmth between my legs, cursing my sex starved body for reacting.

"No," I lied. "And certainly not when the participants are in the next room and totally unaware anyone is watching."

Dylan nodded and looked away from the screens. "Good point. What were you saying?"

I paused for a moment, my brain devoid of anything but porn, made worse by the undeniable heat in Beck's stare. "Uh... oh. Something about Katelyn Huntley. What made you think her turning up has to do with the vote?" I aimed the question at Beck, grasping at that thread of information to keep my mind off the pants and groans coming from the monitors.

"She's been making her interest known," Beck said carefully, his steely gaze locked on me, unblinking. "We speculate she might be tasked with, uh, swaying my vote in favor of Huntley."

My eyes widened and my jaw dropped a little. "You think Graeme sent his *daughter* to fuck you, so you'd vote in favor of Huntley getting a seat on Delta? Why is everything about sex with you people?"

"You people?" Dylan repeated, cocking a brow at me, and I glared back.

"You know what I mean," I snapped, waving my hand at the monitors. "Everything in this fucked up world is sex and money. Does nothing else matter?"

"Power," Beck replied, rubbing his thumb over his lower lip as he continued staring at me.

I glowered. "So Katelyn's been hitting on you at school. I can't even say I'm surprised."

Surprised, no. Angry like I could claw her damn eyes out of her perfect face, yes. What kind of trampy bitch lets her father prostitute her out to win a fucking vote? Oh yeah. The same psychotic bitch who paid some creeps to gang rape me.

"You're not mad?" Beck asked, cocking his head to the side with curiosity.

From the speakers, we heard the blonde woman wailing her climax, punctuated with *"I'm coming, I'm coming!"* just in case we weren't already well aware. Sadly, the senator still looked to be going strong, so I refocused on Beck.

"No, why would I be?"

His brows raised just a fraction. "If I found out some guy had been trying to seduce you, I'd have ripped his head off with my bare hands."

The thought should have made me mad. It was altogether way too possessive and macho. So why then did my core clench with excitement and butterflies spasm in my gut?

"That's because you're insecure, Beck," I snapped, and Dylan covered his mouth with his hand to smother a laugh.

Beck shot his best friend a glare and opened his mouth to say something but was interrupted by Senator Green's voice over the speakers, telling his blonde to *"Suck it like the greedy little whore you are, Lilianne. That's right, milk my dick. Swallow. My. Load."* Those last three words were said with such effort, followed by an unmistakable gagging sound that I didn't need to look at the monitor to know he was done.

Thank fuck.

"Sounds like they're finished," Dylan snickered and bravely looked up at the screens. "We should be out of here soon. Is that file transfer finished?"

Suddenly, the boys were all business again, Beck checking that he had the relevant recordings copied to his flash drive, then ejecting it from the system.

"I'll just need to erase any footage showing us creeping around the office," he muttered, tapping away at the keyboard again. "I'll need to leave this newest one, though, or he'll know someone's been here."

Conversation ceased while he worked, and I watched the screen as Senator Green and his actress put their clothes back on and left the office.

"We're clear," I announced once the lights had been turned off and the door closed.

"I told the boys to return to the party a while ago," Dylan advised us. "All five of us missing for that long was going to raise suspicions."

"Good thinking," Beck replied then frowned at the two of us. "You two go ahead, I'll erase the footage of you leaving."

"Well then how will you get out?" I countered, letting Dylan help me up from the floor.

Beck gave me a smug smirk and winked. "Don't underestimate my skills, Butterfly."

Rolling my eyes, I decided not to argue any further and followed Dylan out of the hidden room and through the dark office. It smelled of sex and sweat, and I couldn't totally decide if I was thoroughly disgusted or a little bit turned on. Both? Maybe.

"Come on." Dylan tugged on my hand after checking down the hall in both directions. We had no look outs now that Jasper and Evan had gone back to the party, so we needed to haul ass out of the restricted area.

We made it all the way down the darkened corridor and had just stepped over the "no access" rope and rounded the corner when we heard voices coming our way.

Panicked, I grabbed Dylan and did the first thing I could think of.

I kissed him.

Chapter 19

"**H**ey! You two!" The sharp voice of the smartly suited security guard saw me jumping out of Dylan's embrace like I'd been electrocuted. "What are you two doing up here, this is off limits to guests."

"Oh, uh, sorry," I stammered, feeling my cheeks blazing. "We were just, uh..."

"Yeah, we're well aware of what you were doing." One of the guards smirked. "Go and make out in a bathroom like everyone else, this is a restricted access area."

I flicked my gaze to Dylan, but he was just gaping at me like I'd hit his reset button, so I turned my very best contrite smile to the guards. "Yes, sorry, we didn't mean to ... uh ... we were just looking for..."

As I stumbled over my words, playing the part of a drunk girl caught making out with some guy, the guard's attention shifted over my shoulder just a second before Beck's hands slipped around my waist.

"There you are, baby," he said, turning me in his grip and crushing his lips to mine. For a second, time stopped and all that mattered was the way Beck moved his mouth, the way he forced his way past my teeth and claimed my damn soul. That was, until someone cleared their throat and I squeaked in fright.

Beck—of course—was much slower to release me than Dylan had been, and when he did it was only to glare at the guards. His hands still clasped my waist tightly, and when I spun around to face our company, I could feel his hard length pressed against my back.

"Can we help you, gentlemen?" he demanded of the guards in an ice cold voice.

The one who'd scolded me was just gaping in confusion, so the other one cleared his throat. "Uh, you're in a restricted area, Mr. Beckett. Would you mind taking this party elsewhere?"

There was a long, crazy awkward pause, then Beck huffed a sound of irritation. "Maybe you should signpost these things better. Come on." He shifted me so I was tucked into his side with his arm around my shoulders then brushed past the guards with Dylan tight on his other side.

When we were well clear of the office wing—and the guards—Beck stopped abruptly and whirled around, pinning me to the wall.

"Beck—" Dylan started to say, but cut short when Beck's death glare landed on him.

"Go back to the party, Dylan," he said with no outward showing of emotion, but it was very clearly a command and there was *zero* room for arguments in his tone. "Here, take this." He held out the flash drive, which

Dylan took with a reluctant glance in my direction. "Now fuck off. Riley and I need to chat."

Beck's steely glare turned back to me, and I caught Dylan mouthing "sorry" at me from over his broad shoulder.

I tightened my jaw and raised my chin to meet Beck's glare. He was trying to intimidate me, and I'd be damned if I let him.

"Did you have something to say?" I asked him in what was supposed to be a sassy, sarcastic way. Instead it came out as a provocative whisper, and I wholeheartedly blamed our front row seats to the senator's sex show.

He was in no hurry to reply to me, letting the tension build between us until my nerves were wound tighter than a violin bow.

"Riley," he finally said in a voice like sin. "Did I just see you kissing Dylan?"

Dread rippled through me, and I sucked in a sharp breath to defend myself. But *shit*! How could I backtrack out of this one?

"Before you say anything," he continued, in that dangerous, seductive tone, "I'll remind you that although we may be fighting right now, I have in *no way* relinquished my claim on you. And I have no intention of *ever* doing so. You belong to me, Butterfly, and you fucking well know it."

His caveman routine turned me right the fuck on, but it also got my back up. "Excuse me?" I demanded, letting my anger boil up and embracing it. "I don't belong to anyone but myself, you misogynistic prick. I'm not a possession to own, and if I choose to kiss Dylan then that's my fucking choice, *Beck*." I practically growled his nickname at him, stubbornly refusing to call him Sebastian like I had when we were on better terms.

The fact that I'd kissed Dylan to give us a plausible excuse for being where we weren't supposed to be, well that was beside the point.

He glowered at my words, his jaw ticking with barely concealed fury. Sucking in a deep breath, he leaned in closer to me. His hands were braced on the wall either side of me, my back flat on the wallpaper, and his face was just inches from mine. I had nowhere to run to ... even if I wanted to.

"That's where you're wrong, Butterfly," he whispered with dark promise, "I do own you." He paused and leaned in closer still, until our lips were just a breath away. "Just like you own me."

Blame it on the martini, the sex scene we'd all witness, or temporary insanity, but I totally lost control. At his whispered confession that I owned him, I closed the distance between us and kissed him with all the pent up anger and frustration of the past month.

Our tongues met, tangling together in a frenzy of emotion, our teeth clashing and our lips devouring. My hands found the back of his neck, gripping tight and demanding more as his body crushed me into the wall. Every inch of me was pressed to him as we drank each other in, and I moaned against his mouth.

Conflicting emotions swirled through me, fighting for supremacy but all I wanted was to pretend none of it existed. We had our issues—by God we had our issues—but just for a few minutes I wanted to forget all the betrayals and the pain and the goddamn infuriating control-freak bullshit. All I wanted, was to get lost in Sebastian Roman Beckett and deal with the rest later.

"Sebastian," I groaned as he kissed down my neck, and he froze. "What?" I demanded, feeling panic flare at the sudden loss of contact.

"Say it again," he ordered, his lips hovering over my skin. His breath was warm against my damp skin, and every exhale sent lightning bolts of sensation flickering through me.

A smile curved my lips, realizing what I'd just said. Fuck it, if that's what he needed...

"Sebastian," I breathed again.

This time, it was like a switch had been flipped. His mouth returned to mine, kissing me with bruising intensity as he lifted me clean off my feet and hitched my legs up around his waist. Thank fuck for the dramatic split in my dress, or that move would have surely ripped it. Not that I gave a shit, it would be worth it.

My eyes were closed, my entire existence consisting of Beck and *nothing else* so I barely even noticed when he moved with me in his arms, opening the door we had been stopped beside and walking us inside.

"That was convenient," I murmured as he set me down on the bathroom vanity and leaned back to flick the lock on the door. He just shot me a cocky smirk, then reclaimed my mouth in yet another demanding kiss that set my whole body on fire.

My legs spread, and I used my heels hooked around Beck to pull him closer to me. Ever since he'd kissed me in front of the guards—fuck, okay, well before that—I'd been craving his touch, and I was beyond the point of waiting.

"Fuck, Butterfly," he groaned, grinding his hardness against me and biting down on the fleshy part of my neck. "You drive me insane."

I let out a small laugh as my hands found his belt and made quick work of opening it. "The feeling is entirely mutual, Sebastian Beckett." I bit my lip as my hand found the velvety smooth skin of his cock and wrapped around the length of it.

He hissed as my fist stroked him up and down, but it was only the briefest moment until he was back in control. There was an urgency hanging over us, and I knew he could feel it too. Not only had we already been gone long enough to arouse suspicion, but we both knew our shit hadn't been resolved. How long until one of us—probably me—decided this was an awful mistake and called it all off?

"Baby," he breathed, his hand shoving the length of my dress out of the way and hooking his fingers in the lace of my panties, pulling them aside. "I missed you." His fingers sank inside me, his thumb finding my clit and rubbing quick circles until I was quivering with need.

"Shut up," I told him. "This is not make up sex. It's just sex."

He snorted, but didn't argue. "Birth control?"

"On it and all good," I groaned back, not wanting him to stop for a second.

He withdrew his fingers and quickly replaced them with his rigid cock. In one harsh thrust, he was fully inside me, and my pussy spasmed around him. It hadn't been all that difficult, I was already so wet before we'd even entered the bathroom, and he damn well knew it.

Whispered curses slipped from my lips as he began to move, fucking me with that same angry intensity that had started all of this. Desperate for more, wanting him deeper, I tilted my hips forward and crossed my ankles behind him.

"Fuck yes," I encouraged. "Harder, Sebastian. Harder." My words dissolved into a wanton moan, and he gave me what I wanted, pounding me so hard my head bounced against the mirror behind me.

His hand snaked down between us, tweaking at my clit until I couldn't hold it back any longer. I screamed my release as my pussy clenched and pulsed, locking his throbbing cock in a vice grip as I came. *Hard.*

"Shit, Riley," he panted, placing another open mouthed kiss against my neck as I rode out my orgasm, my legs shaking and heart racing. "You kill me, baby." Seconds later, his pelvis slammed into mine a few more times as he came.

For a long moment, we just ... remained frozen. My head rested against the mirror and Beck's sweaty forehead pressed to my neck. He was still sheathed inside me, and for a really, really long minute I never wanted that to change.

But, reality, that *bitch,* was waiting right there to slam back down on me and remind me why I'd been pushing Beck away in the first place.

He must have sensed me withdrawing again, because he shifted back and adjusted his clothing. I did the same, grabbing some tissues from beside the basin to wipe myself up as much as I could before righting my panties and letting my skirt fall back over my legs. Not that my pathetic, soaking wet lace thong would do much of anything to stop the wetness of Beck's cum sliding down my thighs, but it was better than nothing.

"We should get back," I murmured, avoiding his gaze as I tidied my hair in the mirror. He said nothing, so I flicked the lock to leave.

"Butterfly," he said, grabbing my wrist and halting my very literal attempt to flee whatever had just passed between us. Not the sex—that part was pretty obvious—it was all the emotional baggage I was running from. "We should talk."

"Mm hmm," I agreed. "We should. But now isn't the time."

He couldn't disagree with me on that, so after a moment he just released my wrist and let me rush out of the bathroom and back to the party.

It was a futile effort. I knew this. But just for a little longer, I wanted to run from all those heavy, dark, painful emotions. I wasn't ready to bare my soul to him, even if he was.

Tonight of all nights, I was grateful for that small favor.

Chapter 20

BECK

After the gala, an exhausted Riley drifted off in seconds, and I watched her like the fucking obsessed creeper I was, long after the tense lines of her face smoothed out. My hands tangled gently in her hair before I could stop myself; I needed to touch her. At all times. It was a need, that for the first time, I could not control. We'd fucked tonight and after so long, all that did, was make me crave her harder. There was something beyond intoxicating about Riley. It had been there from the first time I'd seen her, that defiant, stunningly beautiful face as she schooled us on chicks in car racing.

Riley was effortlessly sexy without even trying.

I'd known I was screwed that first night, but like the dumb fuck I was, I kept trying to fight the inevitable.

A noise outside our room caught my attention, and a darkness settled in my veins as I slowly slipped from the bed, taking care not to wake her.

She made a few whimpering noises, but when I slid my pillow under her arms, she buried her face in it and calmed down.

My chest went tight as I tried not to examine how that made me feel.

I heard his voice again, and I realized that it was time now for me to set a few things straight. Before I ended up having to destroy one of the only people in the world who meant anything to me.

Dylan was waiting on the edge of darkness, and I wondered who he'd been talking to, but then I heard Evan singing his fucking anime songs in the shower. He had zero ability to hold a tune, but that never stopped him.

It made me wish I had a guitar in my hands; I needed to soothe some of the dark anger in my soul, and music was one of the only things that worked for me.

Music and Riley.

"We need to talk," I said quietly to Dylan, a low undercurrent of pissed off leaking into my words.

He just nodded and gestured for us to head into the soundproof music room that I used at times when I had to play at midnight and didn't want to disturb the guys. Maybe he hoped I'd be less violent around my prized possessions.

"You waited up for me?" I asked without inflection. "Knew this little chat was coming, hey?"

Dylan shrugged. "It's Riley," he said as way of explanation.

Her name leaving his lips had my hands clenched into fists at my side. Watching that brief kiss between them had brought out the worst kind of possessive bastard in me.

"She kissed me," Dylan said straight up. "But … I wasn't complaining."

A derisive snort left me. "I noticed."

There was a beat of silence, where both of us sized each other up. Dylan sort of deflated after that. "I'm not gonna lie, Riley … she fucks something up inside of me. In a good way. Sometimes when she stares at me with those blue as fuck eyes, all I can think about is touching her."

Part of me wanted to punch the shit out of him. But a larger part understood. Riley had a way about her, and it didn't surprise me that my best friend felt the same way as me.

"She's mine," I said, letting those words slide across my tongue, dark and dangerous. "You're my brother, Dylan, but if it comes down to it, I will kick your fucking ass if you step over the line with her."

Some of the fire that his parents had tried to destroy inside of him flared to life. "What if she chose me? I mean, you're not exactly her favorite person these days."

I had an instant memory of her when we fucked in the bathroom. The way her pussy contracted on my cock as she shattered in my arms. Her eyes as she stared dead into mine, not blinking, just giving me every part of her. I understood what Dylan meant. Sometimes it felt like I was staring right the fuck into her soul, and it was everything light and beautiful in the world. Unlike mine.

When I was fucking Riley, I had no doubt that I was the only person on her mind. But Dylan had a shit load to offer as well, and if Riley decided he was it for her, I wasn't sure what the fuck I would do.

I wasn't going to let him know that though.

Crossing my arms, I nudged my shoulder against the wall, and shot him my "are you fucking serious, asshole?" look. It was a look that had caused lesser men to cry.

"When has Riley ever gone to you?"

I was being a dick, especially since I could tell that he cared for her. Not as much as I did, but enough to make this one difficult situation. Because I wanted someone to love Dylan, he deserved that and so much more, but it couldn't be Riley.

The melancholy faded from Dylan's face and he straightened. "We really don't need to have this conversation, Beck. I know Riley is yours. Fuck. The girl is so gone on you, even when she was mad as hell at us. I don't begrudge you having her. It's just a thing ... I'll get over it."

The smallest niggle of tension remained between us, and I tried to figure out what to say to make it better, but I was starting to think there was nothing I could say. Only time would help with this. Time where Dylan hopefully didn't fall more in love with my captivating girl.

"You wanna play some music?" Dylan asked, suddenly. I schooled my face, something I'd been able to do since I was a young child, but that request worried me. It had been a long time since he'd asked me to play for him. A long time since his demons had almost destroyed him and he barely slept. Back when we were younger, I'd play music for him all the time. It was about the only time he slept.

"Sure," I said easily, striding over to grab my favorite at our place here: a vintage Gibson Hummingbird. I spent a few minutes tuning it before I settled back into one of the padded arm chairs.

"Any requests?" I asked him, my head already down as I strummed.

Dylan dropped into a chair across from me. "*Jesse's Girl?*" he said, shooting me a shit-eater grin.

A low chuckled left me. "Appropriate." I knew he'd been somewhat joking, but I strummed the opening chords anyway. I'd always had a natural ear for music, something my father had tried to beat out of me, because that was for "fuckboys that wear eyeliner and live on a street corner." And maybe it was this reason I'd pushed so hard to keep going with lessons. Why I'd threatened to kill him in his sleep if he ever touched any of my guitars. Anything to piss off senior Beckett.

But, truthfully, I was pretty sure I'd lose my mind without it in my life.

I started to sing and Dylan leaned back and closed his eyes. I didn't look at him, preferring to go into my own head when I sang. Although, I also couldn't help but remember the last time when Riley had heard me.

The look on her face made me want to sing for fucking ever. Just so I could see that look again.

Fuck. That girl had me tied up in knots. She was ripping the fabric of my world to shreds, and I couldn't even find it in myself to care anymore.

Whatever it brought, I would take this time with Riley. It would be worth the bloodshed that I knew was in my future.

When I finished *Jesse's Girl*, I didn't pause, transitioning straight into another one of Dylan's favorites: *November Rain*.

His breathing started to deepen when I was halfway through that song, and it was just like when I kept Riley's dreams at bay. There was a deep seated satisfaction in doing something non-violent to help the people I cared about.

My entire life was one fucked up circumstance, violence, death, fear, threats, money. That was it. Then there were moments like these, and I wondered if we'd ever get out. Whether there would be more than just a few glimpses of light in all of the darkness. Before Riley, I'd resigned myself to Delta. To this world.

But now it wasn't enough.

It wasn't good enough for her.

I just had to figure out how to get us out without the elders destroying us all.

Chapter 21

The morning after the gala, I woke in Beck's arms, and the fissure which had appeared in my chest last night, after I'd lost control with him, increased. All of the emotions I'd worked to conceal, they were leaking from me, and I couldn't quite figure out how to cram them back inside again.

Sneaking out of the bed, I crept through the penthouse and stepped out onto the huge balcony, closing the door behind me to give me some privacy.

My phone trembled in my hands when I lifted it and dialed a familiar number.

"Riles…" Dante's voice was rough. "Is everything okay?"

I swallowed hard. "I— I'm fucking this up, Dante."

It sounded like he was changing positions in bed. "Fucking what up? Has something happened?"

I hadn't told him about the almost gang-rape, because I was afraid that he would infiltrate the school and kill everyone involved. Well, all of those not in the hospital from Beck already.

This wasn't about that though. This was me ... slipping back into my old life. The one that had almost destroyed me. I needed my best friend to knock some sense into me.

"They're worming their way back into my life. Into my emotions. I'm scared. I know it's stupid to trust them, they're definitely going to hurt me again, that's inevitable, but I can't seem to help it."

Dante took a moment to answer, and I started to pace, the freezing air biting into my skin. "I think you're okay to let this go, Riley," he finally said, and I almost dropped the phone.

"What?" That advice was the opposite of knocking sense into me.

"People fuck up," he said softly. "Sometimes they get caught up in surviving, and then shit gets out of hand, and then people get hurt. I don't think they did it deliberately, they just had no choice."

There was something odd in Dante's voice, something I hadn't ever heard before, and it sent a jolt of unease through my body. That unease settled in low, and for a moment, I wondered if maybe he knew more than he was saying. This didn't feel just like random advice. It didn't even feel like advice connected to the specific incident I was talking about.

"What do you know?" I pressed, more bite in my tone. I trusted my best friend more than any living person in this world, and I knew him very well, which was how I knew he was keeping something from me.

Dante's voice was suddenly clearer, as if he'd sat up. "Riles, seriously, you don't need to worry about me. I've got your back, always. I mean ... I think I'm finally getting my life under control, taking back my power, and once I do that, no one will ever fuck with us again."

Again his words were confusing, and I was almost certain we were no longer talking about Beck and the shooting incident.

Before I could say anything more, the door slid open behind me, and I spun to find Evan there. "You should come inside before your nipples freeze off, Spare," he said, eyes dropping to the thin sleep top I was wearing.

I wrinkled my nose and turned my back on him. "I gotta go, Dante," I said into the phone. "Will I see you soon?"

"Yep," he replied. "I'll be out in the next week or so for your birthday. I'll keep you updated."

Birthday, right, that was soon.

"Bye, love you," I told him before hanging up the phone.

Evan was gone, so I stepped inside and beelined straight for the shower. Thankfully it was empty, and I managed to shower, dress, and get back out for room service breakfast in record time.

The five of us sat, and I held my hand out for coffee, because there was no way they could have forgotten how badly I needed that to function. Beck placed it in my hand, and as I stared down at my mug, the one with the queen on it, my eyes burned.

"I figured we needed a little unity," Beck said softly, taking the seat on my right side, pulling it very close as his dark gaze devoured me.

I looked around, and sure enough, everyone had their personalized cups. Fucker. He knew exactly what buttons to press in my stupidly sentimental body. It had meant everything to me to feel like I was one of them, especially after their early efforts to push me the fuck out of their lives. I'd finally felt like I'd made it, only to have it all ripped away in one moment.

My hands trembled, and for a second I didn't know if I was going to smash the cup. That would have been very dramatic and symbolic of my current anger, but I couldn't quite bring myself to break it. Not yet.

Instead I took a sip of perfectly brewed coffee.

My groan was low and breathy, and I ignored Beck and Dylan as they chuckled at my expense. "Let her enjoy her coffee," Jasper said. "She's much less of a bitch when she has it."

I flipped him off without even opening my eyes. The second sip was just as perfect.

Everyone started to eat, there was a huge spread of food, but my stomach was in knots from Beck, and everything else that had happened in New York, so I just sat back and watched them. In unguarded moments like this, it was the time I learned the most about all four of them.

They left all of the crunchy bacon for Evan, because that was the only way he ate it, and the scrambled eggs were Dylan's while Jasper preferred fried. Beck devoured French toast like it was the best thing he'd ever eaten, the more syrup and fruit the better. They all drank coffee, and it was often Dylan who acted as the house bitch and refilled their cups.

Each of them was so in sync that they didn't even have to speak. They just handed the food around, shared their life, and had each other's backs. The loyalty I could see between the four of them … it said a lot. It told me that they were not the type to betray someone they cared about. Not easily at least.

More of Beck's argument from last time ran through my head. He'd said it was Dante or me, and he chose me.

I understood that. I really did. But why couldn't they have talked to me?

Warned me at least so I was a tiny bit prepared.

"It really hurt me," I said suddenly, and their conversations immediately ceased. Suddenly, I was their sole focus. "Not that I had to kill someone and you all didn't give me a heads-up, but that I had to go through it alone. I'd thought we were a team. Stupidly. I trusted you four, even when everything in the world was telling me that you were bad news, and then you proved the fucking universe right by screwing me." I eyed Beck. "One of you literally."

He opened his mouth, but I cut him off before he could speak. "I've never run from the darkness in your world. If anything, I have embraced the assassination attempts, almost dying, being hunted down like animals, dealing with Catherine, and every other fucked up part of this world. I embraced it all because from the moment that plane crashed into the forest, I haven't felt alone."

My voice broke, and I tried my hardest to get it together, but I couldn't seem to. "My parents were ripped out of my world in an instant. A split second, some black ice, and I was an orphan. Alone. Even having Dante in my life couldn't come close to healing the hole that left in my soul, but you four … you made me feel like I had a family again."

I broke off, my head falling forward as tears dripped onto my clenched hands. "I'm not sure I can let you all back in like that again. I won't survive losing you a second time."

I could practically feel Beck vibrating at my side. Dylan was doing the same, and when I looked up, Evan and Jasper were wearing twin expressions of devastation. Until this point I wasn't sure any of them quite understood how much they had hurt me. How far they had broken me with their actions.

But … it seemed they might finally understand.

"We don't deserve your forgiveness," Dylan said softly, his voice rough. "There was nothing we could have done to stop you from having to cater to Delta's fucked up world, but we could have prepared you. We could have stood at your side instead of on the opposite side. That is on us."

Beck nodded. "I thought I was protecting you," he said, his voice a wash of dark emotions. "That if you went in blind you wouldn't do anything to raise Delta's suspicions. You wouldn't do anything to get yourself hurt."

I had to look at him, I couldn't help myself. His eyes were boring into mine.

"I never for a second thought you would assume we'd deliberately lured you into our world. I thought you would trust in us. That you'd know we were doing everything we could to protect you, while not raising our parents' suspicions."

I'd hurt Beck as well, that much was clear as he sat there, looking a little broken, too.

"Dante was not the smartest move," I told him softly, my tears finally drying up. "My anger over that … it clouded my judgement."

Fire flared in Beck's gaze, and I was confused for a beat as I tried to figure out what had triggered that. "Dante was the best choice," he said coldly. "Not only is he aware of this world and the mess of rules we have to follow, he was the one guaranteed to make you act fast and not fuck around. Our parents are insane, and they would have hurt you to get their own way."

Aware of this world. Did Beck mean simply because I was part of Delta and had shared some things with my best friend. Or because he was a bit of a fan of their company and its rise to power? Or maybe even a slight reference to the Grims and his place there?

Or was there something else…?

"You know you're one of us, Riley," Evan said seriously, that more subdued side that he hid so well in public, appearing again. "It doesn't matter what you do, or say, or how many ways you fuck up. You're always one of us."

"Unconditional," Beck added. "Our bond is unconditional."

The four of them reached out to me, almost like they were sealing that statement with one huge handshake. I hesitated, but only for a heartbeat. Unconditional was pretty rare in life, and if they were offering me that, then I could meet them all halfway.

"Unconditional," I murmured, my hand joining theirs. My eyes met Beck's. "We still need to talk," I told him, and he nodded, looking more relaxed than I'd seen him in a long time.

After that I managed to eat and drink my coffee, the mug lovingly packed back in the box Beck had brought with him. "I know we could get them for every house," Dylan said, as he wrapped each one gently, "but then it kind of loses that special touch."

I snorted. "You're all a bunch of softies underneath, aren't you?"

Leaning down, he pressed a kiss to the top of my head. "Only around you, Riles."

He stared down at me for a beat longer than was necessary in this situation, and I recalled the stunned way he's acted after I'd ambushed him with a kiss last night. I was just about to ask him if everything was okay with us, when we were interrupted by Evan.

"Car's ready," he said as he passed by. "Bomb squad has been over it, and the area is secure. We can head on down."

I jerked back, watching his broad shoulders as they disappeared down the hall. "Did he just say bomb squad?"

Dylan laughed. "Yeah, we haven't managed to ditch the security team when we're in New York. Too many of our competitors here for us to be complacent."

I must have looked nervous, because he wrapped an arm around me. "Don't stress. I'll double check it myself."

"What?" I gasped. "You can detect bombs too?"

Was there any fucking thing that Dylan couldn't do?

He shrugged. "Yeah, I've had training in it. Wouldn't call myself an expert, but I don't risk my friends without double checking things myself."

Apparently Beck had the same training, because he joined Dylan as they walked the perimeter of our car. Checking it over. Poking and prodding some shit. "I want all of you to stand back until it's started," Beck said, waving us toward the elevators.

"Fuck no," I said, stepping close to him. "We're all in this together, dude, and I'm not moving."

He shook his head. "Stubborn like the rest of them."

Jasper chuckled. "Beck always tries to pull the 'I'll start the dangerous car while you all wait in safety' move. It hasn't worked yet."

Beck nailed Jasper with a glare. "Figured you fuckers might be more cautious now that we have Riley, but apparently not."

"You're not blowing yourself up and leaving us to deal with Delta alone," Dylan said. He didn't sound like he was joking.

Beck didn't argue, he just swung around and climbed into the back, letting Jasper take his place behind the wheel. I ended up in the middle again, and sinking back between the guys, I held my breath as the car started. When there was no explosion, Jasper shifted it into reverse, and we left the parking lot.

It felt different in the car today, less tense, more of a companionable silence. My little speech this morning had knocked all of us around, and while it was definitely more emotional than we were most of the time, all of us had needed it. Step one to healing.

When we got outside of New York, Jasper cranked the music, and I spent the rest of the trip screaming old school Eminem songs, rap battling it out with Jasper, who knew every single fucking word to every song.

"Fancy yourself as a rapper, I see," I said to him when I stopped to catch my breath.

Dude was Slim Shady junior.

All too quickly Jasper pulled up at my place, and I blinked when they all got out. "What are you doing?" I asked. "Don't you guys have to get home…?"

Jasper snorted. "We are home, babe. We now own this entire building."

Okay then. "You moved fast on that," I said, surprised.

He shrugged. "I mean, not everyone is out yet, but all of your floor is vacant, and the rest should be out in the next few days."

Two days ago that would have pissed me off so bad, especially since they'd emptied the entire building. But now … now I was happy and excited. This was the best of both worlds. I got my independence from Catherine, the evil bitch, and still had the protection of my very well trained friends around me.

"Well, then," I said, jumping out onto the sidewalk. "Better pick out your apartments."

Chapter 22

If I ever ended up back in my poor neighborhood, I would probably be astonished when it took people thirty days to buy a place and two days to move in. By the time we left for school on Monday, all four of the guys had an apartment on the same floor as me. Fully decked out with sweet as fuck furniture, and looking like they'd lived there for years, rather than hours.

"There are some parts of this world I could get used to," I said as Beck drove me to school. "The money definitely opens a lot of doors for you."

It felt weird to be alone with Beck, even though I'd seen him quite a bit yesterday helping to move furniture and picking out the thick quilt and cover for his room. He'd even managed to set a room up with guitars. I was pretty sure they were all new, his originals back in his mansion, but I loved that an important part of who Beck was, got to come along to this new place. I'd tried my best to forget that song he sang when he thought I was asleep, but there were nights, when I closed my eyes, that the music would be in my head. His beautiful voice. Destroying me note by note.

"I've always had money, and I'd definitely struggle without its power, but at the same time, it's fucking soul destroying. People kill their families for it. They lie and steal and hurt, and maybe it's never that I've had that desperation, but part of me wishes that all of the money would just disappear."

I hesitated to ask the question, one which had been hovering in my mind for days now. "Do you think we could visit my brother's grave?"

Beck was silent, his hands tense on the steering wheel, and for a moment, I thought he was going to just completely ignore me.

"Yeah, it's been too long for me as well," he finally said, pulling into the school. "We can go this afternoon."

I nodded, relieved that he hadn't bitten my head off. Oscar was a touchy subject for all of them, and I really knew fuck all about my brother. Part of me wondered if I was just a morbid freak, because his death was often on my mind. It felt like there were pieces missing. Not just for me either, because the police had never figured out whether it was murder or suicide.

Maybe when we were at the grave, Beck would be more willing to talk.

The others joined us in the parking lot, and the five of us walked in together. A united front. Game faces on.

Katelyn was center stage, holding court with her minions. All of them watched as we walked past, and for the first time, I didn't bother to hide my hatred for her. I met her gaze with one of my own, a slight smirk on my lips.

Her smug expression faltered, and as her gaze ran across the five of us, the way we walked so close together. In sync again. I saw the red tinge her cheeks as her eyes blazed. She was not happy about that, and it made me happy to know that we'd ruined her morning.

"Claws in, pussy"—Jasper paused, and I rolled my eyes at him—"cat," he finished. "That bitch will get what's coming to her, don't you worry."

I turned so I could see him better. "What does that mean? What do you have planned?"

Beck shook his head then, reaching out and threading his fingers through mine. "Not at school, Butterfly."

Fair enough, but I wasn't letting them get away with any more deceptive behavior. If there was shit going down, I wanted in on it.

CLASS PASSED UNEVENTFULLY. EVAN WAS my escort for the day, and with his help during study period, I even managed to catch up on some of the school work I'd been missing. When the bell was about to ring, my phone buzzed.

Eddy: Hey, girl. Is everything okay? Haven't seen you for a few days. Jasper moved out?!?

Me: We definitely need to catch up soon. Jasper moved into my building. You should see about getting an apartment there too. Or you can share with me.

I almost deleted the last part, but then I realized that if I was forgiving the guys, I sure as fuck was forgiving Eddy. She hadn't even done anything. And I was worried about her living in that place with her toxic parents and no Jasper to keep an eye on things.

Eddy: Fuck yes. Okay, I'm asking now. If Jasper is there, they really shouldn't say no.

There was a brief pause and I got another text.

Eddy: And btw, there is a party this Friday that you're going to. Don't argue with me. *It's been too long since we let loose.*

I really hadn't been in the mood to party since everything went to shit in my life, but maybe it was a good idea. I could use a night to let off steam, and watching a peep show of some skeezebag politician didn't count. Even though I definitely had let off some tension that night.

Me: *Let's do it.*

I could already picture Eddy squealing when she got that text. I then shot one off to Dante telling him about the party on Friday. Not only was it my birthday, but he had a thing for Eddy, so he'd no doubt be there. I still wasn't sure how I felt about their "thing", because I was trying my best to keep Dante out of Delta bullshit, but I also knew he'd treat Eddy right, and that was important to me.

After class, Evan and I were met in the parking lot by the other three guys.

"Everything okay?" I asked, looking between them.

Jasper nodded. "Beck told us that you're wanting to visit Oscar's grave, and we figured that it was time for all of us to have a moment with him."

My hands were clammy, my heart doing weird palpitations at the thought of visiting Oscar's grave. "I just ... he was my brother," I said softly. "It feels like I should at least meet him."

Evan coughed and rubbed a hand over his face, like he was desperate to hide his emotions. Stepping forward, I wrapped my hand around his and pulled him along to Jasper's SUV. It felt important that all of us went together.

The drive to the cemetery was silent; I was still nervous as fuck about this moment.

Jefferson cemetery was on the opposite side of town to the Delta compound, and it was really pretty. As a place to bury dead bodies went. White iron gates, that were propped open, trellises of roses that splashed reds and pinks across the green foliage, and so much land that it disappeared into the horizon.

"This has been Jefferson's sole cemetery for a long time," Dylan said quietly, all of us paused at the front gate like we were afraid to take the final steps through. "We all have a lot of family buried here."

"But Oscar and Nat are the most important," Jasper cut in.

I paused. "Who's Nat?"

Silence. No one said a word, and I found myself looking at Beck. His jaw was doing that rigid thing, his eyes were doing the stormy thing, and my heart was galloping a million miles an hour, because I had this feeling this was Beck's great loss.

"Nat was my sister," Dylan told me, and I blinked, because I had not expected that. "Remember how I said my father had an affair with the nanny?"

I nodded.

He let out a derisive chuckle. "Well, we needed a nanny because I was not his first child. Nat was nine months older than me, and she was the legitimate heir. Even though they would never quite acknowledge that … the old 'needs a penis to sit on the Delta board' tradition was even stronger back then."

I gasped, not quite sure how to take this new information. I could feel his pain though—Beck's too—and I waited patiently for more of the story.

"She was a perfect child," Dylan continued. "White skin, like he preferred, blonde curls, and huge blue eyes that could get her anything she wanted."

A single tear traced along Dylan's cheek, and my heart ached like someone was actually squeezing it. "She was run over in our driveway," he finished suddenly. "When she was ten, and I was nine. One minute there and the next gone."

"She was not cut out for this world," Beck said softly. "We should have done a better job protecting her."

I tried to clear my throat. "That's why you were such an asshole to me when I first arrived?"

Beck nodded. "Yeah, I loved Nat like a little sister, and when she was killed…"

I swallowed my tears. "I'm so sorry," I said, stepping forward to wrap one arm around Beck and the other around Dylan. "I'm so sorry for your loss."

Dylan dropped his head, burying it in my neck, and I could have sworn more tears fell. "It was my fault," he whispered. "Her mother was trying to run me down and Nat jumped in the way. She got hit instead."

I gasped, jerking my head back so I could see his face.

"Are you serious?"

He nodded. "Yes. I'm the reason my sister is dead. She was the only one to give a fuck about me, and it got her killed."

I was just staring at him, my eyes wide, my breath ragged. "What in the fuck…?"

How could this be their lives? How could there be so much loss and pain and destruction in the twenty plus years they'd been alive.

"That was not your fault, Dylan," I said seriously, reaching up to hold his face so he couldn't turn away. "I never want to hear you say that again."

His expression shuttered, but he didn't argue with me.

Looking between the four of them, I'd never felt so happy that I'd moved out of the compound and forced the four of them to follow me. Their families were all toxic and deadly. Each of them more insane than the last.

"We should get inside," Evan said quietly, and we all moved to follow him.

The guys stopped at Nat's grave first, which was part of her family plot. The guys explained that all five Delta families had their own huge plots, with mausoleum looking structures and multiple large tombstones. Even in death they wanted to stand out and splash their money around.

Beck and Dylan crouched down on either side of her white marble grave topper, and placed their hands on top of it. They didn't bring flowers, or anything else, and I knew that wasn't their style. They were just here to remember her.

"Hey, big sis," Dylan said, voice somber. "Sorry I haven't been back for a while."

He cleared his throat before falling silent. His head lowered, and I ached to hug him. I'd stayed back with Evan and Jasper, who clearly had not been as close as Dylan and Beck were to her, and it was so hard not to step forward and offer them comfort.

Beck didn't say anything out loud, but he lowered his head as well, and I noted the white knuckles on his right hand that was gripping the side of the stone.

"Rest easy, little one," he murmured, right before he stood.

Part of me hated that they'd had a female as part of their group before me. Eddy had told me there was never a female in Delta, and I realized she hadn't quite lied, because she'd meant that the adult heirs of Delta, the five of them with Oscar, had never allowed a woman into their inner sanctum. But there had been a female they cared about. Another sister. One who was clearly closer to them than Eddy and Evan's sister must have been.

Nat.

Staring down at her grave, I had a strange sense of foreboding, which I pushed down as hard as I could. Worrying about my possible death because of this fucked up world was just a normal part of my daily anxiety these days, but now wasn't the time.

"Let's go to Oscar," Dylan said, and I was grateful for the distraction.

I nodded and then followed them as they wove us through the Grant section of the cemetery, past Langham, and then it was Deboise. There were a dozen or more fancy graves already in this area—Oscar's was right near the end of the taken plots.

The five of us stood at the base of his marble grave—it was black, with flecks of gold and white inlay. There was a fancy statue at the head, carved like four angels, harps in hand. His name was huge and the dates of his life carved beneath. There was a single phrase across it: *Rest easy, for your work here is done.*

Suddenly my throat was tight, my eyes burning, and I had to press a hand to my mouth to stop a sob from escaping. I'd had a brother. A real, blood brother, who might have been a part of my family, if I'd ever been given the chance to know him.

"Oscar was the funny one," Beck said, breaking the silence. "Always making a joke. We learned to never leave him alone in our rooms or houses, because there would be some bullshit prank waiting for us when we least expected it."

"He was such a fucker," Jasper said with a choked laugh. "I still remember the time he dyed my dog purple. I swear he gave her fleas just so I would have to use the powder."

Their laughter died off, but the silence didn't feel quite as heavy this time.

"Tell me more about him," I said, managing not to sob.

"He was shorter than you," Evan chimed in. "Shortest of us all, which he hated, but he liked to say he had the biggest guns."

"Not fucking likely," Beck cut in.

I chuckled, because it was hard to imagine anyone having larger arms than Beck and Dylan.

"He was up for absolutely anything," Dylan added, and the mood was somber again. "It didn't matter if you phoned him at three in the morning, Oscar was always the perfect wingman. He would never let you down."

"Never," Evan whispered. "He was the one who introduced me to anime, so it makes perfect sense that his sister would share the same love."

The tears couldn't be stopped any longer, and I decided just to let them fall. I might not have "known" Oscar, but through these four, I felt the connection.

"He was our best friend," Jasper added. "And the fact that I still don't know what happened to him, kills me every fucking day."

The silence pressed onto me, questions hovering on the tip of my tongue. "Do you think he killed himself?" I finally asked, my voice a breathless quiver of sound in the still air. "Is that possible? We know there's no other way out of Delta."

I waited for their anger, because it felt disrespectful to suggest such a thing when they all had such fond memories of him. But I knew that suicide, depression, grief … it didn't just happen to poor, lonely, sad people. It happened to people from all walks of life.

It happened to anyone and everyone without prejudice.

"Oscar had times when he was introverted," Dylan said, kneeling down then, pressing his hand to Oscar's grave, as he had done with his sister. "Where he would retreat from us, go into his own head, and be aloof for a few days. We always just knew that was his way, and we'd let him go. Giving him the time and space he needed."

"And he always came back," Beck added, voice growly. "Always. Until we got that call."

"So you think he did kill himself?" I pushed, needing to clarify it.

"Not a chance," Beck bit back, crouching down next to Dylan. "Oscar was murdered. I'm certain of it, and I'm equally as certain that it was someone in Delta that did it."

Chapter 23

I couldn't get anything else out of them about Oscar's death, so I instead spent the rest of my time there, silently talking to my brother. It was much more painful than I'd expected, and by the time we left, I was emotionally spent.

The five of us ate dinner together in my apartment, because it seemed to be the central gathering point, and then I crawled into bed, only to be joined by Beck ten minutes later.

He held me close, and even though we didn't talk, there was some more healing happening between us. I ended up sleeping soundly for most of the night, and it was only when I woke that I realized how long it had been since I had a nightmare.

The next day at school passed quickly, and just as I was wandering across the parking lot with Evan, Eddy sprinted out of the school and pretty much tackled me into the grass next to the front stairs.

"Jesus fucking Christ, Edith," Evan cursed, peeling her off me so I could stand up again. "Riles still has bruises and shit, ease up you psycho."

Eddy rolled her eyes at him, like he was another annoying brother, and plucked some grass off my plaid skirt. "Sorry, girl. I was just so freaking excited!" She demonstrated this by bouncing up and down a little with a grin so wide it showed almost all her teeth. "I'm moving in!"

My jaw dropped. "What? Holy shit! That was quick!" I'd only mentioned it to her the day before.

Eddy beamed. "I know! I really didn't think they'd say yes but with Jasper already living there, they didn't have much to say. But also, like, they don't care that much about me." She shrugged, as though that fact didn't bother her. "I mean, I have to live in *his* apartment. But at least we're on the same floor, right?"

"Good enough!" I agreed, returning her hug on impulse. I wasn't a big hugger ... like, at all. But it was hard not to get caught up in Eddy's excitement.

"What did I miss?" Jasper called out, jogging up to us and grinning. "Why are we all hugging? I'll take one if they're going free." He snatched me out of Eddy's embrace and snuggled me tight, making me laugh.

Evan answered for us. "Eddy's moving into your apartment," he informed Jasper. "Didn't you know?"

Jasper froze, but didn't release me. Not that I minded, Jasper gave great hugs and these days I found I was craving that caring human contact more than ever before. Maybe it was having to live without them for so long. Having to hold onto that anger which ate away at my insides.

That shit was so behind me.

"Eddy's doing fucking what now?" he demanded, turning what-the-fuck eyes on his sister.

She smirked at him, with more than a touch of evil. "Eddy's moving into your bachelor pad, big brother."

Jasper gasped dramatically and buried his face in my hair, pretending to sob as he wailed "Noooooooo!"

We were all laughing at his expense when Beck approached and peeled me out of Jasper's grip and tucked me into his side. I was just about to make a comment about how I was getting tossed around like a dog chew toy when—

"Slut," someone spat, and my head snapped around to see who it was.

There. Walking past us was a group of cheerleaders, with Katelyn Huntley's shining blonde head in the thick of them all.

"Excuse me?" I snapped back at them, unsure who had actually delivered the insult.

None of them seemed so brave as to further their insults while Beck, Jasper and Evan were all staring right at them, but the looks I got were pure poison.

"They're getting bolder," Evan murmured as the girls continued across the parking lot to their own cars. "Katelyn's influence, no doubt."

Beck grunted a pissed off sort of sound. "We need to handle her. Sooner, rather than later."

"Handle her how?" I asked, frowning up at them. Damn. Why were these boys all so damn tall, even when I was in heels? "What do you mean by that?"

"Undecided," Beck murmured, then turned to Eddy. "I hear you're moving in with Jasper, huh? This is going to be fun."

"What? How does he know and I didn't?" Jasper grumbled, pouting and stuffing his hands in his pockets as we all headed for the cars.

Eddy snickered a laugh. "Because it was more fun to blindside you. Hey, we should have a housewarming party! Like a giant one, for all of the apartments!"

Jasper gave his sister a light, playful whack on the back of her head. "Security, dipshit. No parties, no guests."

Eddy let out a groan. "I thought the rules would be different away from the compound. Come on, Jazzy, one little party couldn't hurt." She put on her very best puppy dog eyes, but I could have told her she was barking up the wrong tree on this one.

"The answer is no, Edith," Beck said in response to her pleading. "If anything, security needs to be even tighter now that we're out of the compound. There has already been a death threat sent against Riley, and need we remind you of the incident here at school just last week?"

Eddy's face fell, and she gave me a guilty smile. "Good point. Sorry, I was just caught up in the excitement."

"Don't stress," I replied. "We can just party it up at someone else's place and leave them to clean up the mess instead. It'll be great."

This seemed to cheer her back up a bit. "Oh yeah, Friday night. Sick. Okay, I'm gonna grab clothes from Mom and Dad's place and head over. You wanna come with?"

Just as I opened my mouth to accept, Jasper cut me off. "No, she can't. I already booked Riley for Mario this afternoon."

"Ugh, you suck!" She whined at her brother, but eventually got in her car and took off with a wave and a promise to be over soon.

"Mario?" I questioned Jasper. Beck still hadn't let go of me, and if I was being honest I wasn't really in any hurry to detach his arm from my waist any time soon. "I hope you either mean Mario's Pizza or Mario Kart. Or both."

Jasper grinned, and Evan laughed.

"I like the way you think, Spare," Evan complimented me. "Both sounds fucking epic. I'll swing past Mario's Pizza and meet you guys back in Riley's apartment, yeah?"

The boys all said their goodbyes and I—shockingly—ended up strapped into the passenger seat of Beck's Bugatti. A seat I was beginning to think of as *my* seat, which was probably another item to discuss with my therapist, whenever I got around to that.

Neither of us spoke for the drive home, but the way he drove—taking the long route, slamming through corners and far exceeding the speed limit—was deliberate. By the time we pulled up in front of our building, I was practically trembling with adrenaline. Among other things.

Fucking Beck. Everything he did lately seemed to just be proving how well he knew me, and god fucking damn if he hadn't just got me all kinds of hot and bothered right before we were supposed to hang out with the whole gang.

"Everything okay, Butterfly?" he asked with total faked innocence when we stepped into the elevator. My arms were folded under my breasts and my thighs were clenched tight, but still I gave him a tight smile like nothing was wrong.

"Of course, why wouldn't it be?" I lied.

A small smile played at his lips. Smug fuck. "Okay, well if you need a hand with anything ... just let me know." His wink told me exactly where that *hand* would go if I accepted.

Beck pressed the button for our floor and as the doors slid closed, my resolve crumbled.

I threw myself at him in a flurry of motion, my school skirt was bunched around my waist, my panties discarded, and Beck's long fingers were buried deep inside my aching pussy.

I moaned, long and way too loud as he skillfully finger fucked me against the wall of the elevator, sending me crashing over the edge into a dizzying orgasm right before we reached our floor.

Thankfully, no one was in the corridor outside the elevators when the door slid open, because although he'd gotten me off with the speed of light, I was still riding the aftershocks of my climax as he smoothed my skirt back down and pocketed my underwear.

Beck's strong arm around my waist was the only thing that kept me on my stupid stiletto heels as I wobbled out of the elevator, my knees like jelly and glow worms still dancing across my vision. Still, neither of us spoke until we reached my front door and he claimed my mouth in a bruising kiss.

"I should get changed, and so should you. The boys will be here any minute," I warned him, and a devilish look crossed his face.

"Do me a favor?" he asked, and silly me with my post-orgasm euphoria, just nodded. "Don't wear any panties," he whispered, his voice dark and dirty and full of promise.

I should have told him to go shove it, that we couldn't just go back to playing happy families because we'd had one little group heart to heart. I should have told him that sex was not the answer to our problems, and that it was only confusing the situation more. I *should* have told him that I wasn't interested in letting him toy with me, in allowing the sexual anticipation and excitement near drown me until the rest of the guys fucked off later that night.

I should have. But instead I just gave him a smirk of my own and let myself into my apartment, leaving him out in the hall without an answer.

Which, really, was answer enough.

Chapter 24

As it turned out, letting my libido rule my actions was a terrible idea. Or an excellent one. The jury was still out on that case. I'd not only followed Beck's instructions of leaving my panties off, I'd gone one step further and changed into a casual sweater dress, rather than the sweats I'd been planning on.

While I was perfectly safe sitting in one of my twin recliners to whoop Jasper's ass in Mario Kart—proving I was a better driver than him on and off the roads—it was when I relinquished the controller to Evan, and Beck pulled me into his lap on the couch, that I was in trouble.

He wasn't even subtle about toying with me, either. Eventually it was getting all too heated, and I excused myself to get a glass of water from the kitchen.

And by glass of water, I meant that I needed to go stick my head in the freezer for a quick second.

"Hey," Dylan said from behind me as I was neck deep inside my ice box, and I jumped with fright. "Sorry, didn't mean to startle you," he apologized with a knowing smile. "Looking for ice cream?"

"Huh?" I blinked at him for a second. "Oh, uh, yes. Yes, that's what I'm doing. Looking for ... ice cream." I chewed my lip and avoided eye contact so he wouldn't see the clear lie. Not that he probably hadn't already worked it out. Ugh, I badly needed to work on a Delta face of my own.

"So what's up?" I asked him, grabbing the first carton of ice cream I could touch from my freezer and plonking it down on the counter to grab a spoon.

Dylan started to say something, then stopped himself and scratched the back of his head uncomfortably. "I just wanted to check you were okay," he finally said. "The other night at the gala—" *when I kissed him...*

"I'm fine," I assured him, cutting off whatever else he was going to say. "We're cool, right?"

He frowned at me for a long moment, concern evident on his face. "Yeah, always. Just so long as Beck didn't—"

"I'm fine," I said again. I didn't really want to hear what he thought Beck might have done after seeing me kiss his best friend, but I was pretty sure fucking me fast and dirty in the bathroom wasn't it. What could I say? We had issues.

Dylan nodded, seeming to accept my answer. "Okay, cool. I just wanted to touch base. I know all this shit with Delta and everything that happened last week has been a lot. You know you can talk to me if you ever need to?"

I smiled at his genuine offer, despite the fact that Dylan wasn't exactly the most talkative of my new friends. "Thanks, Dylan," I said with sincerity. "I appreciate it."

From the living room, loud voices spiked, and we both glanced in their direction.

"Sounds like Jasper's cheating," Dylan commented, heading back through to investigate.

I laughed. "He does that often?"

"Way too often," Dylan replied with a long suffering sigh then waded in to break up the heated argument between Jasper and Evan, which Beck was just sitting back and watching with an amused smile on his face.

While Dylan tried to mediate the argument between the two friends, Beck caught my eye and jerked his head in the direction of my bedroom. Then got up and sauntered his sexy ass in there all casual as anything, like he didn't have a hard as fuck boner showing through his sweats. Then again, the other three were so deeply embroiled in their argument they probably didn't notice a damn thing.

Fuck it.

Leaving them to their debate over whether it was cheating to interfere with the other player's controller or not, I crossed the room and slipped inside my bedroom.

In a second Beck's lips were on mine, his hands all over my body just like I'd been craving all evening. He picked me up and dropped me onto the bed without once breaking our kiss, pressing all of his hard body into mine as I almost silently moaned my encouragement. The guys were just in the next room, but if we were quiet enough we might have a shot...

Right up until my front door banged open and Eddy stepped inside my room, announcing loudly, "I'm here for my sleepover! Beck, that means you're outta here."

We froze where we were, my legs spread, Beck's erection grinding into my naked crotch and his mouth on mine.

"Come on," Eddy snapped, whacking Beck on the shoulder. "Move it. It's girls' night."

"It is?" I asked, pulling back from Beck just a fraction.

"Since when?" he demanded, turning a glare over his shoulder at Eddy.

Typical of my new best friend, she just propped her hands on her hips and glared right back at him. "Since you all stole my girl for pizza and video games instead of letting her help me move. Now shoo. Go take a cold shower or jack off or something."

I needed to cover my mouth to hide the startled laugh that escaped me at her suggestion. Beck glowered and turned back to me with a look of disbelief on his face, but I just shrugged.

"You heard her," I chuckled, wiggling out from under him and making sure my vagina was covered before I flashed it at Eddy.

Beck grumbled something under his breath, but reluctantly stood up and adjusted his pants before glaring at Eddy again. "Never knew you to be such a cockblocker, Edith," he muttered, but I could tell he was mostly joking. Mostly.

Eddy just shrugged and grinned. "'Kay, have fun with your hand tonight, Beck."

"Think of me!" I suggested oh so helpfully as he stalked back out of my room.

Eddy dissolved into a puddle of laughter as the boys all left my apartment, and I whacked her with a pillow. Hard.

"Ow, what was that for?" she complained, still laughing.

"That." I whacked her again. "Was for being a pussyblocker! Now I'm horny as shit, you asshole."

This only seemed to make her laugh harder, but she rolled off my bed and grabbed a professionally wrapped gift box from on top of her bag. "Good thing I came bearing housewarming gifts then, isn't it?" She winked, and I opened the box with suspicion, then started laughing myself.

"A vibrator? You bought me a vibrator as a housewarming gift?" I leveled an amused stare at her. "I can't decide if you're the best friend a girl ever had or the worst."

She made a sound of mock outrage. "Clearly the best. It's waterproof. Go take a shower and relieve some of that Beck induced tension so we can actually have a proper girls' night."

I had no idea what to do with the absurdity that was Edith Langham, so I just shook my head and went to do what she said. Why not, right?

SCHOOL THE NEXT DAY WAS uneventful; it had been a quiet week on the old bullying front. There were still a few slut-coughs which probably wasn't helped by the fact that all four boys seemed totally comfortable hugging me, holding my hand, generally shadowing me freaking *everywhere*. Then again, I didn't much give a shit about what other academy students thought of me.

"Hey, how come there hasn't been any blow back from the school admin about ... last week?" I asked Beck and Dylan after school while we waited for the other guys, and Eddy, to join us.

I hugged my arms around myself and shivered. I wasn't really ready to discuss and dissect it but it had been playing on my mind that the whole school was acting like nothing had happened. I mean, Beck almost killed at least one student. There was no way the faculty didn't know about it. It also made me wonder just where the hell all those teachers were during my attack.

"We had it handled," Dylan replied, cryptic as fuck.

I scowled. "What happened to no more secrets?"

He nodded and sighed as he stuffed his hands in his pockets. "Okay, Delta made some threats, then softened it with a sizable donation to the school. In about a month, they'll be breaking ground on a brand new Olympic grade polo stadium."

My jaw dropped. "It's that easy? Katelyn pays some guys to try and gang rape me in a classroom, then Beck puts them all in the hospital, and it's all swept under the rug with money?"

Beck tilted his head to the side as he watched me. His back was against the side of his car and he looked totally relaxed, despite the content of our conversation. "Did you want to file criminal charges against them, Butterfly? We probably should have asked you instead of just assuming."

"What?" I shook my head, frowning. "That's not what I meant. And no, I don't want to file charges and do the whole court hearing bullshit. Pretty sure they got what was coming to them anyway. Is that revolting cretin still alive, by the way?" By that, I meant Todd who'd clearly been the one leading the attack. I had a small hope that he'd eventually died from his injuries.

"For now," Dylan murmured. "Oh look, here's Eddy."

I huffed, but let the subject drop seeing as I knew they wouldn't discuss Delta around Eddy. Not that she didn't already know way more than they realized. But whatever. Appearances.

"What's the plan tonight?" she asked, bouncing up to us with Jasper and Evan not far behind her. "Movies and Indian food?"

My belly growled, but Beck shook his head. "Not for me, I've been called in for a Delta meeting." He looked as happy about that as I imagined.

Just then, my phone buzzed with a message, and I swiped the screen to check it.

Richard: Riley, would you be able to stop by the house this evening? Catherine is away in New York. I promise you won't see her.

"Apparently I'm popping by the Delta compound for dinner with Richard," I told everyone.

"I'll drop you over," Evan offered, "I need to go check on my mom anyway."

We all split up into our respective vehicles and headed out of the academy parking lot. I wasn't super chatty with Evan, but there was a lot weighing on my mind. What Delta was calling Beck in for, and even stronger, what Richard wanted to discuss that couldn't be done with Catherine home. Whatever it was, surely couldn't be good or he would have just called.

Chapter 25

Walking back into the Deboise mansion felt ... weird. I'd only had my apartment for a week and a half and it was already a million times homier than this soulless estate.

"Hello?" I called out, hesitating in the foyer. I was still a stranger in this house, blood ties or not. "Richard? It's Riley."

I didn't know why I announced myself like that. As if any other teen girl would be wandering into the Deboise manor uninvited.

My biological father—who I honestly knew about as well as Stewart, the butler—came through from another room and smiled broadly when he saw me.

"Riley," he greeted me, "It's so good to see you. I heard about the unpleasantness last week. Are you doing okay?"

His casual mention of my gang rape attempt had me taken back, and I stumbled over some kind of neutral response without really hearing what I was saying. But what the fuck? Richard knew about that and never reached out to me? Obviously he was my father by DNA only but *still*...

Then again, just because Catherine held his seat by proxy now, didn't mean Richard wasn't the true Delta member. Maybe I'd been giving him too much credit as a nice person.

"Are you hungry?" he asked, leading me through to the dining room, "Of course you are, you're a teenager. I remember what Oscar was like at eighteen, he never seemed to be full." He started to smile at the fond memory, then his face crumpled with grief.

Awkwardly, I sat down at the seat he indicated and cleared my throat. "I, um, went to see him the other day," I said softly, not wanting to upset him any further. "I hope that's okay. I just wanted to..." I shrugged "... I don't really know. It just felt right to visit."

Richard nodded. "He would have liked that. He would have liked *you*. I'm so sorry you never got the chance to know him."

His words got me a bit choked up, and I needed to swallow the lump in my throat before I could respond. "Me too," I whispered.

As if by unspoken agreement, we both rushed to change the subject to more neutral topics.

Throughout dinner, which Stew served, we remained on safe conversation. School assignments, sports teams, movies. It wasn't until Stew had cleared our dessert bowls that Richard got to the point of why he'd asked me over.

"Riley, I know I'm not currently an acting member on Delta's council," Richard began, handing me a crystal cut glass of whiskey as we relocated to the sitting room. "But that's by my own choice. After Oscar's death, I didn't feel like I was of a sound enough mind to handle the decisions and votes which are required of a Delta sitting council member."

I snorted quietly with contempt. "But Catherine is?"

Richard's lips tightened. "Catherine ..." He sighed heavily. "Catherine is a very smart, very calculating woman. When she sets her mind to something..." he trailed off again, then shook his head like he was saying too much. "Anyway, what I was saying, is that although I've allowed Catherine to proxy my position, I am still aware of everything going on. I was kept well informed of your mission with the other successors on the weekend, and given a full report on your success. I wanted to tell you how proud I was of you."

I narrowed my eyes at him. "For ... breaking into a senator's office and stealing his illegal sex tape? Strange thing to be proud of your daughter for, but whatever." That was mostly muttered to myself, and I took a long sip of the amber spirit to stop running my mouth further.

"Yes, well. Strange world we live in." Richard just shrugged it off. "Here's the thing, though." He paused, like he was trying to decide if he should continue or not. "Somehow, Huntley also obtained the same recording."

My brows shot up in surprise. "How?"

"Well, that's what I'd like to figure out," he said softly, his gaze all too sharp on me for comfort. "What can you tell me about that night, Riley? Could anyone else have gained access to that recording room? Made a copy of the flash drive, perhaps?"

I blinked at him a couple of times, comprehending his question while I took another sip of the whiskey. "You mean... did Dylan or Beck make a copy?" I was already shaking my head. "There's no way, they had one copy and it was handed off immediately."

Richard just shrugged again, his face neutral and non-threatening. For some reason, that scared me more than any of the other Delta members I'd met. "Not just Dylan and Beck ... anyone at all?"

Frowning, I shook my head again before belatedly noticing how fuzzy it felt. "No, I was with them the whole time. Beck only had the one flash drive, then he gave it to Dylan to take to Catherine. And no one else was in the room with us."

Richard nodded slowly. "I see. And you saw Dylan hand the flash drive to Catherine, then?"

"No, I..." I scrubbed at my eyes with the heel of my hand. "I was fucking Beck in the bathroom." I frowned, hearing those words come out of my mouth. *What in the world?* "Did you..." A sick feeling of dread washed through me as the room began to spin. "Did you drug me?"

Richard shrugged again, a gesture I was fast coming to despise. "Just a little something to loosen your tongue, dear. It won't have any long term effects, I promise. Now, to be clear, you said Sebastian handed the flash drive to Dylan, but you never actually saw him give it to Catherine?"

"No, but he did." I scowled and tried to stand up, but my legs turned to liquid and I fell back into my seat in an awkward sprawl. "Fuck you, Richard," I snarled. "You never actually stepped down from Delta, did you?"

A smile creased his features, which were blurring a bit. "Oh, I did. In a way. My son's murder required investigation, and it was so much easier to fly under the radar when everyone writes you off as a grieving father on the brink of breakdown. And now here I am, investigating a mole. Tell me, Riley ... are *you* that mole?"

His tone was so light, so matter of fact, I wouldn't have been shocked if he decided to shoot me in the head right here in his sitting room. Fuck. Me. The rest of the council combined didn't have *shit* on Richard Deboise, he was one scary ass motherfucker.

"No," I snapped back, "and neither are Dylan or Beck. If you want to find a mole, maybe look at the other people who knew about our mission." Namely—the entire Delta council and whoever else was involved with our operation that night. Especially Catherine Deboise, who had a very close tie to the head of Huntley.

Richard smiled again. A creepy, soulless smile. "I believe *you* believe that. Thank you, dear. It's been lovely getting to know you better. Stewart will see you home."

I could no longer feel my limbs, and my vision was both blurring and spinning, but I still noticed when Stewart gathered me up in his arms and started walking out of the sitting room.

"Oh, and Riley?" Richard called after us, causing Stew to pause. "I trust you won't share this chat with anyone. It would be so sad if Beckett lost their heir so close to his succession, and when you've clearly formed such a close bond with the young man too."

"Fuck you, Richard," I tried to snarl back, but it came out a bit slurred.

Stewart started walking with me again, and just before I passed out, I could have sworn I heard Richard mutter something more from close by.

"You should have taken the IDs and run while you could, stupid girl," he said, but instead of sounding threatening, his voice was full of ... regret and despair. Something soft brushed across my forehead, but I was already dropping into unconsciousness.

SUNLIGHT BEAT DOWN OVER MY face, and I groaned. Why did my head feel like I'd been put through a meat grinder and who the fuck left my curtains open?

"What the hell?" I mumbled, my tongue thick and heavy like I'd been drinking all night. Picking up my phone from the night stand, I checked the time ... then groaned. My alarm was set to go off in six minutes, and it was a school day.

My head was pounding. Utterly thumping. Cringing with every movement, I staggered over to my bathroom and busted in without taking notice of the fact that the shower was running.

Why was my shower running?

Ugh, too hard to look.

I turned the sink faucet on and splashed a couple of handfuls of cold water on my face then patted it dry with a washcloth as the shower turned off.

My eyes opened just in time to see the reflection of a very wet, very naked Sebastian Beckett stepping out of my shower.

"Sebastian." I frowned, still fuzzy headed and confused. "Why are you in my shower? I don't remember..." I was going to say that I didn't remember going to bed with him, but really I didn't remember *anything*.

He grinned, taking his sweet ass time to pick up a towel and *slowly* dry off. It was like getting front row tickets to the Magic Mike show ... if Mike ditched the G-string. "I'm not surprised you don't remember," he said with a low laugh. "You were passed out cold when Stewart brought you home. Hit the Scotch a bit too hard with Richard, huh?"

"Huh?" I wrinkled my nose, then all of a sudden the night before came flooding back to me, and I gasped. "Holy shit," I whispered, covering my face with my hands. Richard ... he'd *drugged* me! What kind of sick, deranged, messed up...? But of course he was unstable. All of them were. It had to be scientifically impossible to maintain total sanity in the fucked up world Delta operated within.

"Butterfly?" Beck tucked his towel around his waist and stroked my hair. "Are you okay?"

My lips parted to tell him everything. All of it. Richard's questions, the fact that he suspected a mole, the fact that I may have inadvertently cast suspicion on Dylan, the fact that he'd been working for Delta all along, conducting investigations into...

But I couldn't tell him. Richard's threat came slamming back to me, and I had to swallow several times to keep from throwing up. Not just because the threat had been really fucked up, but because I'd been mad at them for keeping secrets, and now I was doing the same fucking thing. And using the same excuse.

To protect him.

Beck would be pissed too, but that was just something I'd have to deal with. Keeping him alive was my number one priority.

"Uh huh," I lied, giving him a tight smile. "Just, uh, really hungover. I guess."

He cupped my cheek in one of his huge hands, peering into my eyes like he could read my soul, and secretly I hoped he could. Maybe then he'd have a heads-up on everything and be able to ... I didn't know. Save himself?

"Okay," he finally said, accepting my bullshit. "Get ready for school and I'll grab you some aspirin. One of us should have warned you how heavily Richard can drink." He said this last with a chuckle, and ice formed down my spine. Had Richard pulled this same trick on him at some stage? Except he didn't remember it?

The whole thing was turning my stomach, so I just gave him a tight nod of acceptance.

"Sebastian, wait," I blurted as he started to leave the bathroom. He turned back to me with interest in his gaze, and before I could second guess myself, I grabbed his face and planted a quick kiss on his lips.

It had caught him by surprise, no doubt, but not so much that he didn't grab me back before I could pull away, deepening the kiss to something much hotter than I'd intended.

"I don't know what's going on with you this morning, Butterfly," he whispered in a husky, lust filled voice. "But I like it." He pressed another kiss to my swollen lips. "I'll be back with those aspirin in a sec."

He left the bathroom, and I hurried to shower and dress for the day. Beck had left the aspirin on the bathroom counter along with a glass of water so I gulped them down while blow-drying my hair. By the time I emerged ready for school, I was already feeling better.

"Coffee," Beck said when I met him in the kitchen. He placed a steaming mug—my queen mug—in my hand, and dropped another quick kiss on my lips. "I just need to grab something from Dylan, I'll meet you at the car?"

"Yep." I nodded and took a long sip. Holy damn, Beck made an orgasmic cup of coffee. I might just keep him around to make me coffee for the rest of my life ... among other things. He bent down to pull his boots on, and I didn't even try to pretend I wasn't checking his ass out. He had a really great ass.

He glanced back, catching me staring, and I just shrugged.

After he left, I allowed myself a couple more minutes to drink my coffee while Richard's threat echoed through my head. There were two major things I could take away from what he'd said.

One, Oscar had been murdered, and I think he suspected another council member. Just like Beck did. And two, I was sort of falling in love with Beck. Okay, fine. It had already happened, but my anger toward him had masked it all. Hearing his life threatened in such a callous way had sent such potent, soul crushing fear through me, that I couldn't keep burying my head in the sand.

So now what the hell did I do?

Panic, I guess? For today, though, I would allow myself a little indulgence. Would it really be so terrible to drop my guard around him for one day and just see what it was like? After all, Dante himself had told me to let it go...

Lost in thought, and practically buzzing with butterflies in my belly, I made my way down to the parking garage. I was so distracted, I didn't see the dark figure waiting between the cars until it was almost too late.

As it was, it was my heel catching in a drain grate that saved me when the person took a swing with his knife. Terrified, I let out a scream and ducked out of the way when he stabbed at me again. He didn't get a chance to try a third time as a shot rang out with a deafening crack, and my attacker crumpled to the ground in a lifeless heap.

"Riley." Beck rushed over, his gun still in his hand and his eyes darting all around us, even as he crouched beside me. "Are you okay? Did he hurt you?" He must have been satisfied that there was no one else jumping out of the shadows, because he tucked his gun away and pulled out his phone instead. "Dylan, parking garage, now."

"What the fuck just happened?" I squeaked, staring wide eyed at the dead man. Blood had begun pooling under him and was slowly crawling toward the drain that had saved my life.

Beck gathered me up in his arms and stood, carrying me away from the body and placing me gently down on the fire escape stairs. "Riley, baby," he coaxed. "Tell me if he hurt you anywhere. Did he hit you? Cut you?"

I shook my head, numb. "N-no. No. I caught my heel and tripped…" I waved a hand at the drain grate which was now stained red with my attacker's blood. "He just came out of nowhere. What the fuck just happened, Beck?"

His face tightened, the skin around his eyes pinching as he cringed. "Please don't, baby. Please don't shut me out again. I'm so sorry. I shouldn't have left you alone." He wrapped his arms back around me, hugging me tight to his chest. His heart was thundering, and the way he stroked my hair it seemed like he was shaking a little.

I frowned, confused, then it clicked. I'd called him Beck again, and he'd taken it as a sign that our earlier progress was ruined.

"Hey." I pushed back from him just far enough that he could see my face, see the sincerity in my eyes. "Sebastian. I'm fine, I promise. That scared the shit out of me, no joke. But it's pretty far from the worst that's happened in the last few months, you know?"

He looked unconvinced, but Dylan arrived then and it was suddenly all business again.

"Did he say anything to you?" Dylan asked, after he'd checked behind every car, pillar, and shadow in the whole damn parking garage. "Anything at all?"

I shook my head, hugging my knees as I remained on the steps where Beck had put me. "Nothing at all. Just popped up out of nowhere and started swinging his knife."

Dylan and Beck exchanged a look. "He was trying to be quiet," Beck said gruffly. "A gunshot would have alerted us. He was no amateur."

Dylan shook his head. "They're getting bolder. They really want Riley out of the way, but I can't figure out why."

I eyed Beck closely. "So Katelyn can have Beck. It's the only explanation."

Huntley was desperate to secure their second vote.

Beck looked extra pissed and disgusted then. "I've called the cleanup crew," Dylan advised, distracting us. "I'll wait here until they arrive. You two should get to school."

"What?" I exclaimed. "Just ... go to school after someone tried to murder me?"

Beck nodded. "He's right. If Katelyn had anything to do with this, we want to see her reaction when you turn up alive and well."

I gaped at him. "But what if one of you guys were the intended victim?" I changed my story. "It was your car he was hiding beside." I might have just been the unlucky one to come out first.

"True, but considering all the threats sent to Delta recently have been centered around you, it's a pretty safe guess that this was an attack on you." Dylan shrugged like it was so fucking common to get death threats—or attempts.

"Wait, what?" I blurted, "All the threats? There have been more than one? What the Hell, Sebastian? You told me about one!"

Dylan grinned at us both. "Sounds like you two are back on good terms, *Sebastian*." He dodged just in time to avoid the punch Beck was about to deliver to his midsection, and backed up a few steps—still smirking. "Go on, I've got this handled here. You two sniff around Ducis and see if any blondes are acting suspicious."

Without really giving me any opportunity to delay further, Beck did a quick check of his car, and then had me bundled into it and out on the road in no time. The short drive to Ducis Academy gave me just enough time to reel at what my life had become. It wasn't even nine in the morning and already I'd fought off a drug hangover, seen a totally naked, totally gorgeous man coming out of my shower, had a coffee, been almost murdered, and seen a guy shot.

"Fuck," I swore as Beck parked in front of the Academy. "I forgot to do my English assignment."

Beck just shot me a puzzled glance, and I burst out in borderline hysterical laughter.

Someone had just *tried to kill me* and I was worried about my English assignment.

Yep, another one on the list for my future therapist.

Chapter 26

School passed uneventfully again. Katelyn didn't seem to register any shock at seeing me alive so she was either the best actress in the world, or innocent—in this case.

I did, however, get called in to a meeting with the academy guidance counselor just before the end of the day.

"You're failing," she told me, when I sat down in front of her.

I blinked a few times while this sunk in. "Sorry, what?"

"You're failing," she repeated, slower this time, like I was an idiot.

"How?" I demanded. "I know I've missed a couple of assignments and taken some time off but you don't understand everything that's—"

The guidance counselor held up a hand to stop me. "Miss Deboise, you're absolutely right. I don't understand what's going on with you, nor do I want to understand. The mere fact that the teachers here have been paid an exorbitant 'bonus' to give you passing grades regardless of attendance is enough to tell me I don't have a single clue about you or your life." Her lips pursed and she frowned at me. "I could be fired for even having this conversation with you, but I'm going out on a limb here, Riley. When you arrived at Ducis Academy, your grades were stellar. For all intents and purposes, you seemed to be a model student. Now..." She shrugged, looking severely disappointed. "I'm taking a chance here that I'll still have a job to return to tomorrow. But *you* needed to be aware that despite the fact that you will graduate—your family's bribes have seen to that—you don't deserve to. Not the way things are right now. Is that what you want?"

Was it? Hell no! I'd always been so proud of my GPA, of the fact that I'd been on a track for a decent scholarship. But when it came down to it, staying alive had become more urgent than learning trigonometry.

"Thank you for letting me know," I replied in a shocked whisper. "I had no idea about ... the bribes. I'm sorry that you feel threatened, and I assure you that I won't tell Catherine about this."

She nodded, her gaze wary. "And your school work?"

Sucking a breath, I released it in a heavy sigh. "Honestly, I want to tell you that I'll do better, and that I'll spend the rest of the school year making up for it."

Her brow arched. "But you won't?"

I met her gaze head on, going out on a limb like she had for me. "Last week a group of boys here at this school dragged me into a classroom, beat me, and tried to gang rape me. Almost two months ago I was in a plane crash and nearly died. This morning, someone again tried to murder me. It's not that I won't try. It's that I physically *can't*." The guidance counselor's face was pale and drawn, her eyes full of fear and pity. "I'm doing my best, here, but I'm not Superwoman."

We sat there and stared at each other for a long moment before she cleared her throat and looked down at her hands. "Yes, well. I'd say you're coping better than Superwoman."

Her genuine compliment brought tears to my eyes, and I bit the inside of my cheek to keep them at bay. "Thank you for your concern. I really will try harder, when I can."

She nodded again, not looking back up at me until I stood to leave. "Riley," she said, halting my exit. "If you ever need to just *talk* to someone..." Her offer stood clear, even as a tear rolled down her cheek.

"I'll know where to find you, Ms. Hewlett. Thank you." I gave her a small smile, and let myself out of her office before I had a mental breakdown and told her my whole sad story. As it was, I'd said too much, but something about her seemed trustworthy.

"Everything okay?" Jasper asked when I joined him in the hallway. He was my shadow for the day, and a damn fun one at that.

I nodded, falling into step with him as the final bell chimed. "Yep, all good. Just discussing grades."

Jasper wrinkled his nose. "But why?"

"Oh, I don't know." I glared at him. "Maybe because I have higher aspirations in life than to end up as someone's trophy wife with nothing more than a high school diploma that she didn't earn?"

Jasper threw an arm around my shoulders and grinned. "Aw, come on Riles. As if Beck would ever call you his *trophy wife*."

I elbowed him in the side and tried really hard not to picture myself as

Mrs. Beckett. "Shut up, you. I really do need to study a bit harder. All this Delta shit has made me lose sight of my own goals."

He kept grinning at me, but he nodded his agreement. "That's fair enough. I'll help you study for some classes if you want? I don't know if you know this, but I'm actually kinda brilliant."

"Hah! I had no idea. Thank you for informing me." The sarcasm was heavy, but all in good humor. One thing I was coming to count on, was that Jasper could cheer me up pretty much always. Beck knew what he was doing by assigning him as my shadow today.

"Seriously!" he insisted. "In fact, let's get you caught up on class work tonight. What's your worst subject?"

"All of them," I muttered with a pout, and he rolled his eyes. "Okay, fine. Probably biology?"

Jasper cringed. "Yuck. Okay, I'll call Evan. He can help you on that one."

THAT EVENING TURNED OUT TO be shockingly normal. Evan came over and put me through a crash course on everything my biology class had already covered, and we even had enough time for Jasper to help me finish my English assignment. It would be late, but at least I would have learned something.

Dylan and Beck didn't come by until after we'd finished dinner—homemade enchiladas, courtesy of Eddy. Both of them seemed moody and quiet, but I didn't press them for information. No doubt they'd discovered something about the early morning assassination attempt and I was enjoying the "normal" evening we were having, so didn't want to ruin it.

It wasn't until later that night, when Beck slipped into my bed in nothing but his boxers, that I broached the subject.

"You found something out, huh?"

He let out a long sigh, wrapping his arms around me so that I was snuggled to his hard chest. "Yep."

"Anything I need to be worried about?" I asked, tracing my fingertips over one of the tattoos on his ribs.

"Nope," he replied, sounding confident. "I have to meet with Delta about it tomorrow, though, so I won't be on campus."

"Okay," I said, not pushing it any further. My meeting with Ms. Hewlett had given me a whole lot to think about, and seriously given me some perspective. I'd been so caught up in everything Delta—despite my insistence that I wanted nothing to do with it—that I was practically drowning in the intrigue. If I was really serious about getting out, about not just rolling over and becoming their obedient little lap dog, then I needed to stop involving myself.

So it had been me who was attacked, but Beck and Dylan were handling it. There was absolutely no need for me to go off all Nancy Drew, investigating it myself and probably ending up in an even worse position.

"That's it?" Beck asked, disbelieving when I said nothing more.

"Yep," I responded, snuggling down into the blankets a bit more and closing my eyes. "Good night, Sebastian."

He stroked my hair for a few minutes before whispering back, "Sweet dreams, Butterfly." I felt the briefest press of a kiss to my lips. "And happy birthday for tomorrow morning, since I won't be able to tell you until after school. I have a Delta meeting in the morning."

My eyes flew open again. "You know it's my birthday tomorrow?"

He snorted, his hand brushing down my side and sending tingles across my skin. "Of course I know. I haven't forgotten anything about you."

My body was warm, my chest aching in a good way. "It's my first birthday without my parents," I confessed my pain. "And even though they never made a big deal about birthdays, it still hurts like a fucking bitch." Somehow, I wasn't crying, even when my eyes burned. "I planned on forgetting it completely, but deep down I know they wouldn't want me to do that."

"I'm so sorry, Riles," Beck said, his deep voice wrapping around me almost like a protective blanket. "You're right though, your parents would want you to celebrate your birthday, because you deserve to celebrate every perfect moment."

The tears finally came, and they were different to the last few times I'd cried about my parents. Healing, almost.

I was coming to see that Beck was more than just the guy who kept my nightmares away. He was also the one who was slowly healing me, piece by piece.

I'd never be over my parents' deaths, but maybe one day I would be able to function okay in this world without them.

Hopefully.

BECK WAS GONE WHEN I woke up, but the bed was still warm beside me so he could have only just left. Sure enough, when I wandered out to my kitchen, I found a fresh, hot mug of coffee waiting along with a note that simply said "Happy birthday, Butterfly. Stay out of trouble - S" which seemed innocent enough but set my belly fluttering.

Stupid hormones.

A polite knock at the door clued me in to who my shadow was for the day, and I happily welcomed Dylan inside.

"I'll just be five minutes, cool?" I called out as I hurried back to my bedroom to finish getting dressed. It was Friday and tonight I was going to party with Eddy and Dante, so I was eager to get through the day.

When I re-emerged, fully dressed in my Ducis uniform, Dylan gave me a sheepish look and presented a gift box from behind his back.

"You didn't think I forgot, did you?" he teased when I just stood there gaping with my mouth open.

"Uh ... actually I didn't think you knew at all," I admitted. I should have known after Beck mentioned it last night, but for some reason, I thought it was only him that knew.

Dylan gave me a small frown. "You told us your birth date on pretty much the first day we met. But even if you hadn't, one of us would have looked it up."

My jaw dropped a little at the idea that he'd *remembered* such a small detail from when they were all hating on me. "Well, you still didn't have to get me anything," I murmured, accepting the box nonetheless.

It was all white, tied with an expensive looking satin bow and when I opened it up, I needed to dig through layer upon layer of tissue paper to reach the gift inside. When I finally got to it, I pulled it out and inspected it—speechless.

"It's..." I trailed off, turning the clutch bag around to look at it from all sides. It was small, the sort of thing I'd use if I was going on a date, but instead of a normal clasp at the top, there were four loops with huge precious stones on top of each. So if I were to carry it, it'd look like I was wearing rings on all four of those fingers. "It's stunning, and way, *way* too expensive."

I knew designer and high quality when I saw it these days.

Dylan smiled. "It's not just a vanity item," he informed me. "Look." He slid the fingers of my right hand into the loops and positioned the clutch bag in my palm. "Now, what would you do if someone attacked you?"

"Huh?" I frowned up at him and he just waited patiently for me to click on. "Oh, my god. You bought me a knuckle duster purse?" I burst out laughing and simulated a punch to his face with the bejeweled bag. "Dylan, this is seriously the most amazing present."

He nodded, satisfied. "Not to mention functional."

Not wanting to let go of my awesome new bag, I gave him a quick one armed hug and kissed him on the cheek. "Thanks, Dylan. You're the best."

"Careful, Riles," he teased, but there was an edge of tension in his face. "I really don't need another lecture from Beck about getting too friendly with you."

I gasped, mortified. "He didn't. Did he?"

Dylan grimaced, and shrugged. "Come on, let's get to school. Jasper filled me in on your new determination to pass classes legitimately, so we should stop skipping."

"Fair point," I agreed. I tucked my awesome present back in the tissue paper and left it on the counter top to fetch my school bag. "Let's roll."

"Hopefully we can make it through your whole birthday without anyone dying," Dylan muttered as he followed me out of my apartment. It seemed like sort of an odd thing to say, but then again ... this was Delta.

Chapter 27

During study period, Dylan joined me in a quiet corner of the library and peered over my shoulder at my open laptop screen.

"Ah, I remember that assignment," he commented, coming around the table and taking the seat opposite me. "Can't believe Mr. Matherson hasn't changed his course material."

I smiled. "Well then, would you care to read over what I have so far?" I turned my laptop around and pushed it toward him. "I'll be back in a sec."

"Why? Where are you going?" He made as if to get out of his seat and join me, but I waved him off.

"To pee, shadowmaster. I highly doubt Beck would appreciate you holding my hand while I did that." I snickered at the thought, and Dylan cringed.

"Fair point," he agreed, relaxing back into his chair. "Be quick though, or I'm coming to check on you."

Totally straight faced, I nodded. "So, don't take my time on a huge poop then?"

The look of abject horror on Dylan's face kept me chuckling all the way out of the library and down the corridor to the nearest restroom. Right up until I pushed open the door and found Katelyn Huntley holding court with her minions.

"Yay, my favorite person," I muttered with heavy sarcasm when she glared daggers at me. It probably would have been smarter to just turn the fuck around and walk away, but stupid me was all buzzed on how pleasant my birthday had been so far. That, and I was pretty confident Katelyn would never actually get her own hands dirty in trying to tear me down.

"Where do you think *you're* going, slut?" Brittley sneered, stepping in front of me when I made to pass her.

I took a deep breath to try and calm myself before replying. "To pee, Brittley. That's what you usually do in restrooms. Not stand around and compare lip gloss shades." I flicked a contemptuous look at Katelyn, who was currently applying another coat to her lips, as I said this.

"You're going to want to mind your manners, Riley *Jameson*," Katelyn said, smirking at me in the mirror. "You don't have your lap dogs in here to protect you."

I met her gaze dead on, not a single ounce of fear projected from me. "I don't need them."

The other chick, who I hadn't had the pleasure of meeting, turned to join Britters and Katelyn. Great, three against one. Were these bitches actually serious?

I had a brief eight-second daydream about Dylan busting in here and using his kung fu skills on the three of their perfect bitch-faces, but then I remembered that I was a strong, confident chick, with half a day of fight training. I'd survived a lot lately, and I would survive these bitches.

"Where's Sebastian?" Katelyn said, and all of a sudden I was fucking pissed. I called him Sebastian. She could call him nothing, because she shouldn't even say his name.

"None of your fucking business."

She smirked harder. "Oh, I wasn't asking because I didn't know. I was just pointing out that he's been gone a lot lately and you should maybe find out why that is."

Her implication that he was out fucking someone else was very clear.

"I know exactly where *Sebastian* is, and I don't have any worries when he's not here, because we trust each other."

Saying it out loud cemented that truth for me. I really did trust them again, maybe I'd never stopped—I'd mostly been pissed by their actions, but I was coming to learn that was a part of being in Delta. Not everything was above board, and now that I was a Delta heir, I had to readjust my expectations of life.

Fury pulsed through me as I pushed closer. "What sort of woman pays a group of guys to gang rape someone? You should have your tits ripped off and your vag glued closed. You've officially lost your chick card."

Brittley gasped, swinging her head to stare at Katelyn. "I thought you said they were just going to scare her?"

I snorted. "Word of advice, Britters. Don't trust bottle-blondes who wear permanent smirks. It's like the 101 of surviving a psychopath."

Katelyn was no longer smiling. "I'm going to laugh at your funeral," she said quietly. "Then I'll fuck Sebastian. Just to prove I can. Bad things are coming for you and Delta, and if I was you, I'd run now. It won't do you any good, but at least you'll feel like you had a chance."

I laughed. Because I really couldn't let her threat settle inside of me. I had to take it as a joke because that was the only way I would survive.

Her face creased into angry lines, and she lunged forward for me. I'd been waiting for it though, and I channeled Dylan and Beck, and instead of backing up, I pushed forward, aiming for her throat with an open handed punch.

She'd clearly had some fight training as well, because her movements were smooth as she dodged my punch, swinging her arm around to crack me in the side of the head. *Fuck.*

I didn't let that stop me though, and my next hit was a solid smash into her nose. She hadn't expected it. She'd thought hitting me would be enough to stop me. But I'd been hurt a lot recently, and I was pretty sure my pain threshold was at a new high. "Are you bitches going to help?" Katelyn snarled.

Brittley shook her head. "I'm out. This shit is insane."

She rushed from the room, and the other chick followed soon after. Leaving Katelyn and me alone.

"Now, you should run," I advised, even though my stomach was still churning at everything she'd said. I was damn fucking good at false bravado. "We all know the head bitch can't fight her own fights ... your squad has bailed."

The bathroom door slammed open then, and my heart sank until I turned to find Dylan framed in the doorway. Now it was my turn to smirk. "You're fucked now," I said cheerfully.

Katelyn backed up, clearly well aware of the deadly skills of my guys. "Get out," he said without inflection, and she was gone in a flash.

"Thanks, dude," I said cheerfully, ignoring the feeling of dread in my gut. "I still gotta pee though, so can you stand guard."

Dylan nodded, his face hard and unyielding. He was not happy, and I couldn't blame him. This might have ended differently; Katelyn was a complete psycho and she could have had a gun or anything.

When I was done, hands washed, I joined Dylan who had not moved from the doorway, keeping out any other students.

There was a line of glaring chicks when we got out; I must have missed the bell ringing for next class. When they noticed Dylan with me though, they stopped glaring and started drooling. This was half the reason I got hate, because everyone wanted the Delta boys, and they fucking hated that I appeared to have them.

"Riley!" Eddy shouted, distracting me as she rushed down the hall. "Did you fight with Katelyn?"

I blinked. "Heard that already, huh?"

Her pretty face looked darker and angrier than usual. "I'm gonna kick her ass," she said.

I shook my head. "Don't even stress on it. There was hardly any fight, and I managed to crack her in the nose, so I'll take that as a win."

Eddy let out a huff. "I should have been there. No more going to the bathroom alone, okay?"

Dylan let out a huff of his own, arms crossed over his chest. He'd barely said a word since busting into the bathroom, and I knew he was mad at himself for letting me get ambushed.

"It's not your fault," I said, reaching out to wrap my hand around his arm. "I went on my own, and told you not to worry. In hindsight, it was fucking stupid. I should have left you outside, so I could have at least screamed."

Not that I'd have given her the satisfaction. I'd rather take the beat down, but if there had been a group of guys waiting for me, then at least I would have had a chance with Dylan. After my almost gang rape, I really had to be smarter about my own safety.

"How much longer can this go on?" I asked softly, my head spinning at everything that had happened recently.

Beck appeared then, moving with deadly grace through the crowds. I recognized that look on his face. "You told, Beck?" I said, narrowing my eyes on Dylan.

He shot me a pair of raised eyebrows and a smirk. "Of course I fucking did. If he found out later and we didn't mention anything, he would lose it badly. I like my face too much to continue letting him pound on it."

I must have looked disbelieving because he shook his head. "I'm not sure you realize just how much you mean to him, Riles. He would kill or die for you in a heartbeat. There are not many people in the world on Beck's list, but you're one of them."

My heart was practically bursting from my chest at this point, and I found myself running toward Beck. At that action from me, some of that feral anger in Beck's eyes faded, and there was a moment of shock. I hadn't run to him like this in so long, and there was no doubt some sort of symbolic bullshit going on right now. Like ... we were moving forward with forgiveness and trust and blah blah.

It all boiled down to one thing: I needed Sebastian Beckett.

His arms closed around me, and some of the darkness inside faded. It was kind of ironic that the darkest guy I knew, was the source of my light.

But there you had it.

"Are you okay, baby?"

I nodded against his chest, just taking a second to breathe him in. "Yeah, she just said some asshole things, tried to intimidate me, and then smacked me in the head."

He stilled. "She hit you?"

Oh shit. That tone was his scary one. "Yeah, but I hit her back, so we're even."

"Not even fucking close," he murmured before he dropped my feet so I landed back on the ground. "Come on, Riles, we're out of here."

"School isn't finished," I said, letting him lead me along the hall.

"It is for you," he said shortly, and I turned to see Dylan and Eddy hurrying along behind us.

We took separate cars back home, and Beck drove directly into the underground parking lot.

When he pulled to a stop, he turned in his seat to face me. "I'm sorry I had to leave you today," he said softly. "On your birthday."

My lips twitched. "It's not a big deal. Like I said, my parents never even made it a big deal." I shrugged, "Besides, you said it was Delta business, right? Not like it was something you could refuse."

He nodded. "Delta, and … something else."

That reminded me briefly of what Katelyn had said in the bathroom, but I decided not to push. I would just trust and accept that if he needed me to know, he would tell me.

"Happy birthday, baby," he said, wrapping his arms around me. I sank into him, only slightly awkward trying to lean across the car. "Never again will you have a birthday that is not a big deal. You deserve so much fucking better than that, Riles."

Before I could reply, he tightened his hold and somehow yanked me out of my seat and onto his lap without completely smashing my head on the roof. I groaned, immediately pressing my aching body against his.

"Now this is the sort of special surprise I like on my birthday," I murmured, breathless.

Beck was too tall for us to easily, or comfortably, fuck in his car, but I could tell by the look on his face, that something as insignificant as "no room to move" was not going to deter him. My panties were pushed aside, and his fingers moved inside me in the same instant. I rode them until my body burned and Beck's lap was wet from me.

Under his pants, there was no underwear barrier, and I wiggled up so I could let his cock free, my eyes greedily devouring the thick length. Sliding down on it, we both groaned, and my head fell back as his fingers bit into my hips, moving me. I started out somewhat graceful, but by the end I was just smashing myself against him, needing more. Needing it to be harder than ever. There was probably going to be a Riley sized dent in the roof from my head, but we were both too far gone to care about that.

"Beck, fuck," I groaned. "Fuck me harder."

The look on his face, it was almost my undoing, as an orgasm screamed toward me. He shifted down farther in the seat, which moved our positions and allowed him to hold me up slightly, so that he was now the one slamming up into me. I was immobile, unable to do anything but hold on to him with one hand and the roof with the other.

I all but screamed out as my orgasm hit hard, and Beck pulled my lips to his, taking every cry into his mouth. He groaned as his body jerked inside of me, over and over, both of us riding that orgasm out for many long minutes.

"Happy fucking birthday to me," I gasped, trying to get my heart rate and pulse back under control. If Beck kept fucking me like that, he was definitely going to give me a heart attack one day.

Beck laughed softly, his hands gently tracing across my back as I collapsed against him. "This isn't your present, Riley Jameson. This is just the prelude."

I snorted. "Give me five minutes before the main act, because I'm not sure I'll survive it."

That had him laughing again, and I felt stupidly proud that I could make Beck laugh.

When we were both recovered, I lifted myself off him, and managed to open the door and scramble out. Getting out of the car like that was almost more awkward than fucking in the car. As I fixed my panties and skirt, I lifted my head, and across in my parking space, a familiar shiny door panel caught my eye.

My gasp was long and loud. "What?" I took a step closer, unsure if I was seeing things correctly.

Beck's heat pressed into my back. "That's the second reason I had to bail early this morning. Happy birthday, Butterfly," he said.

I pressed my hand to my mouth, mostly to stop a sob from escaping. Crying over a car was probably the stupidest thing ever, but … he'd brought my butterfly back.

Stumbling closer, I ran my hands along every perfect, undented panel. My sticker still in the back window, and the blue paint gleamed like it had when she was brand new.

"You kept her," I said, turning watery eyes on Beck. "Why did you do that? You hated me then?"

His hand crept into the back of my hair, tangling in the strands as he pulled me into his side. An engine broke through the silence, and he briefly checked it was only Dylan—they must have taken their time because Beck had this surprise planned—before turning his full attention back to me.

"I never hated you, Riley. I feared what another female Delta heir meant. I feared what I felt. I knew you were going to have the power to fucking destroy me, and I did everything to stop you before you started."

I snorted. "Yeah, I'm like a wrecking ball. You ain't gonna get rid of me until I destroy everything first."

Beck shook his head as Dylan and Eddy got out of the car. "Turns out you're the opposite of destructive; you're the light in the fucking darkness."

I jerked my head toward him, surprised he'd used a similar analogy to me. I'd thought the same thing about Beck only an hour earlier.

He kissed me again, softly this time, and I whimpered as I pressed up to him. The result of our last fuck was still running down my thighs, and I couldn't help but want him again. I was addicted and not ashamed to admit it.

Chapter 28

At Eddy's shriek, I pulled away from Beck. "Your car," she yelled, dashing forward, an expert at running in heels. She smirked at Beck. "Look at you being all sentimental. Definitely not like you, Sebastian Beckett."

I pressed my hand into his firm chest, knowing that there was a ton more going on under his hard-ass outer persona. Eddy had clearly never been in the inner circle before, so she didn't know. But I did.

Eddy admired the butterfly for a moment before spinning around to hug me. "Happy birthday, bestie. My present is upstairs. I didn't want to drag it to school today."

I sniffed. "I've never had this much attention on a birthday before. Even Dante forgets it most years."

"Dante is a fucking idiot," Beck growled. "He's got more than one thing to atone for."

I blinked at him. "What does that mean? You keep hinting at these things with Dante, but you never come right out and say anything."

Beck shook his head, but I didn't let him get away with it this time. "Tell me, Sebastian. What do you know?"

He cupped my face. "I won't lie to you, Riles. But I also don't have the evidence yet to prove my suspicions."

I shook my head. "Dante can't be involved in Delta business, right? I mean ... how?"

Beck's lips were close to mine as he leaned down. "You're blind to his faults. You love him unconditionally. I'm just not sure he deserves it."

Eddy popped her head up near ours. "Dante is a decent guy," she said seriously. "I have a pretty good eye for assholes, after spending my years around you all."

Dylan appeared to be on Beck's side with this though. "I would keep an eye on him. There's something there. I noticed it the first time we met him, and it was even worse when he was taken to ensure Riley's cooperation. He ... wasn't surprised by that. Like he knew it was coming and was way too accepting of his part in it all. I've never seen someone react that way."

Beck nodded. "He wasn't surprised at all, and he took my beatings like a man with sins to atone for."

"Who suggested Dante be the one?" I asked, having assumed all this time it was Beck. He'd known better than anyone how much Dante meant to me.

"Catherine," Beck said. "She insisted that only Dante would convince you. I argued against it, because he was all you had in the world. I told Catherine that you'd save anyone innocent and that it wasn't worth using Dante and pissing off his gang, but she wouldn't budge."

Catherine. I should have shot her that day. Something I'd regretted many times over the past few weeks.

Eddy looked between the three of us with confusion, and I realized we'd just openly talked about Delta business in front of her, but she was smart enough not to ask questions. Eddy definitely knew more than she let on ... more than she should.

The four of us remained there, silent and somber.

"We should head upstairs," Eddy finally said, and no one disagreed.

I followed along, Beck at my side, and as I turned back for one last look at my butterfly, my phone buzzed in my pocket. Pulling it out, there was a text.

Dante: Will be there tonight, Riles. Wouldn't miss your birthday.

Normally that would have made me happy as fuck. He was visiting. I'd have my best friend by my side on my birthday. But now I was filled with doubt and worry. Could Dante know more than he was saying? Had he known about this Delta bullshit before my parents died? I mean, he'd never kept it a secret that he was interested in Militant Delta and their rise to riches, but I'd thought that was more along the lines of "I watched a Netflix documentary and now think I'm an expert," not an actual real life connection.

I was so lost in thought that when I walked into my apartment, I missed the initial "surprise!" shouted at me, and it wasn't until Jasper lifted me off my feet and twirled me around in a hug that I noticed the room.

It was full of balloons, hundreds of them, floating across the ceiling, in a wash of gold, silver and pink. My dining table was set up beautifully— on top of the gold tablecloth there was a huge white cake, covered in blue butterflies. Jasper let me down and I stumbled closer, my chest tight and shit.

Fuck. I had no idea they had been planning this.

"Happy birthday, Riley," Evan said from close by. I spun to him and wrapped my arms around his broad frame. "Thank you," I murmured back.

The cake wasn't the only thing they had. There was expensive champagne, to get the pre-party started, as Eddy put it. "We wanted to celebrate here with you first," Dylan said, smiling broadly for once. "Before we head out to the party tonight."

Eddy pushed the guys aside and thrust a brightly wrapped package at me. "Best friends first," she declared before glaring at Beck and Dylan. "I'm already mad at you two fuckers for beating me to this."

I snorted before I ripped open the package to find a pair of heels that exactly matched the bag Dylan had given me. "This designer doesn't normally do heels," she said, leaning closer. "But I convinced him to make you a pair specially. You can't have that fucking stunning bag, without the matching shoes."

The jewels were embedded across the round, enclosed toe, in the same formation as the knuckle duster bag. There were other similarities, and I immediately fell in love with the dark vibe of this brand. *Designer.* Jesus. How my life had changed since my last birthday.

Jasper was next, and I was slightly nervous to open it, expecting to find something vaguely inappropriate and embarrassing inside. Only he surprised me. It was a framed photo, one I hadn't even known had been taken, when I was driving his Lambo. The black and white still showcased my face the moment I crossed the finish line first, and there was a unique blend of pride and joy written across my features.

"Jasper," I breathed, staring down at it. "I ... thank you."

He shrugged, like it wasn't a big deal. "One of my friends snapped this on his phone and sent it to me, and with a little help, I turned it into something for you to keep."

I brushed my fingertip across the black and white image. "This was the moment I found some of myself again. You know, after losing my parents." I sniffled. "That first race, I froze up and lost control, because all I could think about was the crash. All I could remember was the screeching sound and the dread in my gut. But when I raced for you…" I lifted my head. "…it was as if some of the old Riley appeared again."

He'd probably never know how much this image meant to me.

Evan made a low rumbling sound. "I can't believe I have to go last after all of you fuckers were so sentimental."

I laughed, shaking my head and turning to him. "I will love whatever you've given me," I said. "Even if it's just a hug."

Evan rolled his eyes before turning away to grab a small bag off the table. I took it, marveling at how expensive the bag looked. It was one of those off white, thick embossed bags. It was only small, and when I reached in and pulled out the small white box, I was almost certain that this was jewelry.

I kind of wanted to joke about him proposing, but when I looked up, it was to find his nervous expression on mine, and I shut my mouth. This was no time to joke. He'd tried to find me something special and now he was worried it wouldn't measure up to everyone else's.

Slowly, I opened the box and stared down at the piece nestled there in a red velvet. It was a necklace, a thick gold chain, and there was a word that joined the ends together. It said "Bulma."

I snorted and my eyes watered at the same time. I immediately knew what this necklace meant. Evan was reminding me of two things … one, our moment bonding over Dragon Ball Z, which was something I also cherished, and two, Bulma was married to Vegeta. We'd both eventually agreed that Beck was Vegeta. So this meant even more to me.

"I love it," I said, shooting him a full smile. "Thank you." I hugged him hard. "Will you help me put it on?"

He nodded, and stepping forward, fumbled at the back of my neck for a beat before he got the clasp clicked into place. It was heavy and expensive, that much I knew for sure, and the "Bulma" hung just above my breasts. I noticed that there were diamonds embedded along the L, and I just loved everything about it.

Beck strolled closer, his eyes glued to my chest. "Bulma? What does that mean?"

I snorted, and Evan and I shared a brief amused look before I turned back to Beck. "It means that I'm the coolest Dragon Ball character, and you all better watch out when I get pissed off."

Dylan and Jasper both laughed out loud. "Looks like you finally found a nerdy friend, Evan," Jasper said, holding his sides. "I'm happy for you."

Evan just flipped them all off, and I stepped into Beck, who shot my necklace one last look before wrapping his arms around me.

Eddy popped champagne nearby. "Time for a drink," she shouted, breaking the mood.

I laughed. Oh yeah, there were parts of this life I could definitely get used to.

THE PRE-PARTY WITH MY FRIENDS turned out to be a ton better than the main event. I was currently wishing we'd never left our apartment. The main party was being held at some kid called Brian's house—mansion— and the whole place was packed with drunken, sweaty college kids from the neighboring town. A mid-twenties dude with designer stubble attempted to DJ but really just played tracks from his iPod while wearing headphones and chatting up chicks.

"This party sucks," Dante observed as we sipped from solo cups and watched a wasted guy egg his friend on to jump in the pool fully clothed.

"Agreed," Eddy cringed. "Brian's parties used to be way better than this."

Not to mention that Beck and the guys had been waylaid the moment we got there, and I'd barely had a chance to see them. Sure, they were close, always keeping an eye on me, but I wanted them even closer. I didn't like all of the darkness—and assassination attempts—hovering around us; it made me nervous.

"We should at least dance," Eddy said, jumping to her feet. "Right after I get another drink."

She looked between Dante and me. "You two want a refill?"

We both nodded, and when I went to follow her, she shook her head. "All good, I'll be right back."

There was a moment of awkward silence, and I couldn't get my suspicions under control. Dante was my oldest friend. I could barely remember a time when he wasn't in my life.

Speaking of…

"Do you remember how we first met?"

I'd been young and my memories of those days weren't that clear. It sort of just seemed like one day Dante was there. Hanging out wherever I was in our neighborhood

His green eyes were confused as he met my gaze. "I mean … I don't really know. We lived in the same neighborhood, and you were outside all the time, and I just started to hang out with you."

He'd repeated my thoughts almost exactly, but there was something I was missing.

"Yeah," I nodded, having no idea why I was asking this anyway.

"Is something wrong, Riles?" he asked, turning to face me fully, legs slightly spread as he rested both elbows on his knees. "You've been really quiet ever since I showed up. I know birthdays are not your favorite time, and this is your first one without your parents, but … is there something else?"

Questions bubbled up, as I desperately tried to ignore his words. I couldn't think about the fact that my parents weren't here today. I'd break down into a sobbing screaming mess if I did that.

"Nah, all good. Was just feeling slightly sentimental."

Dante smirked. "Happens with old age."

"Did you know that Beck fixed up the butterfly?" I sat a little straighter. "She's beautiful. Not a mark on her."

Dante's smile faded. "He did? I asked him a while ago what happened to her, hoping I could find it for you, but he wasn't exactly forthcoming with the answer."

I snorted. "Sounds like Beck."

"What sounds like me?" he said, sliding in behind me, legs on either side of me as he pulled me back into him. I relaxed against him.

"Just discussing how you're a control freak," I teased, leaning back to see his face.

He pressed his lips to mine, and Dante coughed. I turned to find him glaring. "You didn't tell me that this was back on again," he said, sounding a little too accusatory for someone who'd basically told me to forgive and forget.

"You're going to have to let the jealousy go," Beck drawled. "Riley belongs to me."

I smacked Beck's arm before turning back to Dante. "I thought you'd figure it out after our last conversation. I told you I was losing my battle in being angry at them. You told me to forgive and forget, and ... I took your advice. The guys explained everything that happened, and I ... I guess I understand why they did what they did."

Dante shook his head. "Forgiving them isn't the same as jumping straight back into bed with Beck. You five are a team that should stick together, but the romance part just complicates everything."

"You would know, wouldn't you?" Beck said darkly, his eyes locked on Dante. "You've been mixing business with pleasure for years."

I waited for Dante to tell him to fuck off or something. That wasn't the sort of accusation he'd normally let slide, but he just got to his feet, muttered something about needing a drink, and hurried away.

My heart was pounding hard in my chest, my palms clammy. That hadn't looked good.

I spun to see Beck. "He's definitely part of something," I said softly. "Or he at least knows a hell of a lot more than he's letting on. I know Dante better than almost anybody, and that was not the face of an innocent person."

Beck cupped my cheek, his fingers rough as they tightened against my skin, pulling me into him. I forgot about Dante as I slid up so I was straddling Beck. By the time he was finished kissing me, I could barely remember my name.

"Whatever game Dante is playing, we'll figure it out together," he said softly.

He was just leaning back in for another kiss, when his phone started to vibrate under my thigh. With a scowl, he half-lifted me and pulled it from his pocket.

Beck never liked to let the phone go, just in case it was one of his friends needing help. He glanced at the screen and grumbled. "Fucking Delta," he said before he slid the screen and answered the call.

"What?" he said roughly, his free hands caressing my lips before trailing down to my chin to stroke across my necklace. For a second I worried he was going to rip it from me, because Evan had placed it on my body, and I wasn't fully comfortable explaining that Bulma was married to Vegeta and that Beck was my Vegeta, because that was quite a heavy conversation. Which meant Beck didn't really know the full significance of this name.

Thankfully he didn't break it, just letting the chain fall before he continued to run gentle fingers over my thin black top. When his thumbs brushed my nipples, I squirmed against him.

"When did that happen?" Beck suddenly asked, distracting me. His hand stilled on my body, and that's when I started paying closer attention too. I could hear the other person talking fast on the line, but I didn't know what they were saying.

"Yep, I'll be there," Beck finally said before he hung up the phone.

"What happened?" I asked.

His face was hard and unyielding. "Someone destroyed Oscar's grave."

I stilled. "What do you mean?"

"They smashed the marble, and there's possible damage to the coffin."

"You going to check it out right now?" I asked.

He nodded. "Yeah, I need to make sure that nothing else has been destroyed in our plots. There are some family secrets out there that need to stay buried."

I nodded, sliding off him and standing tall on my new heels. "I'll come with you."

He shook his head. "Nah, Butterfly. You stay here and enjoy the party. It's your birthday."

"I'd rather be with you," I said honestly.

He stood, towering over me, his body leaning down into mine as our lips met again. "I'd rather be with you as well, but the entire fucking council is there, and I really don't want those bastards around you any longer than is absolutely required. You've not been called, so I'm keeping you out of it."

I shuddered at the thought of going near them. "Yeah, okay. Will the other guys stay?"

He nodded. "Yeah, that's the only reason I'm comfortable enough to leave you."

I didn't argue anymore; accepting that Beck didn't solely belong to me was an important step in our relationship. I would always have to share him with Delta and his responsibilities there. At least until I could figure out how to end them.

Chapter 29

Beck made sure that Dylan, Evan, and Jasper were nearby before he left. He hadn't been drinking, so he was driving the Bugatti. Once he was gone, I was a sad bitch, so Eddy dragged me onto the dance floor, all the while plying me with more drinks than was safe for me to consume. Dante reappeared at some point, and it was almost like the entire scene with Beck hadn't even happened. He smiled and laughed and flirted with Eddy. I tried my best to get lost in the beat and alcohol, but I was uneasy, never able to fully relax.

"He'll be fine, right?" I asked Dylan, who was propped against a nearby wall, not drinking either. "Why would anyone destroy a grave? That's so fucking weird."

Dylan wrapped his arm around me, pulling me closer. "Beck is fine. But he says there's something unusual going on with the grave. He didn't want to say anything more over the phone, but he'll be back in an hour or so to fill us in."

Knowing he'd be back soon was enough for me to head onto the dancefloor and try and enjoy what remained of my birthday. "Everything okay?" Dante asked. I nodded, smiling.

"Yeah, just a weird Delta thing. You know how it is."

He balked. "What the fuck is that supposed to mean?" he snapped suddenly. "I don't know shit, and I never thought you'd stoop to these low, underhanded accusations. That's more Beck's speed."

Eddy had stopped dancing, both of us staring at him. "I just meant because of your," I lowered my voice, "gang stuff. There's always something weird and fucked up going on."

Dante was pale, and I didn't like the sweaty brow he was sporting. "Is there something you need to tell me?" I asked him, giving him this one chance to confess. I wasn't sure what I would do if I found out Dante was involved in this world somehow.

"I don't have anything to tell you, Riles," he said, visibly calming. "It was just … you know … a hangover from Beck before."

I probably would have pressed him a little harder, because there was something there, only an idiot wouldn't see it, but a large shove in the back distracted me before I could say anything else.

Spinning around, I glared at Katelyn, who stood in a tiny white dress, her long blonde hair dead straight and gleaming.

"Whoops," she said, smirking at me. "Didn't see you there. You blend right into the floor with that outfit on."

I had on a black shirt and skinny jeans. Nothing fancy, that was for sure, but I hardly looked as bad as her expression implied.

"This party is off limits to Huntley trash," Eddy snapped, stepping in close to me. "How the fuck did you even get in here?"

Katelyn leveled a glare on her. "Edith," she spat. "I keep hoping to read about your untimely death, but you somehow keep kicking."

Eddy smirked. "You'll probably be dead before me, bitch. Remember who's an heir here. No one gains anything by killing me."

I looked around then wondering if we should be having this sort of conversation in public. Luckily, most people hadn't noticed the fight going down in their midst, but that quickly changed when Katelyn snarled and reached out to grab Eddy's hair. She yanked it hard, and my friend started cursing and throwing punches in an attempt to dislodge her.

"Girl fight!" Some dickhead nearby yelled, and the crowds closed in around us, effectively blocking Dylan, Evan, and Jasper, who had been heading in our direction. In an attempt to help Eddy, I got smacked in the face by a flailing arm, and with a chuckle, Dante reached out one of his long arms, and yanked Katelyn up and off Eddy. There was a shriek as more than a little of Eddy's hair went with her, but Dante didn't care. He just held Katelyn up, practically by her throat.

"Stay the fuck away from Eddy and Riley," he snarled, all humor lost. "If I catch you near either of them again, I promise that you won't have to worry about a little hair pulling. You have no idea who I am, bitch, and it's best you don't find out."

She snarled, swinging at him. "I will kill you, you piece of shit ganger."

Dante's laugh was dark, cold. "You should be more careful who you threaten. You have no idea what I can do to you," he said, his voice thundering with anger. "I would end you without a second fucking thought."

Then he basically threw her ass across to where some of her minions waited, and they managed to catch her before she slammed into the ground. People started shouting and cheering, and Dante got a few dark looks, but no one stepped in because he was tall, scary, and obviously well known as a member of the Jersey gang world. "Thanks," Eddy said, and I stepped closer to help her fix her hair. "She has quite the grip on her."

Dante shrugged. "Yeah, no big deal." He ran a hand over his shaved head, the tattoos flashing in the low light. I was struck by how many times I'd seen him do that same move. It was so familiar, and everything inside hurt, because there was a divide between us. It had slowly been forming ever since I lost my parents, and it was breaking my heart.

"I need some air," Dante muttered, and he turned and pushed through the crowd. I went to go after him but Jasper got to me first. "You okay, Riles?" he asked, using his bulk to stop me from getting knocked around.

"What about me, asshole?" Eddy said, smacking him. "I'm the one who got half my hair ripped out."

He ruffled her hair, and she shot him the darkest look ever. "You're always fine, little sister."

Eddy flipped him off before she stormed off toward the bar.

"I'm okay," I said, smiling as Evan and Dylan made it to my side. "Just a little cat fight."

Dylan's face was thunderous. "That stupid bitch needs to be taken down. She's been in our territory for too long."

"I don't understand why Huntley is here at all. I mean, how come Delta hasn't kicked them out."

"It's the vote," Jasper bit out. "All rules are off until this fucking vote is over."

"How long until this vote again?" I asked.

Evan sounded tired. "One month. One more fucking month of that stupid bitch, and Graeme Huntley around town."

I hadn't seen her father at all, but it sounded like he was here as well.

"I'm going to find Dante," I said, meeting their eyes. "Check he's okay … maybe ask him what the fuck is going on."

Dylan wrapped his hand around my wrist. "Do you think it's safe to be alone with him?"

For the first time I hesitated before answering. "Dante would never hurt me." At least not physically anyway. Emotionally was another story.

"Maybe you don't know him as well as you think you do?" Jasper said, not moving to let me past. "At least let us stay in sight."

I finally agreed, and the four of us walked around the party while I tried to spot Dante. I finally saw him at the end of the long driveway. "You wait here," I said to them. "He won't talk to me unless we're alone."

None of them looked happy about it, but they didn't argue. They already knew Dante was a touchy subject for me, especially after they'd hurt him.

Hurrying along the path, I kept an eye on my feet, because the ground was pretty uneven, and in the dark, there were a lot of hazards—empty beer bottles, glass, trash. It wasn't until I finally looked up when I was almost at him that I realized he was on the phone. His back was partially to me, but from what I could see of his face, he didn't look happy.

"I'm fucking done," he snarled. "She knows, Catherine."

My entire world fell out from under me then, and I must have stood there for many minutes just staring at him, trying to comprehend what I'd just heard.

He'd said Catherine. I was almost certain of it.

I had to be in shock, because I couldn't move closer to him, even though I needed answers. Dylan was shouting now, and I wanted to listen to his words, but I couldn't hear anything. There was a weird, echoing ring in my head, and I finally stumbled back before spinning and running. Straight into Dylan's arms.

"What happened?" he said.

I shook my head, throat tight, eyes burning. There had to be another explanation. Catherine wasn't an uncommon name; maybe he was talking to someone else. Someone in the gang or maybe an old friend.

She knows. That could mean anything too, right? *She* could be anyone.

"Riley!" Dylan gently shook me. "Snap out of it. We can't help you if you don't tell us."

"Let's just kill him now," Jasper suggested, already heading toward Dante.

All of our phones buzzed at the same time, which stopped him in his tracks. I was in no frame of mind to read mine, so I let them all fill me in on whatever horrible shit had occurred in our world. Phones going off at the same time was never a good sign.

"Beck's not coming here now. He wants us at the cemetery," Dylan said, still keeping me somewhat propped up.

I hadn't taken my eyes off Dante, who appeared to be off the phone now, but he was still staring out into the darkness around him. I couldn't tell if it was a blessing or not that he hadn't seen me yet.

Dylan's words finally registered with me. "Cemetery? What? Why?"

"Guess we'll find out when we get there," Evan replied, tucking his own phone back into his pants pocket. "Let's roll."

"Wait, what about Eddy? We can't just ditch her here," I protested. I'd come to the party with Eddy and Dante but now that Dante seemed like a snake in the grass ... I couldn't run out on my only other friend.

The guys exchanged a look, doing their silent communication thing before Dylan nodded to Jasper and grabbed my hand. "You come with me and Evan, Riles. Jasper will grab Eddy and drop her home on his way to the cemetery."

"Okay, that works," I agreed, letting Dylan hurry me down the drive in the direction of his car.

Jasper turned and went back inside, searching for his sister, and the urgency of Beck's message almost had me forgetting about the betrayal from my best friend.

"Riles!" Dante called out as we hurried past him. "What's wrong? Where are you going?"

My breath sucked in with a harsh gasp, all that broken hearted betrayal I'd felt just moments ago slamming back into me.

"Evan," Dylan snapped. "Deal with him. We'll meet you there."

We'd just reached Dylan's car, and I gratefully slipped inside and slammed the door shut while Evan stepped in front of Dante and blocked him. I couldn't deal with Dante. Not yet. Not when something was going down at Oscar's grave and the pain was still so fresh.

She knows, Catherine.

His words echoed in my head, and I clenched my eyes tightly shut as Dylan gunned his engine and carried us away from that *awful* party.

Chapter 30

Beck was alone when we arrived. He waited beside the wrought iron gates of the Jefferson Cemetery with his strong arms folded across his chest and his face like a thunderstorm.

"Where are the guys?" he demanded when only Dylan and I got out of the car.

"Coming," Dylan replied, succinct as ever. "Council gone?"

Beck nodded. "Yeah, they saw all they needed to see. I didn't want you all hearing this over the phone or from one of them, though."

A chill traveled through me and I rubbed my arms. "That sounds ominous," I murmured, and Beck just looked a bit … disturbed.

Seconds later, Jasper's yellow Lambo pulled in behind Dylan, and both he and Evan hopped out.

"That was fast," I commented, frowning. "Eddy okay?"

Jasper shot me a sly grin. "Uh, more than okay. She was tonsils deep in some preppy dick from Jefferson U and basically threatened me with castration if I tried to take her home." He shrugged. "Guess she's more like me than I realized."

I rolled my eyes. "Fair enough. So long as she's okay." *And not hooking up with Dante, that two faced, lying piece of shit.*

"Come on," Beck said, bringing our attention back to why we were all there. "You guys need to see something."

He led the way into the dark graveyard, and I quickened my pace to catch up with him. Biting my lip to keep from babbling nervously, I wrapped my hand around his and snuggled into his side. Because, *fuck*, cemeteries were creepy at night.

Somewhere above us, an owl hooted, and I was embarrassed to admit a small squeak of fright slipped out of me. Beck chuckled softly before he tightened his grip on my fingers. His thumb stroked over the back of my hand, and I pushed all my focus into that touch, so I didn't look at the shadow which could have easily been a zombie or vampire or something.

"Oh shit," Evan breathed as we came to a stop, and I gaped.

I'd been so focused on the scary shit around the graveyard, I hadn't noticed we'd arrived at Oscar's plot. Or… what was left of it.

"What the fuck?" Jasper cursed, crouching down to take a better look. Not that he needed to get any closer. It was pretty fucking obvious from where I stood—someone had taken Oscar's corpse.

"Who would do this?" I whispered in abject horror. The whole grave was dug up, dirt piled haphazardly on the neighboring plots, and the stained, silk lined coffin sat open.

Open and very empty.

"That's what Delta wants to know," Beck said softly, just barely hiding the grief all over his face. "That's what *I* want to know. Why dig him up? Why now?"

"And what was in there?" Dylan added, pointing down at the small wooden box—also empty—which sat at the foot of the casket. "I don't remember seeing that during the funeral."

Jasper's phone started playing Taylor Swift and everyone glared at him as he hurried to turn it off.

"Sorry," he muttered, his cheeks flaming, "Eddy keeps changing her ringtone on my phone."

Despite the current creepy situation, I couldn't help but send out a bit of love for my fucked up best friend. Maybe the only person in my life not to betray me so far. It wouldn't surprise me at this point, if my adopted parents were in on some nefarious scheme as well.

"Anyone else think it's a pretty fucked up coincidence that the first time we visit Oscar's grave since his death, it's basically ransacked a few days later?" Evan asked as he paced around the open plot.

"First time?" I asked.

They all nodded. "We were here at the funeral, and then I've been back one more time," Beck added. "But that was the first time we've all come together like that."

"We weren't dealing very well with it," Dylan said softly, his voice filled with a dark anger that was even scarier than a cemetery at night.

And it had only been a few months, because Oscar died not long before my parents. Which was another fucked up coincidence I didn't want to look at for too long.

"This has got to strengthen the murder argument, right?" I finally said, unable to look at the empty grave any longer. Instead I looked at my guys, right into each of their faces, letting that comfort me. "Someone came here for something. Taking whatever was in the box and the body, screams of a cover up. Someone didn't want us to ever exhume his body, because there might have been evidence on it."

No one laughed, or even offered up another plausible explanation; they all kind of seemed to agree with me.

"Is there any way to get the police investigation?" Dylan asked, turning to Beck. "I know you tried before, but we didn't push very hard, because we weren't sure there was anything to investigate."

Beck's eyes were that of a burning man. Furious. Hurting. Out of control.

"I let this slip through my fingers because I was too fucking afraid of what I might find," he said softly. "But they didn't let us have an open casket. The council declared that. So that police file might be the only place we get a good look at the body."

Dylan nudged the box with his hands, only touching the very edge as he knocked it over. "I remember this from Oscar's room," he said. "He kept it on one of his shelves, I'm almost certain."

It was definitely a memorable piece. Old and thick wood, with brass decals on the corners and in the center where it could press into a locking mechanism. At the moment it was open and filled with dirt, but there had to be something in there that was worth burying him with.

"Richard might know," I said, knowing I couldn't just avoid my creepy birth father when he might have answers we needed. "Or even Stewart."

The five of us moved closer together, standing at the foot of his grave.

"First thing is the police," Beck said without inflection. "Then we pay the Deboise estate a visit. Riley can enter and go about that place like it's her own, and I plan on taking advantage of that."

I shuddered. "As long as I don't have to go there alone, I'm cool with that."

Beck shot me a probing stare, and I tried not to let all of the fucked up mess that was my emotions out. I wouldn't risk his life, not when Richard Deboise was such a fucking unknown piece of insanity.

"We'll start tomorro—"

Dylan was cut off by Jasper's phone ringing again, and he scowled down. 'For fuck's sake, Edith, could your timing be any worse."

I pushed closer to him. "Was that her before as well?"

He nodded.

With a glare, I yanked his phone off him and put it on speaker. "Eddy, you okay, girl?" I asked.

A sob echoed down the line, and Jasper was immediately on high alert. His annoyance fading as worry took over. "Eddy, what happened?" he barked out.

"You—" she cleared her throat. "You all need to get back here right now. Some huge shit has gone down. Katelyn Huntley is dead, and they're about to arrest Dante."

The phone went dead, and we were all left staring at it for a few moments.

"Fuck," I said in a rush before I basically threw the phone at Jasper and sprinted toward the cars. They caught up to me in seconds, all of their legs much longer than mine. Not to mention their fitness. We jumped into the cars, and Beck was just about on two wheels as he spun us around to get back onto the main road.

It wasn't like I needed much push to have mad love for the Bugatti, but that night, when it got us back to the party house in minutes, I could have literally kissed her.

Before I could dash along the driveway, Beck wrapped his arm around me, and hauled me back to his side. "There is a killer out here," he said. "Do not run away from me." He spoke in the sort of soft voice I expected a serial killer would use right before they skinned their victims. It was low and deadly.

Scary as fuck.

We started up the drive and were joined by the other guys almost immediately. It wasn't hard to figure out where everything was going down—there was a large crowd gathered around the side of the house, all of them being questioned by police.

"It was definitely the big tatted guy," one chick was saying, tears streaming down her face. "He threatened her and said that he would kill her. We all heard it."

Lots of others agreed, and I cursed Dante for his fucking big mouth. I might have been angrier at him than I'd ever been, but I hadn't even had a chance to confront him about Catherine yet. I hadn't given him a chance to explain what he was doing. If I'd learned anything from my fight with the heirs of Delta, it was that there were two sides to every story, and sometimes hearing the other side, changed your perception.

Dylan and Evan started chatting with a police officer, one they clearly knew well, but I didn't stop. I couldn't stop. A force beyond my control was pushing me forward. Katelyn's body was taped off, but they hadn't covered her up yet.

"What happened?" I asked a chick who was pressed right against the yellow tape. From my angle, all I could see was blonde hair, spread out everywhere.

"Stabbed. Ten times," she said, not even looking my way. "She might have been raped too. Her underwear is missing."

"Doubt she even wears underwear," I said, honestly. It was probably not nice to think ill of the dead, but ... to be honest, Katelyn was a bitch, and I wasn't going to pretend otherwise just because she was now dead.

"There's Dante," Beck said from behind me

"Where?" I asked, not seeing him.

My head was spinning as I tried to see between the police and medical people. Beck tilted my head to the right, and I gasped as Dante came into sight. Dante was framed by two burly officers, his hands cuffed behind his back, a stoic expression on his face.

Without another thought, I raced toward him. "Dante," I called, and for the first time, something like pain crossed his face. He turned in my direction, and I couldn't stop the tears. "Wait," I called. "You have the wrong person. Dante would never kill her."

For the first time I wasn't quite sure that was the truth, but it didn't stop me from defending my oldest friend.

The officers stopped and eyed me closely before their gazes lifted to meet Beck's eyes. "She yours, Beck?" the younger of the two said.

I made an angry growling sound. "I'm a fucking person. I don't belong to anyone."

"She's Delta," Beck said over the top of me.

Both officers eyed me with new interest. "Why are you arresting him?" I said quickly. "You can't have any evidence."

"How about the threats he made toward the victim earlier in the night?"

the young officer said. "Or the fact that he was found with multiple blades illegally concealed on him."

"Were any of them the murder weapon?" I asked, almost terrified of the answer.

The officers exchanged a look, and I figured they weren't going to tell me anything more, until Beck cleared his throat. They met his gaze again, and then immediately answered. "No. None of them match the blade marks, but we only have preliminary forensics. For now, Dante will need to answer some more questions down at the station."

It took everything inside of me not to reach out and try and yank my friend out of their hands. "I didn't do it, Riley," he said, his eyes boring into mine. He was imploring me to believe him, and in this regard, I pretty much did.

"I know," I said quickly. "We'll get lawyers for you. Don't say anything until they show up."

Dante nodded. The officers started to lead him away again, and I would have faltered if Beck hadn't kept me upright. Dante looked back. "I'm so sorry, Riley. So fucking sorry."

I didn't know what he was apologizing for exactly, but it was destroying me nonetheless.

"Dante," I called, crumpling forward.

He was almost at the closest police car then, and I could only just see him when he shouted. "Stay away from Catherine. Don't trust a thing she says—"

Anything else was muffled as he was pushed down into the back of the car.

I broke apart then, and it was only Beck's arms around me that kept me standing. He held me while I sobbed against his shirt.

"Dante works for Catherine, doesn't he?" I said, choking on the words.

Beck didn't speak. "How long?" I said, pulling back, my hands twisted in his shirt front. "How long has he been working for her? From the start?"

Beck hesitated. "It would make sense. She probably never wanted to lose touch with you, just in case. Dante was the perfect mole. Who would have expected a kid to be a double agent?"

All a lie. Every fucking moment with Dante from the first time he "found me" in his neighborhood had been a lie.

But ... could it all be a lie? He'd expressed real emotions to me more than once; demonstrated his caring. He loved me in his own way, I was sure of that.

He'd have to be a damn good actor if it was *all* a lie.

And maybe he was. Maybe it was naive of me to think that this was anything other than a careful ruse orchestrated by my fucking bitch of a birth mother.

Another way for her to control my life. To control me.

I was still holding onto Beck, staring up at him, tears filling my eyes. I wasn't really seeing him though, stuck in my own head, as I tried to comprehend it all.

"What's wrong with Riley?" Dylan asked from nearby.

Beck didn't answer him, his dark gaze still on me, murder in his eyes.

"Riley," Dylan said, closer to my face. "Snap out of it for a minute, because if you don't, Beck is going to go postal and start hurting people."

I swallowed hard, trying to stop the rapid in and out breathing I was doing—sounding like a dog panting. I couldn't seem to get myself under control.

"Dante," I choked out. "He's been Catherine's mole the entire time. All the fucking time. My entire fucking life. It's all been a lie."

How much more could Catherine take from me? How much more could she extract before there was nothing left inside?

Beck made a low rumbling sound, his chest and arms shaking, and I somehow managed to calm my own freak out, so I could wrap my arms around him. "It's okay, Sebastian," I said, using his name in an attempt to snap him out of it. "I'm okay. We'll figure this out."

His hold was rough, almost painful as he yanked me into his body. "It's going to be okay, Butterfly," he said close to my ear. "I promise you, Catherine will pay."

He didn't have to tell me that, I was already planning it in my head.

This time when I pulled the trigger, she would be the one in my sights.

Chapter 31

Jefferson police station was not that large, nothing like the ones back in Jersey. It had a sterile, tiled sitting area at the front, a long desk with screens and bars, and a door that led back into whatever was beyond the sitting area.

I had started pacing ten minutes ago, much to the annoyance of the middle-aged chick behind the desk.

"Miss, if you take a seat, I will let you know when you can see your friend."

I swung a glare in her direction. "I'll sit down when you tell me something. For now, I'm pacing, okay?"

She shut her mouth and continued with whatever paperwork was in front of her. It was almost 4:00 a.m., and I'd been waiting here for two hours. Delta lawyers arrived just before us, and they were back there now with Dante. So far we hadn't heard a thing.

"Riles, sweetheart, maybe we should wait at home. Meredith here will call us as soon as there's news, right?"

Dylan turned his dark eyes on her, and she almost wilted. "Of course, Mr. Grant. I will phone the second I hear anything."

Everyone was exhausted; I felt like I was literally dead on my feet. So much fucking stuff had happened today that it was hard to believe it had only been twelve hours since I was drinking champers with my friends and family to celebrate my eighteenth.

"Okay," I finally agreed. "Our apartment is not far from here, so we can be back in a few minutes."

Dylan, Jasper and Evan looked relieved. Beck's expression hadn't shifted in hours. He was still wearing a scary mask that gave nothing away and at the same time made me afraid to leave him alone. He was plotting something. Something big.

Shit was going to go down.

He held my hand as we left the station though, only letting it go so we could get into the Bugatti before he took it again. He parked next to my butterfly, and I could barely look at her, because all she did was remind me of Dante. All of the times we took her out, raced her, won together.

All fucking lies.

Once we were inside, I convinced Dylan, Evan, and Jasper to go to their own apartments—they wanted to stay with me, but they needed sleep, and my couch was not big enough for the three of them. Beck never left, and I never suggested he should. We got ready for bed silently—I didn't even bother to find pjs, just stripping down to my underwear, peeing, brushing my teeth, and then crawling into bed. I'd worry about dirty sheets tomorrow.

"Whatever happened to my gun?" I asked Beck as the darkness closed around us and we snuggled together.

"It's in your drawer," he said in that same expressionless tone. "Right next to you."

I chuckled dryly, finally able to be amused by the way he just broke into my apartment whenever he wanted.

Rolling over, I faced him. "Talk to me," I said softly.

He wrapped me into his arms, bringing me closer to him. "If you'd seen your face, you wouldn't be wondering what's wrong," he said. "I've never seen devastation like that, not even when you found out about the Delta tapes."

I struggled not to cry again, waiting until I could speak without sobbing. "Because I knew, deep down, that you guys didn't really betray me. I knew that Delta forced your hand, but I was so mad that I got caught up in that bullshit, that I needed someone to be angry with. You four made an easy target."

"Still think you let us off too easy," Beck murmured, some of the ice melting in his tone. "We fucking deserved to grovel."

I smiled, even though he couldn't see me in the darkness. "You did grovel. And it hurt me to keep you all at arm's length. Especially you, Beck."

His lips found mine, and for a brief moment, I forgot about my pain and grief. Beck had a way about him. He could wipe everything else from my mind. Erase my worries and stresses with his simple presence.

But there was one niggling question that wouldn't fade. Did Dante betray me completely? Was he actually working for Catherine from the start, or did she do something to force his hand recently?

I had to know. And there was only one way to find out. I needed to confront Catherine, and I needed to do it in a way where she felt free to confess all of her sins. Which meant I could not take Beck or any of my guys with me.

That's why I asked about the gun. Because Catherine was psychotic and unstable and I was going to walk right into her lair and accuse her of a lot of shit. I might not come back from this, but even that knowledge wasn't enough to stop me from going.

This showdown had been a long time coming.

First though, I was going to love Beck like this was our last time together. Just in case it was.

"Butterfly," he murmured, his lips brushing over my pulse point in my neck and his breath warming my skin. "Why are you asking about your gun?"

"No reason," I lied smoothly. "Just sentimental attachment. It's the first gift you ever gave me, you know?" A pang of guilt forced my eyes shut, just in case he caught me out. The ease at which I'd just lied to him almost scared me. Delta was changing me.

Beck pulled back from me a fraction. Just enough to look me in the eyes when he used his thumb and forefinger to bring my face to his. My lids flickered open, and I held my breath, waiting for him to call me out.

For a long moment, he just stared back at me. Neither of us blinked, and the only movement was the rise and fall of our chests together.

"What did I do right in a previous life to deserve you?" he finally whispered. His voice was full of emotion, and my eyes dampened. He held so much self-loathing for who he was, when none of it was his fault. He didn't ask to be born into Delta any more than I did. The only difference between us was that I got the opportunity to grow up as a normal kid.

Really, I should be thanking Catherine for giving me away. She did me the biggest favor of all, allowing me the love and support of real parents for almost eighteen years. The loss of my parents still cut like a knife but fuck if I would change anything. I had something that Beck, or any of the guys, had never had.

I *should* thank her, but I was probably going to kill her.

How oddly appropriate that she turned me into a killer, allowing me to even entertain the idea of shooting her right in her Botox-filled face.

"Who says it was a previous life?" I whispered back to him, stroking my thumb over his rough, stubbled cheek. "I think we're pretty damn perfect for each other just the way we are."

His cheek twitched, and I silenced what was sure to be a disagreement by pressing my lips to his. It was a gentle kiss at first, tender and... dare I say, *loving*? But Beck and I didn't really have the sweet, tender sort of relationship of romance novels and our kiss quickly deepened, turning hot and possessive as he rolled me on top of him and slid his hands up my rib cage to cup my breasts.

His thumbs skimmed across my hard nipples, and I let out a little whimper of encouragement. The lace of my bra was thin enough that it may as well have not been there at all, but still...

"Beck," I started, but cut off with a groan as his mouth closed over one of my nipples through the gauzy fabric. He sucked and nipped at me, his fingers toying with the other one until I was writhing all over his hardened shaft and desperate for more.

Finally, he reached around behind me and unhooked my bra, releasing me long enough that I could slip it off and toss it across the room. His warm hands were back on my breasts right as my lips found his again, and I hissed with the sheer pleasure of his skin against mine.

"Damn, Butterfly," he murmured between teasing kisses. "Did I ever tell you how perfect your tits are?" He rolled my nipples between his fingers again, driving me wild. "Because they seriously are."

I quirked a grin as I slipped from his grip and shimmied down his body. "You're no slouch yourself, Sebastian Roman Beckett." I licked my lips in what I hoped was a really sexy way as I peeled his boxers down and eyed his cock.

"Riley Jameson, are you—" his silly question cut off as I ran my tongue up the length of him and swirled around the tip. "Yep. Yeah you are. Fucking shit." His words dissolved into a groan as his fingers tangled in my hair, and I closed my lips over his dick and sucked.

His control issues were only going to allow me so long, but I made the most of it while I could. My hand worked his lower shaft while my lips, tongue and sometimes a little bit of teeth took care of the rest. His tight hold on my hair—controlling me—pushed the limits of my gag reflex, but instead of feeling dirty and cruel, it turned me on harder. I loved that feeling of him taking what he wanted, even though it was me blowing him.

Right when I thought I had him, when I thought he was about to lose it, he hauled me up and flipped us in a tangle of limbs. Next thing I knew, my face was against a pillow while my ass was high in the air, my naked cunt exposed to the cool night air.

Where the hell had my panties gone, and how did he just get them off me so fast? It was dizzying, but there was no time to ask silly questions. Beck's mouth closed over my pussy, and I moaned, long and low.

Apparently, he was in the mood for revenge. His strong hands held my ass, spreading me wide and allowing him unhindered access to lick and suck me to the point of trembling. But even so, he wasn't done. Right as I was sure my orgasm was going to hit, he stopped.

But then...

"Is that—?" I blurted at the distinctive sound of something vibrating.

Confirmation came quickly as Beck toyed with me, running the buzzing head of my new vibrator over my aching lips and dipping it in and out of me with infuriating shallowness.

"I found this in your drawer earlier, when I put your gun there," he commented as he teased me. "How long have you had this, hmm?"

My response just came as a strangled squeak as he pushed the vibrator deeper and delivered a quick lick over my clit. "Uh, not long?" I replied when he withdrew it, even though I was silently *begging* him to keep going. "Eddy gave it to me as a housewarming gift."

He hummed a thoughtful sound under his breath, but obliged my mental pleas by pumping the purple silicone toy in and out of me a few more times.

"Well then," he murmured, his breath hot on my throbbing pussy. "Remind me to thank her later."

His weight shifted on the bed, and I craned my neck just in time to see him stroking a fist down his erection. He caught me looking, and just smirked at me before pulling the vibrator out and replacing it with his huge cock.

"Fuck," I halfway screamed as he slammed the whole way in. He was a clear sight bigger than the toy Eddy had given me, so that first thrust held an edge of pain while my walls stretched and adjusted to accommodate the new intrusion. It was a pain I craved, though, and I writhed under his grip, praying that he'd move.

Beck let out a small, self-satisfied laugh as I whimpered and squirmed, but his hands were tight on my hips—holding me still. "I'm really getting the impression you like it rough, Butterfly."

"Fuck yes," I gasped, totally past the point of discretion. "Sebastian, please, *please*, fuck me hard."

Thank all the deities and stars and whatever the fuck else, he didn't require any more encouragement. In fact, he stepped it up a notch by bringing his hand down—open palm—on my ass cheek and making me yell.

Fuck me. What was it about that sharp sting of pain that just drenched my cunt?

Beck fucked me exactly how I wanted him to. Hard, fast, dirty and possessive. When he ran the vibrator over my clit, I exploded in a screaming, thrashing mess.

"Holy fucking shit," I breathed. "Shit. Holy wow."

A strangled sort of grunt came from Beck as he held my hips tight and kissed my spine. His cock was still lodged deep within me, and it quickly became clear that he wasn't finished with me yet.

"You good?" he asked, and I nodded into the pillow. "Good."

That was all the warning I got before Beck pulled out, flipped me over onto my back and thrust back inside my still pulsing pussy.

I moaned, long and languid as he started moving again. Slower, this time. All my nerve endings were lit up from my intense orgasm, and I draped my arms around his neck in an almost drunken haze.

Beck kissed me while we fucked. Slow and gentle but still with all that dominant ownership that he held in his eyes every time he looked at me.

Except ... we weren't fucking any more. What he'd done to me doggy style, torturing me with my vibrator and smacking my ass until I came—that was fucking. This...

"Sebastian?" I sighed, loving every inch of skin that touched along our bodies. "Are you...?"

I couldn't even say the words. Yet another thing for my therapist to handle.

"Making love to you?" he murmured back, smoothing my hair back from my face and meeting my heavy lidded eyes. His face was serious and ... vulnerable. It scared the shit out of me, but at the same time it was as though all my bones has started buzzing with excitement.

"Yeah, baby. Because I think something's on your mind, and I just want you to know how I feel..." he trailed off, kissing my lips in little, teasing pecks.

My breath caught in my throat, even as my legs curled around his waist, pulling him deeper. "And how is that?" I pushed, despite the near debilitating fear running through me.

A small smile pulled at his lips, and when he replied it was totally without hesitation.

"I love you, Riley."

The sheer conviction in his voice, the naked honesty on his face ... it was too much.

I panicked, kissing him deeply and continuing to kiss him—preventing any more conversation—until he came inside me. Beck wrapped me in his arms, hugging me tight on just this side of *snuggling* until I wriggled out of his embrace and gave him a sheepish smile.

"Just going to clean up," I explained. "Back in a sec."

Without waiting for a response, I scurried my butt into the bathroom and cranked the shower. But no amount of soap was going to wash away the revelations of the night. Beck loved me. And if I wasn't such a massive pussy, I could have admitted that I loved him too.

BROKEN TRUST

But with all the broken trust and heartache I'd only just started to get over, I wasn't ready to voice those heavy feelings.

Not yet.

Chapter 32

It took hardly any time for Beck to fall asleep, and even though my exhausted body kept pushing me to do the same, this was my only chance to escape without any of them knowing. I knew it was stupid. I was well aware I was the fucking moron heroine in the scary movie that deliberately ran away from the highly trained men that cared about her and were trying to protect her. But I was starting to understand that stupid heroine better, especially with my recent situations.

Sometimes the stupid decision was the best one for sanity, and I needed to know about Catherine and Dante. I needed to know before I lost my fucking mind, and since it didn't appear they were going to let me talk to Dante any time soon, there was only one person who could tell me anything.

Sliding from the bed, I stared down at Beck for a few minutes. Even in sleep there was a coiled lethality about him. I'd have to be very stealthy to even have a chance of getting away; it was only that he was exhausted I even had a shot.

Silently, I opened the drawer and removed the gun and magazine filled with bullets. They slid almost soundlessly together, and I left the room to grab some clothes from my bathroom. Jeans, a hoodie, and my converse was all I needed. Catherine didn't care if I wore a bra when I confronted her about being a lying bitch of a human.

The last thing was my keys. The butterfly and I were going for a drive tonight. As long as I didn't wake any of my guard-dudes.

I made it out of my apartment and into the elevator without incident. As the doors were sliding closed, I kept waiting for someone to shout my name and rush forward, but no one did. When I entered the parking lot, I had the gun ready in my hand, and I was on high alert. I hadn't forgotten about the last assassination attempt.

No one disturbed me, and I got into the butterfly without a problem. I clicked the button to open our automatic gates first, and then I started her up. I really wanted to give her a few minutes to warm up, but the engine was so loud that I was afraid it would somehow alert the guys, so I just carefully backed out and pulled out of the parking lot, closing the gate behind me. It was very early morning, the sun just starting to make itself known to Jefferson, and I was basically the only one on the road. My heart rate picked up as I made my way closer to the Delta estate, and when I pulled into the first set of armed gates, I was sure they could hear the beat from where they stood. "Name?" one said, looking at his sheet and not at me.

"Riley Deboise," I said back.

His head jerked up, and he stepped aside. "Sorry, Miss Deboise. I did not recognize the car."

I waved a hand at him. "No problem. I'm just here to visit my dad."

He smiled, and stepped away. "Have a nice visit."

Not fucking likely, buddy.

When I got closer to the estate, I parked the butterfly beside some bushes, and went the rest of the way on foot. I knew it was going to be next to impossible to surprise her, considering all the security, and the fact that the front guards had probably called my arrival in, but I was at least hoping not to give her too much advance notice. She might take off. Or plan some horrible shit to do to me.

A surprise attack felt like the right move.

Out of the car, I checked that the safety was on on my gun, and slid it into the front pocket of my hoodie. Then, creeping around, I did my best to avoid the camera, knowing the angle where I could stand to be out of sight. I used a stick to press the buttons and unlock the gates.

A lot of my plan was relying on the hope that Richard had not changed the code he'd given me to enter with.

Sure enough, it opened smoothly, and I slipped inside. I wasted no time, sprinting like my life depended on it down the driveway. When I got closer to the house, I silently debated with myself about trying to sneak in, or just knocking on the front door and getting it over with. I'd almost settled on sneaking in, because I might get a shot at looking through Oscar's room first, when something caught my eye.

I hit the ground hard, wincing as the gun rammed into my gut. I shifted to ease off the hard metal, while remaining partially hidden by the rose bushes that lined the circular driveway. Catherine was right there in front of me, on the front stoop, talking to someone who had his back to me. Someone who was definitely not Richard Deboise. The man was tall, standing above her even when she was in five inch heels, and there was something vaguely familiar about him.

I needed to get closer so I could listen in, but I was afraid any movement would draw attention to me, which would limit whatever I could find out from whomever Catherine was meeting so early today. It was probably a lover; wouldn't surprise me at all if she was cheating on Richard.

Sure enough, she reached around and threaded her fingers through the back of his hair, blood red nails flashing as she pulled him closer.

I shook my head at the cliché of it all. Rich woman having an affair. My god.

They kissed for a long time, passionate, pressing their bodies together. Catherine was clutching at him like he was actually important to her, and that shocked me a little. I didn't think there was anyone important to that bitch. As he went to turn, she pulled him back for one last kiss, and he must have said something nice, because she smiled, her face softening.

Then he turned around.

My gasp was muffled, because I'd managed to bury my mouth in my arms just in time.

Holy fuck. Holy fucking fuck and more fucks.

Catherine wasn't just kissing any old random.

It was Graeme Huntley.

Catherine was kissing her brother.

To be continued in...
BROKEN LEGACY

Stay Connected

JAYMIN EVE

Facebook Page: www.facebook.com/jaymineve.author
Facebook Group: www.facebook.com/groups/764055430388751
Website and newsletter: www.jaymineve.com

TATE JAMES

Facebook Page: www.facebook.com/tatejamesfans
Facebook Group: www.facebook.com/groups/tatejames.thefoxhole
Website: www.tatejamesauthor.com
Newsletter: https://mailchi.mp/cd2e798d3bbf/subscribe

Also by JAYMIN EVE

SUPERNATURAL ACADEMY
(URBAN FANTASY/PNR)

Year One

Year Two (2019)

DARK LEGACY
(DARK CONTEMPORARY HIGH SCHOOL ROMANCE)

Broken Wings

Broken Trust

Broken Legacy (2019)

SECRET KEEPERS SERIES
(COMPLETE PNR/URBAN FANTASY)

House of Darken

House of Imperial

House of Leights

House of Royale

STORM PRINCESS SAGA
(COMPLETE HIGH FANTASY)

The Princess Must Die

The Princess Must Strike

The Princess Must Reign

CURSE OF THE GODS SERIES
(COMPLETE REVERSE HAREM FANTASY)

Trickery

Persuasion

Seduction

Strength

Neutral (Novella)

Pain

NYC MECCA SERIES
(COMPLETE - UF SERIES)

Queen Heir

Queen Alpha

Queen Fae

Queen Mecca

A WALKER SAGA
(COMPLETE - YA FANTASY)

First World

Spurn

Crais

Regali

Nephilius

Dronish

Earth

SUPERNATURAL PRISON TRILOGY
(UF SERIES)

Dragon Marked

Dragon Mystics

Dragon Mated

Broken Compass

Magical Compass

Louis

HIVE TRILOGY
(COMPLETE UF/PNR SERIES)

Ash

Anarchy

Annihilate

SINCLAIR STORIES
(STANDALONE CONTEMPORARY ROMANCE)

Songbird

Also by
TATE JAMES

THE ROYAL TRIALS

Imposter

Seeker

Heir (2019)

KIT DAVENPORT

The Vixen's Lead

The Dragon's Wing

The Tiger's Ambush

The Viper's Nest

The Crow's Murder

The Alpha's Pack

The Hellhound's Legion (Novella)

Kit Davenport: The Complete Series (Box Set)

HIJINX HAREM

Elements of Mischief

Elements of Ruin

Elements of Desire

THE WILD HUNT MOTORCYCLE CLUB

Dark Glitter

FOXFIRE BURNING

The Nine

DARK LEGACY

Broken Wings

Broken Trust

Broken Legacy (2019)

Made in United States
Cleveland, OH
10 September 2025